AN

By

Robert Lee Hamburger

This is a work of pure fiction.
Any resemblance to people living or dead is purely co-incidental.

**To my ever-loving and loyal wife, Jane without whose kindness and support,
I would not have known real happiness.**

Chapter 1

The Beginning of the End

Bonnie Winters, a slender, blonde-haired beauty met Robert Schaffer, a tall, handsome, aristocratic-looking athlete on their first day at the University of Michigan. Bonnie, who had large shapely breasts and a firm ass and who had learned to show them off as a high-school cheerleader, grew up on the west side of the picturesque midwestern town of Ann Arbor, Michigan, not far from Veterans Memorial Park. Robert, who had played quarterback on his high-school football team, was brought up on the south side of the town near the University of Michigan Golf Course. Both families emanated from Europe and through hard work and education had accumulated upper middle class American wealth. Schaffer's relatives had immigrated to the States in the mid-1850's from Bavaria on his father's side and from a little town outside of Graz on his mother's side in the last years of the 19th century. Bonnie's grandmother and grandfather arrived in America in 1922 from Gloucestershire, England. Both Robert and Bonnie were the first in their families to attend graduate school and to achieve advanced degrees.

They attended different grade and high schools but remembered seeing each other at parties and football games on more than one occasion before they actually met formally in a freshman English class. Within a few weeks they had their first date and first kiss. Three months later when they'd both had too much to drink, they threw caution to the wind and became lovers in Bonnie's room on the ground floor of her campus accommodation, Betsy Barbour House. Robert had kissed her goodnight on the front steps of the residence hall but armed with Dutch courage and spurred on by an uncontrollable urge to hold her close and stroke her all over, snuck around the back of the building burning with hope that she would let him in through her window. When Bonnie returned to her room she regretted that she had not invited Robert to join her. She needed his big, strong arms around her and was wet from imaging what it would be like to allow him to touch her between her legs and to have him in her. She knew she needed to satisfy the need for an orgasm before she would sleep and decided to fantasize that Robert would be outside her window hoping to see her undress and to pretend he was watching while she made herself come. She was excited by her fantasy and, to make it more real, she did not close the curtains completely and made sure her body was in full view as she took off her clothes and prepared for bed. Robert watched her lay down on her bed and begin touching herself at which point he let his presence be known by tapping on her window. The noise startled her and she quickly removed her hand and rushed to close the window and curtains when she heard Robert say: "Bonnie, darling, it's me."

She let him in and they enjoyed each other's bodies until the early hours of the morning.

Bonnie was an English literature major but spent more time on her minor, modern art that was her true passion. She did inordinately well in both and, when it came time for her year abroad, she decided to follow Robert, who was studying International Relations, to Paris for one term and Rome for another so that she could experience first-hand the creation of European contemporary art in two of the world's most romantic cities. For a few weeks after their arrival in Paris, they tried to find separate accommodation and even lived for a short time with other fellow students. However, one night over dinner in the Latin Quarter in Paris, they decided it would be fun to live together rather than with other friends. They found a great flat a few days later not far from their lecture halls and moved their things in that afternoon. When they had to go to Rome for the next term, living together was not even debated and they took a great little flat in Trastevere and decided to remain living together when they returned to Ann Arbor from their year abroad.

While they graduated at the top of their classes, both Robert and Bonnie knew they would be better off going somewhere else for graduate school. Robert felt an MBA from a top five school would serve him better in his career than another degree from Michigan which was just outside of the top ten so he elected to attend Northwestern University's Kellogg School of Management which was located in Chicago, Illinois. Bonnie decided to pursue a Master of Arts degree also at Northwestern, a program that was one of the best in America. Their sex life had always been good if unimaginative as neither of them were experienced. They also were very fond of each other and were good friends so before moving down to Chicago from Ann Arbor, Robert and Bonnie were married in an elegant church ceremony involving their families and close friends. Their marriage was more a logical next step than an event driven by love and passion.

Schaffer finished the MBA program at the top of his class and chose The Global Banking Corporation from a dozen alternatives. The reasons for accepting the position were that he would have additional practical training at Global's New York Head Office and the promise of a European posting when he successfully completed the bank's training program. He spent his first year mastering corporate finance before graduating number one in his class and, as Bonnie was desperate to do further studies in Italy, Robert accepted the post of Chief Credit Officer for Italy and transferred to GBC's Italian headquarters in Milan in early October 1971. They found a glorious apartment on the top floor of a 300 year old building in Piazza Borromei in Milan's Old City and within a few weeks had furnished it with carefully selected antique looking furniture made just blocks away in the labyrinth of tiny winding streets that surrounded them. They had a small roof terrace and from there and from their bedroom and living room, they had views of the Duomo and its historic steeple and of the heart of Milan. From the opposite side of the apartment, where Robert and Bonnie situated their studies, they had a view of the red tiled roofs of the Old City and of the Alps that lay just 20 miles to the north.

On a clear and crisp late November day Robert arrived at the bank's offices just off of Piazza Meda about 20 minutes earlier than he usually did. He went immediately to his spacious office on the third floor, hung his suit jacket on the back of his chair and then unlocked the small, secure room that adjoined his office. He began to attack the mound of faxes that had arrived on his private fax machine overnight from their head office in New York. Several of the youthful bankers whom he had hired into the bank's credit training program were surprised to see the lights on in his office and knocked on his door to say good morning. Before they could greet him a loud banking sound began to filter through the bank's air conditioning system and into Schaffer's office. "What's that banging?" Schaffer asked the small group of the trainees encircling him.

"I don't hear any banging," said Rudi Cortina, the eldest of the trainees at 24 years old, as the clamor also began to echo down the elevator shaft and into the corridor. Cortina, who came from a little town on the Italian side of the Swiss-Italian border, had a practiced American accent as his father had taken up the position as Italian Consul in the city of Philadelphia when Rudi was about 13 years old. Five years at an elite preparatory school in a wealthy Main Line suburb had enabled Rudi to sound American without actually being even remotely like one, an accent he maintained after returning to Italy for university and graduate school at the renowned Bocconi Institute.

"You can't hear that. What are you deaf?" Schaffer demanded as he made his way along the passageway toward the ever-escalating sound. Rudi hurried after him as the others made themselves scarce. Everyone except Robert knew full well that when he found the source of the commotion it would be best not to be around. Before Rudi could catch him, Schaffer was in the lift so Rudi came in after him. The banging sound had increased in intensity and had become a clanging, banging almost roller coaster melody when the elevator doors opened. As they moved along the corridor and came to a partially open door to the room from the sounds were emanating, Rudi said "You don't need to do this. Let me see what it is and I'll take care of it for you."

But it was too late. "Rudi, you hear that? Someone is screwing in there" Robert announced the obvious and watched as the colour began to drain from Cortina's light skinned, north Italian face. The moans of a woman in the heat of passion filled the room.

"Please, Robert," Rudi pleaded with him. "You don't want to see what's going on in here."

Schaffer came to an abrupt stop as Rudi interposed his mass in the doorway of the room. He looked over his head and in the dim light of the unfinished hallway could just make out a temporary, hand written sign on the door that said "Occupata". "Get out of my way, Rudi," he said to him harshly.

"Robert," Rudi responded in a supplicating voice. "Let me handle it. I think I know who it is and...."

Schaffer fought for words and shouldered his gaunt but stony German tank commander body past Rudi and through the door. The only furniture in the room was a scrawny chair, which was submerged in a mix of men's and women's apparel, and an immense metal cabinet. A woman's bra and pants lay in front of the cabinet whose doors were closed. Despite the cabinets massive dimensions, it was rocking back and forth and seemed to Robert that it might work its way out the room's floor to ceiling bay window where in had been positioned. The cabinet virtually lifted itself from the floor as the moans now turned to a woman's screams of pleasure.

"No, don't," Rudi tried to deter Schaffer from opening the cabinet doors.

But it was no use. Robert's tank had made the running and now he was the determined commander, blonde hair and blue eyes at the ready, in the prime of life in his mid-twenties, only seconds away from ordering his men to join battle. He twisted the metal handle and pulled open the two large grey metal doors to an amazing sight that he will never forget. "Mrs. Gavi!" he exclaimed, at the spectacle of his luscious twenty-six year old, very married with children, Piedmontese secretary, Annarosa Gavi being banged into oblivion by Gianni Resca, one of the bank's senior officers. Her naked legs were opened in the missionary position as she accepted his continued thrusts into her with a cock that looked the size of a horse's penis when Resca withdrew it in preparation for another plunge. To Schaffer's secretary's credit, she tried momentarily to extricate herself but gave up almost instantly as Gianni Resca made his final thrusts and emptied his come in her as he sucked on her enormous nipples.

Schaffer stared in disbelief as Resca got off of her, said "Grazia, Annarosa" slid himself off of the shelf on which they had been copulating and pushed past Schaffer and Cortina to retrieve his clothes and leave the room to get dressed.

Annarosa tried to cover herself with her arms and burst into tears and sobbed uncontrollably. Rudi quickly came to her rescue by moving Robert away from the cabinet and ushering him out of the room.

"What are you going to do, Robert?" queried Rudi as he guided him back to the lift and to his safe little world back down on the third floor.

"Do!" he shouted. "I'm not sure, Rudi but I should have them fired," he hissed as his muscles tightened and his hands turned to molten iron fists. Just the thought of Resca banging his secretary infuriated him. It was irrational, he knew, but it hit him like a personal insult, like he had found him banging Bonnie.

"It's been going on a long time," Schaffer heard somewhere in the distance.

"What?"

"He was screwing her at least a year before you got here," explained Rudi as though he had read Robert's mind.

"Here in the bank?" Robert asked.

"Here, there, everywhere. She's besodden with the guy."

"What about her husband?" Schaffer inquired reasonably.

"He doesn't mind that much, Robert" said Rudi evenly. "Resca gives him a big chunk of the money Gianni makes on his personal foreign exchange dealings."

"Personal foreign exchange dealings, Rudi?" Robert asked suspiciously. What are you talking about?"

"Most of the senior Italian officers of the bank deal in foreign exchange for their own account, Robert. It's normal in Italy."

Robert was shocked. He knew nothing about this activity. "It may be normal, Rudi but it makes me very uncomfortable as it is clearly illegal."

"I understand your view, Robert but if I were you I would do nothing about it."

When Rudi left Robert's office, Schaffer sat at his desk and thought about Annarosa screwing Resca. Moments earlier he had been infuriated by it but his mind had moved him on to the bigger, more serious problem of Rudi's report on foreign exchange dealings. He quickly decided he would do nothing about his secretary's indiscretion and decided to focus on the foreign exchange issue. He grabbed a copy of GBC's *Policies and Procedures Manual* from a shelf next to his desk to see what he had to do about the foreign exchange activity. When he got to the pages dealing with it, he was not surprised to see that it was up to him as Chief Credit Officer of the Country to decide what needed to be reported by officers dealing in foreign currency for their own account. If it were illegal in a local jurisdiction, he had to curtail it immediately. He quickly wrote out a memo to all staff requiring them to report all foreign exchange dealings to him effective immediately and then sat back in his chair and wondered how best to handle Annarosa.

Ten minutes later, Rudi came into his office with a hand written note. "Robert," Rudi said gravely, "here is Annarosa Gavi's letter of resignation."

"Tear it up, Rudi. I don't want her to leave. I will need her to help me look into this foreign exchange dealing issue. Ask her to meet me in the little bar in the arcade below the bank in ten minutes. Will she do that for me?"

"I'll ask her, Robert. She's just collecting her things. She is certain you would have dismissed her if she did not resign."

"I won't dismiss her as long as she meets me for a chat and agrees to stop screwing Resca, in the bank at least."

"I'll ask her but as you can imagine, Robert, she is mortified and embarrassed to see you."

"Just do your best for me, Rudi. I'm going down to the bar now."

Ten minutes later Annarosa came into the bar with Rudi who was giving her emotional support. Dr. Schaffer," she began when she was standing in front of Robert. "I am so, so sorry. I am embarrassed for me and for my husband and my family. I feel that I must leave the bank."

Schaffer turned to Rudi and asked him to leave them on their own. When Rudi had gone, he said "Annarosa, I know you all think I am a square Germanic American but ...."

"Please Dr. Schaffer, Dr. Resca and I, we are to blame," she said in her less than fluent English. "You are a fine man. I am so sorry to have brought this problem on you."

"I don't want you to leave the bank, Annarosa," he said seriously. "I want you to continue as my secretary but if you want to continue to see Resca, it must be outside of the bank."

"Dr. Schaffer I will never see Resca again either inside or outside of the bank. I promise you that. If you are certain that you want me to stay, I would be honoured to stay with you.

"I do, Annarosa and I need you to help me with a problem that Dr. Bogni told me about. I need you to help me review what everyone is doing in foreign exchange."

"Tell me what you want me to do."

This was the beginning of the end of the Lugano foreign exchange insider dealing ring which made history in the 1970's for losing more money for the global banking system than had ever been lost in modern banking history. Robert and his wife, Bonnie with the help of Annarosa did most of the uncovering as the Italian trainees, with the exception of Rudi his wife Maria, thought it too risky to become involved. In fact they considered them mad to get mixed up in the whole affair. But Rudi and Maria, who became life-long friends of the Schaffers, were completely supportive until a few weeks later when their lives were in serious danger.

Based on digging by Annarosa, the four of them went to Lugano on the first Saturday in December 1971 to have lunch and to see what they could learn. Their plan was to observe the weekly luncheon party that Mrs. Gavi discovered took place among key Italian and Swiss foreign exchange dealers from many of the international banks that operated on both sides of the Swiss-Italian border. As Rudi rammed his big green Alfa Sports Coupe into its own unique fifth gear, Robert settled back in the front passenger seat and surveyed the foothills of the Alps peeking through the now dispersing mid-morning mist. The early morning autumn frost had not yet been burned away but he knew it would be by the time they crossed into Switzerland in a half hour's time. He let himself be transported north without comment, listening only to Rudi's clever handling of the gears and to the mix of Italian and English being exchanged in the back seat by their wives.

"Where did you stay when you lived in New York when Robert was in training," Maria asked Bonnie in English.

Robert braced himself for Bonnie's answer. She hated New York and Robert dreaded what she would say especially as a letter from her mother that arrived just before they departed Milan had put her in a foul mood. The letter explained why yet again why she was giving another $100,000 to Bonnie's lay-about brother and why she could not afford to give Bonnie anything.

"A rat infested hole not fit for human habitation," she contended unequivocally. Not a promising beginning, he thought. "Even our dog hated the place," she continued. "He was sick most of the time."

Rudi endeavored to change the subject. Maria had never been to the States and found London to be terrifying so he had an interest in damage limitation as he knew he had to spend at least six months at GBC's headquarters if he were to become an officer. "It's not that bad, Bonnie," he remarked as he glanced into the rear view mirror to catch Bonnie's eyes which Robert knew from experience would be filled with fire.

"Don't try to paint a pretty picture of New York, Rudi," Bonnie answered him sharply. "Maria is best forewarned. You'll never see her the whole time you're there if my time with Robert in that God forsaken hole is anything to go by and it's too dangerous for a woman to go out alone. The last time I did that a guy came up to me on the street and felt me up right in front of Saint Patrick's cathedral. It was horrifying!"

"Bonnie, don't terrify Maria," Robert attempted to restrain the tide. "Rudi has to go to New York regardless."

"Maria doesn't, Robert. She can stay in Milan. With her mother," she added lamely. They all fell silent after that and only found their voices as they approached the Italian/Swiss border.

In 1971 anyone going from Italy into Switzerland was suspected of something, usually of smuggling out gold, silver or increasingly valueless Italian Lira so it could be used to buy Deutschemarks, US Dollars, or Swiss Francs. The Italian border guard stared at them dubiously as Rudi brought the big Alfa to a screeching halt and rolled down his window. The guard strode cautiously over to Rudi's side of the car, touched his military beret in a type of salute and waited for Rudi to say something. Moments passed and the waiting game persisted. Finally, the guard crumbled as Rudi knew he would if only because of the Alfa. "Dottore," began the guard gazing down from on high into Rudi's now relaxed, dark brown eyes. This greeting of respect -- everyone in Italy had a title in those days -- said everything was going to be all right so Rudi decided to award the man his due.

"Capitano," he began, presumably Robert thought, because the guy was at best a sergeant. "We are going to Lugano for a peaceful lunch and maybe to fill up with some economical Swiss petrol!" Robert could not help chuckling at the scene especially as Rudi was admitting to a bit of thievery. In those days, Swiss gas and for that matter food could only be paid for with Swiss money that an Italian couldn't legally possess in any meaningful quantity.

The guard could not conceal a slight smirk, gave the ladies a little salute and sent them happily on their way saying "I should be careful of the Swiss, Professor, they are watering down their gas these days!" Rudi threw back his broad north Italian shoulders while at the same time craning his head and neck forward as he made a little laughing grunt of pleasure and laid rubber all the way to the other side of the border where the Swiss guard merely turned his back as the Alfa roared toward Lugano.

The square where the luncheon parties were said to be held was spectacular in appearance. The Swiss had it all decked out with Italian flags in honor of the ritual evacuation of the wealthy Milanese into southern Switzerland at the weekend. Signs on the ten or so restaurants which enclosed the main square made it clear that today all the best tables were reserved, a dilemma which Robert felt sure could be easily surmounted with a few US Dollars. Even the Swiss coveted the old greenback in those days and their willingness to embrace the US Dollar today made him feel awfully confident about the future. The quandary was finding the "right" table. Somehow they needed to be positioned close to the wheelers and dealers of the world of foreign exchange, a task he had delegated to Rudi.

Within moments of their arrival they were seated in a quite empty place near the center of the piazza. Rudi managed to secure a table on the perimeter of five unoccupied tables that were set for parties of ten. "Now all we do is wait," Rudi declared proudly. "Don't ask how much!" he told Robert emphatically.

Robert studied Maria. She was incredibly beautiful. Her hair jet black was pushed back from her angelic face into a stylish bun revealing perfectly formed ears and an angelic face. Her lips were sensuous and her nose perfectly formed. Her breasts were full and her cleavage, which was very much on display, would draw the attention of any normal man. He had never lusted after a woman, including Bonnie, the way he did Maria. He wondered if she had any feelings at all for him and why she had married Rudi who was anything but good looking.

Bonnie leaned over to Robert and whispered "You're staring at her, Robert."

Schaffer was startled by Bonnie. "I was just wondering if she is aware of the bank's problems, the FX situation," he whispered back to his wife.

"Bull shit," Bonnie whispered to him. "You were looking at her tits and thinking how great it would be to get her in bed.

"We'll, 'yes'," he said and laughed out loud and wondered whether Maria sensed how much he fancied her and what she would be like in bed and what Bonnie's price would be for his indiscretion.

Chapter 2

Lunchtime in Lugano

Robert looked away when his bank's head foreign exchange dealer, Gianni Rinaldi, a small, slim Piedmontese looking man with jet black hair and in his early 30's made his way to the center table which was situated just behind their table. Rinaldi wore a hand-made, autumn coloured, cashmere sports coat with dark brown trousers and a dark orange shirt accompanied by Saville Row especially made dark brown shoes. His clothes cost more than Robert's paycheck for three months' work. All four tables broke into applause and Rinaldi nodded and periodically raised one of his hands in acknowledgement just like a Sicilian Don.

Bonnie leaned over to Robert and said: "He must be the ring leader." They were all so used to their weekly merrymaking and lack of scrutiny that safeguards against snoopers were the last things on their minds. A few years later, after the Schaffers finally blew the lid off of the insider-dealing ring, the following article appeared in the 16 September 1974 edition of *Time* magazine:

"After more than a generation of stability, most of the Western world's bankers and the men who regulate their operations were smugly convinced that the financial chaos of earlier decades was forever behind them. Now, a recent string of bank failures and losses in both the U.S. and Europe has jolted public confidence and raised troubling questions about the supervision, efficiency and even the honesty of international banking. Last week the European financial community received ... more shocks.... Lloyds Bank, Ltd., one of Britain's most prestigious, disclosed that its branch in Lugano, Switzerland, had lost a walloping $79 million because of "unauthorized foreign exchange dealings." Lloyds, one of London banking's Big Four with assets of more than $1 billion, is in no danger of failing....

Meanwhile, the branch manager and money trader, both Swiss, have been suspended and could face criminal charges. Lloyd's officials uncovered the losses only after a chance phone call from another banker, curious about the heavy volume of currency trading being done by the small Lugano branch. It appears that the branch officials were seeking to turn a profit—whether for themselves or the bank is not clear—by speculating in Deutsche Mark and dollars without reporting their trades on the books. Apparently, after losing on some initial misguided trades, they wagered more and more of the bank's money trying to recoup, and the losses snowballed...."

Shortly after this article appeared, the Chairman of one of the largest banks in the world came up to Schaffer at a New York Federal Reserve Bank function, looked him in the eye and said: "You know Schaffer, the guys were making money, we were making money, your bank was making money, everybody was making money, even you could have made a lot of money. Why did you try to fix a boat that wasn't leaking, asshole? People are right about you. You are really seriously brain dead."

Schaffer thought about what he should or could say and decided that he would just shoot from the hip. "You know, I see your point, I really do," he responded, "especially when I see the way my wife looks at the two new Porches that one of your guys, who lives next door to me, got the other day. One for him and one for his wife, he told her. He makes half the salary and bonus that I do and has no family money to fall back on. But hey, if you don't care that he can afford two Porsches and I can't, why the fuck should I? Don't get me wrong, I'm not griping, cause I sleep real well except after a chat like this. So, do me a favour, asshole, fuck off tonight if you can get it up and find a guy who is interested!"

But that was the future and Schaffer hadn't even cracked the ring yet. His back was to the table populated by his bank's head FX dealer but he knew Rinaldi's voice as well as any. He leaned back with a glass of Orvieto Classico to take in the tidings. Bonnie and the Cortinas were no less attentive to what was about to occur and managed to busy themselves with newspapers, magazines and insipid dialogue to shelter their actual mission.

Rudi concluded his examination of the attendees and passed Schaffer a folded napkin on which he had scribbled the outcome of his surveillance. The good and the great were certainly not absent. "What can we do with this?" Schaffer asked him. The name of virtually every bank of any international standing with an office in Milan and its head dealer was on the list not to mention nearly all the Lugano based dealers of the notable American, British and Swiss banks. In those days the Swiss were astute enough to keep their offices out of Italy proper save for that little bit of Italy which was entirely encompassed by Switzerland, Campione d'Italia, a boat ride across the lake from Lugano.

"Probably best to burn it," Rudi responded candidly. As it turns out he was correct but Robert thought the boat was leaking and what U-Boat Commander wouldn't have tried to fix it.

Rinaldi proposed a few toasts and even singled out the Chairman of the Board of their bank whom he called "a man of vision, like Chase's David Rockefeller, only smarter". When he finished the toasts, he carefully surveyed each of his adoring followers and their wives and children who seemed to crave his words. Rinaldi was about twenty feet away from their table, all too close in the circumstance. Rudi nudged Schaffer just before Rinaldi began to use his coffee spoon to thump a sturdy Swiss glass to signal the formal part of his address and to get the absolute attention that he felt he deserved. His rich Piedmonte accent and background did not obscure the banal Milanese message he begin to dispense.

Schaffer would have testified that he heard, albeit in Italian, "Friends, Romans and Countrymen" as an ingredient of his opening commentary but both Rudi and Maria subsequently assured him that he had said "Friends, Thieves and Conspirators". Schaffer didn't quarrel about it, as the deviation in any event in the Italy of the day wasn't vast. "I am honored," he carried on, "to be with you today. We have done well by any gauge but now we must struggle to reach true excellence. Roberto," Rinaldi said as he turned to the stately looking man on his right, "you have attended us skillfully and to you I elevate my glass today to say 'thank you' from all of us for your counsel, leadership and," he paused for effect, "training." A huge roar of laughter greeted his final words. Rinaldi babbled on and by the end of the afternoon almost every male around the four tables had said a few words of thanks to Roberto de Ciano for his immense contribution. What was he being thanked for was the question, although it seemed that the likely answer was for helping to make them all very wealthy.

Schaffer knew the story of Ciano, as did most Americans living in Milan. He was said to be an Italian who had seen hardship and misfortune as a young child in the southern most tip of the boot of Italy despite his noble heritage. He was blessed, however, to have had a mother who saw no future for her or her young son in Italy following the murder of Roberto's father by the Mafia. She was unselfish and courageous enough to search out a life in the New World. Sadly she had died before she was able to see her son's triumphal return to his homeland bearing the wealth he had amassed in America and reclaiming the title and lands which had been lost with his father's death. Ciano drew his lanky, angular, sixty year old frame from the chair he occupied next to Rinaldi and looked out over his adoring listeners. Schaffer glanced at his watch as the first shadows from the late autumn sun, which brought late summer warmth to Lugano's balmy microclimate, commenced their journey across the square. Most of the people in the piazza were beginning to move but not Rinaldi and Ciano's devotees or for that matter Schaffer's little, almost equally attentive party. Ciano, who Schaffer had heard address an audience at the American Chamber of Commerce, conversed in flowery Italian phrases and proverbs. "Gentle people and kind friends, all of you are my family and it is to you that I give thanks for permitting me to bring some solace to the common people of my first and true country. We have been blessed these last few years and now...."

Nothing was untouchable. He even called on his long deceased mother to bless their mission. And yet, even if the authorities had recorded the entire days' proceedings, there was not a jury in the western world that would have convicted anybody of anything. "The real dealings took place," Rudi divulged to us on the way back to Milan, "when they all went to the john just after their Sambucca and coffee."

"What?" exclaimed Bonnie incredulous at the news.

"They did it in the john, the loo, the toilet," he gave us a translation in case we had missed it. "But if they hadn't done it there, they could have done it on the way back to their cars or overlooking the lake. It only takes a few seconds."

"Did what?" asked Bonnie in that low, soft menacing voice that Robert dreaded.

"They decided how to work together to make money on the foreign exchange market for the coming week when they went to thc toilet."

"You mean Rinaldi said 'one fart means sell and two means buy'?" asked Schaffer's wife in a now even more ominous, scornful vein.

"Something like that," replied Rudi.

"Well, Rudi, if that is all there is to it, then even you and Robert ought to be able to figure it out!" she exclaimed.

When they got back to their flat in Milan, Robert expected Bonnie to berate him for his pre-occupation with Maria and was shocked when she did not. In fact, when he had finished his shower and joined her in bed, she said: "Robert, I really need a quickie" and before he could react she moved her head down to his cock, got him hard in seconds, mounted him and came within just a few minutes. "Thanks," was all she said when she was finished, got off him and went straight to sleep.

The next morning Schaffer got into the bank early. It was becoming a habit. Starting time was officially 8:25 AM but he had no idea why. He did inquire and not just once. This was one morning when he was more than just slightly preoccupied to grasp the rationale as he wanted to be able to tell the FBI, CIA, the Bank of Italy and anybody else he could think of about everything and he figured those people would want to know about that. Every other bank in Milan opened at 8:30 AM and here his bank was asking its employees to be there five minutes early.

They even had a time clock that shut down after 8:25 AM. You could work if you wanted to but, by god, there was no way you'd get paid for the day. If you were sick, the bank had to pay and so Robert's bank had the highest sickness rate of any bank in the city and probably in the world. But they had about 20% more employees than they really needed, so the sickness rate did not inhibit getting the required work done. Rather, it just made profits much lower than they should have been. Until he got wind of the foreign exchange dealing, Robert had concluded that five minutes more working time a day made up for it and by having to employ more people, it was just his bank's way of keeping the Italian Government happy. Now he was looking for another motive.

Because Schaffer was an officer, he had his own key to the building. He also had the combination to the main vault. When Robert let himself in, the old time clock said 7:15. He took the lift to his office on the third floor. Robert was an officer but the most junior one in Milan. All the guys with real clout were on the mezzanine or first floor. He knew he would get there in due course, everybody did, but he expected, naively that exposing what Rinaldi and the others were doing would let him pass the first floor completely and put him in one of the wood adorned offices on the mezzanine. He also didn't particularly like crooks, maybe because he just couldn't be one himself. He checked the office next to his for any evidence of Annarosa. Nothing, unless she had organized a way to silently bang old Resca in the cupboard on the top floor. Schaffer's next stop was to be the foreign exchange dealing room where he intended to go through drawers and just nose around to see what he could detect. Bear in mind that he had never entered the bank before about 8:15 in the morning so this was all a fresh episode. The dealing room was situated on the mezzanine level together with the top bankers and until the end of his brief circuit on this momentous morning that had never meant much to him.

When he reached the mezzanine floor via an internal staircase and invaded the inner sanctum of foreign exchange and found every dealer at his desk silently nibbling croissants and paging through the morning newspapers and overnight reports, which had appeared on their Reuters machine, Schaffer almost fell over. The astonishing thing was that they scarcely seemed surprised to see him. Oh, there was an attempt in that direction, presumably just to make him feel more untroubled. An FX dealing room in the early 1970's in Milan or, for that matter, anywhere wasn't very grand so they could hardly disregard him. Rinaldi was the first to take notice. "Boun journo, dottore," he acknowledged Schaffer between sips of black coffee and bites into his slowly vanishing pastry.

"Boun journo, Rinaldi," Schaffer called to him as he stepped over to the Reuters machine and started to go through the reports just to give his intrusion an unspoken objective.

"Won't find anything of benefit in that lot," Rinaldi volunteered after a few minutes.

It all seemed fascinating to Schaffer as he had never bothered reading more than a few pages off of the machine on his floor but he yielded to Rinaldi's intimidation. "Yea, it all looks pretty boring today," Schaffer answered him and strolled over to the small screen that flickered in front of him. A mind-boggling list of US and Italian government bonds reciprocated his gaze. Rinaldi had sketched a small graph on a piece of paper and seemed to be conducting some sort of analysis of the variations.

"Just checking the yields by maturity to get an idea of the trends but it's probably a waste of time as all our," he said the 'our' with serious emphasis, "American bosses ever want to do is sell Lira and buy Deutschemarks or US Dollars. It's not altogether legal but the Bank of Italy doesn't seem to mind because we deposit the Deutschemarks and Dollars with them and they are desperate for any kind of real money deposits with the Lira under such pressure."

Schaffer didn't know what to say? Here Rinaldi was confessing something illegal without the slightest prompting and just sitting there munching away without a care in the world. Schaffer finally managed "you mean our fearless leaders have approved it?"

Rinaldi and the others in the room were overcome with laughter. All the tension came out in one big outburst and, just as their laughter was dying out, Rinaldi rekindled it anew with: "Approved it? You must be smoking something, Robert, they invented it!"

Schaffer left to return to the sanctuary of his third floor office. Christ, he thought, I am way over my head. I should have minded my own business, got promoted, served my time, made a bit of money and earned my pension. But, he concluded, that's just not me. Schaffer called Bonnie and asked her to meet him for a coffee in their favourite cafe in the Galleria, which was mid-way between the bank and his apartment in the old city. Fifteen minutes later they were sipping coffee and debating what to do next. Robert supplemented his coffee with a double Grappa to try to calm his nerves.

"We're over our heads, Robert," opined Bonnie reasonably after hearing what had transpired in the FX room. "One, we don't need this hassle. Two, this could get dangerous. Three, I really need to enjoy life a little."

Her response surprised him. She was a doer, not an enjoyer but he said, "I don't disagree, babe, but we can't just do nothing. We either try to stop it or we need to get out. "

"Get out?"

"Yeah. Out of Italy and probably out of the bank," he said truthfully and tried not to notice the look of discontentment as it passed quickly across her pretty face.

"Not very attractive. We've only been here a few months and I can't stand the thought of you having to embark on the job search all over again and me giving up my art work here." There were other selfish reasons why Bonnie did not want to leave but she could not discuss those with Robert.

"Agreed, but that means we've got to do something. At least I do," he said as an after-thought, "and whatever I do is going to involve you one way or another."

He could see that she was unusually troubled but all she said was "OK, you know I'll be in but we're going to need some help, someone professional."

"Yea, but first we need something that will reduce the danger."

"Like what?"

"Like photos of the key players with girl friends or boyfriends. Something like that."

She studied him and shocked him by saying: "That sounds like fun. Can I be a key player too?"

"You're joking, Bonnie," he said but was not sure that she was.

"Not really," she said matter of factly. "We need to put some spice into our marriage, Robert. Think how much fun you could have with Maria or Annarosa" she said laughing.

Now he knew she was teasing him. "Big talker, Bonnie," he said to her but when she just smiled up at him he began to wonder. This was a side of his wife he had never seen but for the moment he could not take his mind off of Rinaldi's seeming lack of any concern whatsoever about what they and the bank were doing and the fact that he and his entire staff were totally prepared for his early arrival were disconcerting. He managed a smile but forced Bonnie to focus on the seriousness of the situation. He knew that trying to stop whatever was going on wasn't going to be easy, and that it would be dangerous, regardless of any precautions they might take or help they might be afforded.

She had to know that as well, if they were going to stay and fight as opposed to split and run.

"Let's talk about spicing up our married life later, Bonnie. First things first. If we want to stay in Italy, I have to address this insider-dealing problem. If I do nothing and things go wrong and the bank loses money, they'll fire me and it will be difficult for me to ever get another job in the banking industry. So, to stay I need to address the issue and I think the only way I can succeed is to get help and to take some real personal risks, Bonnie," he said seriously. She tried to interrupt but now he knew what had to be done. Seeing her determination to stay in Italy helped him to focus and to see clearly. "It's obvious to me now," he told her "that top management and, who knows how many other bank officers, must be involved in what Rinaldi is up to. He's trying to pass it off like the bank has made some kind of formal decision to carry out illegal foreign exchange activity for its own profit. I haven't been in this country very long but I'd be willing to bet that Rinaldi and anyone else who is involved are getting plenty for their own account, regardless of what the bank is or isn't doing for its own account."

"OK," she said reluctantly. "What do we do now?"

"First, I want to talk with Stephanie and Paolo. Can you see if they are free for an early dinner, say at Al Mercante?"

Bonnie looked worried. "Are you sure we should involve them, Robert? They've been through so much."

"I think they'd relish the prospect of a practical attack on corruption in their country," he answered. They hadn't known the Mancini's long but had been fortunate enough to know them well. They lived in the apartment building next to theirs in the old city and had taken them under their wings shortly after they arrived in Milan from the bank's headquarters in New York.

"You know the Fascists put Stephanie in a concentration camp just before the end of the war," Bonnie protested. "She still has health problems as a result of it." Robert tried to interrupt but Bonnie wasn't finished. "And Paolo's factories are having trouble with the labor unions. He doesn't have time to help us."

"Paolo told me a few days ago that Stephanie's been compiling a dossier on so called, he paused and tried to spit it out the way Paolo did, "'respected people' in government and industry that she thinks are taking kickbacks or engaging in some kind of illegal activity. And I think Paolo would love some help in getting evidence of corruption on the labor union leaders. He told me that all they are really interested in is money in their personal accounts in Switzerland, not in improving working conditions, a comment which says he's prepared to go to a lot of trouble." He looked at her carefully and thought that he was getting through. "It would be a lot easier and take vastly less time and ultimately less money for him to put some money in the labor leader accounts in Switzerland than to resist, Bonnie, you know that."

She looked up and probed his face for a moment. Bonnie knew him well and could tell when he was determined or just wanting to have a debate. They had lived together for four years before they were married. They weren't quite childhood sweethearts but they were damn close to it. "OK," she finally acceded, "but I think we should ask for advice from Paolo and Stephanie, not try to enlist them."

Schaffer decided to leave it at that as he was fairly sure that it would take the proverbial team of wild horses to keep them out of it. "Agreed," he said simply, as he saw her glance at her watch. "You'll be late for your art class." He could sense that she was serious about discussing their married life but that would have to wait.

"That is what I was thinking," she said.

Bonnie gave him a little peck on the lips and waved goodbye when she left the cafe. She loved Robert and wanted to stay married to him but sex had always taken a back seat in their relationship. Everything else, school, career, jobs and everyday living always made them put sex on the back burner. They made love albeit it infrequently but they never had sex or a good shag. Often their lovemaking lasted five minutes or less as was the case the previous night. That was all fine until she discovered just a few weeks after they were in Italy how good sex could be. She had fallen head over heels for her art teacher, a handsome Italian man nearly 20 years older than her and could not resist his advances when they were alone after one of her art lessons. He was a suave Roman from a wealthy family that allowed him to indulge his love of drawing, just enjoying life and teaching others how to do the same. She could not wait for him to teach her more about her body and emotions and to screw her in some new and exciting way. She was wet between her legs just thinking about what he would be doing with her in just a few minutes time. As she came into the little street that housed his studio, her heart began to beat faster. She pushed the bell to his flat and waited.

"Pronto," he said into the speakerphone.

"Sono Io," Bonnie responded.

"Come in, darling," he said in English. I'm desperate for you."

She pushed open the big wooden door that opened onto an inner courtyard that was filled with decades old trees that provided natural shade during the warm Milanese summers. They were now laden with orange and gold autumn leaves that provided the courtyard with a warm, natural carpet. Her lover's flat was on the top floor of a centuries old building on the far side of the courtyard. There was a little lift that opened directly into his flat. When the doors opened, Carlo gave her a welcoming smile, bowed as he took her hand and lifted it to his lips, kissed it gently and then lifted her off her feet and carried her into his bedroom. He was a big, strong man but one who knew how to be gentle. He carefully laid her on the large, brass framed bed that looked out over the old town and the Duomo's incomparable steeple that stood watch over them. Bonnie could not wait for him to be in her once again.

"Take me, darling, Carlo, please make me happy."

Carlo sat down next to her on the bed and started to give her kisses firstly on her forehead and then on her nose and finally on her waiting, parted lips. As he slid his tongue inside her mouth, his hands caressed her full, perfectly formed breasts and, with the skill brought on by years of experience, he quickly removed her shirt and bra and turned his attention to licking her breasts and sucking her nipples. His hands now moved down to her legs and he began to stroke her other open lips that dripped with anticipation. Once she was prepared, he removed his own clothing and lifted her head to his swollen penis and let her lick him and suck him until he was fully erect.

"Turn over, *cara*, and get on your knees."

Her response was immediate.

"*Brava, cara, brava*," he reassured her. "Now put your head down on the pillow. I am going to lick you in both your precious places and then make love to you in a way that you have never experienced before."

Bonnie shuddered when his tongue found her bum hole and when he licked her pussy she could not surpress her first come of the day. Robert had never licked her bum or penetrated it with his tongue and now that she knew how glorious it felt, she could not get enough of it.

"Good girl," he told her. "What a clever woman you are, Bonnie," Carlo whispered into her ear as he now straddled her and began to gently insert himself into her. He had a huge cock and knew exactly how to use it to provide any woman with incomparable pleasure.

"Oh my God, Carlo," she moaned. Oh that feels so wonderful. Never better, darling, never ever." In fact, it was the first time she had a man take her in this way.

"One day we will persuade Robert to join us," he whispered to her as he gently pushed into her, "so that you can experience the pleasure of having two men inside you at the same time."

"That would be wonderful, Carlo," she said and then gasped as he now began to thrust into her with increasing speed. "I'm going to come again, Carlo, give it to me hard now, darling, and spank me just when I do."

As she began to shake from her orgasm, he hit her hard on her ass and pulled out as he started to come and she squirted all over him and the bed.

Chapter 3

Death in the Men's Room

Robert watched her walk down the concourse toward the Cathedral end of the Galleria, paused for her to turn and wave, and then he made his way back to his office where he found Annarosa organizing his morning post. "Good morning, Annarosa." Ever since he saw her on her back in the metal locker with the gallant Resca, he found it difficult to call her Mrs. Gavi and she really couldn't protest.

"Good morning, dottore," she replied.

He could have insisted on being addressed as "professore," as he had a Ph.d., but decided "dottore" had a better ring to it. Most prosperous Italians relish being called "dottore" if at all possible. Even the modern day, north Italian, liberated workingwomen like the sound of "dottoressa", which is the female equivalent. A university degree is all that is required to be addressed in this satisfying way. "Anything interesting?" he enquired, as he gazed at the end of a small white envelope protruding from under her armpit while at the same time noticing she was not wearing a bra.

She saw his stare. "Oh, you mean this?" she questioned him ingenuously as she raised her saucer-like brown eyes into a steady, confident assertion with his. Examining her just then, Schaffer could understand why Resca had risked so much to screw her. "That and anything else that you may have discovered," he said as evenly as he could, as he took the little white envelope and a card that had been tucked alongside it from her now outstretched hand. The card went with the letter which had been opened and indisputably perused by Annarosa despite the fact that the envelope had the words "Personal and Confidential, Addressee Only" emblazoned on it in both English and Italian.

"I'm sorry I opened it, dottore. I was going through all the post quickly and just slit it open with the rest."

"Fine, Annarosa," he managed to reply, knowing that it was senseless to say anything else.

"I hear you arrived early, dottore?" she said with more than just a little cognizance and inquisitiveness in her voice.

"Where did you hear that, Annarosa?" Robert inquired, knowing that it was a miscalculation the instant he said it.

"We'll, from everyone, really," she proposed, hoping that would appease him. His silence said it didn't, so she said, "we'll, from Rinaldi himself and, of course, dottore Resca and from...."

He interrupted her. Her opening assertion was accurate. "All right, Annarosa. Just get me some coffee and let me know what appointments I have today when you return." When she left, he quickly opened the private and confidential letter and nearly fell over when he read it and the attached card, both of which he has kept to this day as reminders to himself of how tricky the Italians can be, a race of people whom he still thinks are cleverer than most others.

He read the letter, which was written in Italian, once quickly and then very carefully to try to understand every word and the overall meaning. It was written in long hand on plain white paper embossed at the top with a gold crest.

> *7 December 1971 Private and Confidential*
>
> *Dr R Schaffer*
> *Vice Directore*
> *Piazza Cordusio 1*
> *Milano, Italia*
>
> *Dear Dr Schaffer:*
>
> *I have been following your most promising career with interest, especially since you arrived in Italy not long ago. Recently it has come to my attention that you are making certain enquiries regarding the foreign exchange activities of banks in Milan and Lugano. Once you have completed these enquiries, I should be most grateful if you would share the results with certain colleagues at the US Embassy in Rome who shall make themselves known in due course.*
>
> *In the interim please accept my best wishes for continued success in all your endeavors.*
>
> *Yours sincerely*
>
> *Roberto de Ciano*
>
> *P.S. I'm having a small party at my villa on Lake Como on Saturday evening 18 December. I do hope you and your wife are able to attend. Her artistic talents are highly regarded by several of my most respected friends and I know you would enjoy seeing key business and government leaders who will be joining us, including your own General Manager, Bob Franco.*

The card, which was about four by four in size and which was made of heavy, rich looking and feeling paperboard, was embossed with the same gold crest as the letter. It seemed to be some sort of coat of arms. The invitation invited Dottore and Dottoressa Schaffer to attend a dinner dance at the Como Villa of Count Roberto de Ciano on the evening of 18 December. Guests were expected at 8:30 pm and dress was formal. Accommodation would be provided for those wishing to spend the night.

As he reread the letter and card for the third time, the emotions that swept through him, when he fully comprehended the full magnitude of Ciano's letter and card, started to sink in. It was less than a week since he had decided to embark on his inquiry and less than two days since he had witnessed the gathering of foreign exchange dealers in Lugano. Here was the apparent initiator of the entire scheme, the teacher from whom the students had learned everything, letting Schaffer know that he knew he and others were investigating him, that he was being watched by the US government, that his ultimate boss in Italy, Bob Franco, seemed to be in on whatever was going down, and that Ciano was a highly respected, noble Italian who could be helpful not only to him but also to his family. Moreover, in the finest traditions of the wisest European royalty which had engineered retention or reclamation of their wealth, Ciano was taking steps to bring the most valuable of those outside the establishment into the privileged few that made it all happen. Even a saint can think of becoming a crook when faced with that kind of temptation.

As usual his immediate impulse was to evaluate it with Bonnie, but as he was dialing his home number, he remembered that she was at the Milan Art Academy for her lesson. Had he known that she was getting her brains shagged out by a 40-year-old Roman, what he did next might not have transpired at all. He decided to clear his head with some fresh air. Once outside the bank it was easy to establish how laborious and, most certainly hazardous, it was going to be to compromise the dealing ring, if there was such a ring. At this stage he only had the information from Rudi, the financial analyst most in need of his benediction in order to advance his own career, and from his less than trustworthy secretary, Annarosa, as confirmation of his own suspicions regarding the dealing ring. What he had heard at the luncheon in Lugano couldn't convict any one of anything and he had no faith whatsoever that Rudi, Maria, or Annarosa would actually reiterate what they knew about the ring to any one of real authority. They had much too much to lose. Moreover, there was no longer any assurance that exposing the ring would further his career. Rather, it seemed that it might well ruin the likelihood of advancement, especially if Bob Franco was in on it, as now seemed more than likely. Doing what he knew he should do, exposing the dealing ring, no longer seduced him, as there was nothing in it for him. Moreover, there was a great deal he could lose, including most everything he truly valued.

With all these weighty thoughts burdening him down, he returned to the bank to discover Bob Franco waiting for him in his office. Robert could immediately see that Franco had looked through the things he had left on his desk, as was obvious from the fact that Franco had left the papers that Robert had put in a neat stack, in disorder. It was also evident because Franco was reading a memo he had received from New York regarding alterations to our credit-training program, a memo that Robert had put on the bottom of the pile. Franco was notorious for going through people's desks and, as a result, rarely found anything worthwhile.

"Morning, Robert," he greeted him cheerfully." He persisted looking at the memo before Schaffer could even respond. "Hope you don't mind me having a look at this memo but I have some budget people in from New York today to review a number of things including some of the cost implications of the changes being made to our credit training program. Mrs. Gavi said you wouldn't mind if I had a look for this memo."

"Sure, Bob," he said. "No problem," as he postulated what else Annarosa had related to him.

"Have you had an opportunity to study this thing?" he asked, as he waived it in Robert's direction.

"Yeah, I spent a good part of the weekend reviewing it," he lied as he watched him shift over to the window and look down into the courtyard that backed up to Robert's side of the building. Franco, an American of Italian origin who was a 25 year bank veteran was a tall, heavy set man in his late forties who had lost most of the hair on the top of his head and had allowed the remainder to grow long in compensation. A thin layer of grease kept it pushed back behind his ears and almost flat against the side of his head. He wore reddish brown, horn-rimmed glasses and today he had on one of the two baggy, thread bear grey suits, that he kept in a special "secret" closet next to his office, and that he put on in the event someone from head office was due to materialize. His hand made, English cashmere suits, of which rumor said he had about thirty, were stashed in the same "secret" closet and were never used when anyone from other branches of the bank were around. His good suits were for meetings with officials of the Bank of Italy and the Italian Government, the few clients that preferred a wealthy as opposed to a poor banker, and for lunches and daytime rendezvous with his girl friend and for dinners with his wife.

"Really?" he interrogated me.

"Yeah, other than a trip to Lugano for lunch with some friends," Robert decided it best to add as it was more rather than less likely that Franco knew he had been there.

He turned away from the window to look Schaffer straight in the eyes and asked in a intimidating way "Learn anything interesting up there?"

Three or four safe responses flashed through his mind but seeing the mess Franco had made of his desk and thinking about what a truly disgusting person he was Robert said, "Frankly, Bob, I did. I think you've got a real mess on your hands...." Schaffer paused for effect and then continued even more forcefully, returning his menacing stare. "I think I'm in the process of uncovering a foreign exchange insider dealing ring which may involve more than one employee of our bank."

Robert scrutinized him closely and to his credit Franco didn't stammer or even blink when he said, "You'd better be able to back that accusation up or you'll wish you and that sweet little wife of yours and the Cortinas were dead."

Robert had just about decided that the best course of action was to do nothing but his mid-west upbringing combined with his Teutonic heritage which makes it difficult to do nothing about something and, in particular, Franco's reference to Bonnie and the Cortinas, stood in the way of the safe course of action. "Don't worry, Bob," Robert said as he took a step toward him with confidence that he did not feel, "you'll be one of the very first to see a copy of the dossier just as soon as it's all tidied up."

"Dossier?" he asked weakly.

"Dossier, Bob, a real work of art. Rudi Cortina helped me put it together. One of the reasons I went up to Lugano was to post a copy to a friend in the States who acts as my family's lawyer. I figured I should take the precaution of having someone I trusted make sure my facts were set out in an informed, dispassionate way, with as much detail as possible. The pictures and tape recordings were the icing on the cake."

Schaffer never saw anyone, before or since, react as Bob Franco did. He sort of aged about ten or fifteen years right before Robert's eyes. The colour drained from his face and then he grabbed his chest and then his stomach, as he began to rock back and forth unsteadily from toe to heel. He tried to speak but the first traces of regurgitation were already on his lips. He looked at his hands as the liquid seeped through them and then he ran out of Schaffer's office and raced down the corridor to the men's room without saying a word or uttering a sound other than an uncontrolled retching. Mrs. Gavi must have seen him, and almost crashed into Robert as she came out of her office to see what was going on as Robert tried to follow Franco. "I think he's having a heart attack," Robert shouted at her. "You'd better call for an ambulance."

After that, there was chaos. The buildings' alarm bells sounded within a matter of 30 seconds. Annarosa had tried to call for an ambulance but the emergency telephone number was busy so she pulled every alarm in sight figuring that someone who could be helpful would eventually arrive. Everyone in the building rushed to do something, to be seen by someone to be doing something but in the end there was nothing to be done. Bob Franco died in the third floor men's room from what the coroner later determined was lack of oxygen not poisoning as many had assumed. It looked as though his tie had caught on a piece of pre-World War II plumbing in the men's room, which Franco himself had decided, only a few months previously, was more than adequate for the bank's staff, and that he had suffocated as he retched into the toilet bowl.

Chapter 4

Party Time at Lake Como

To this day no one is really certain who killed Bob Franco. But, three things are clear. He didn't strangle himself in the third floor loo and he didn't die of a heart attack, massive or otherwise. Franco also wasn't missed by anyone in the bank or, for that matter, by his wife or girl friend. Most everyone in the bank thinks the killer was Gianni Rinaldi on the orders of Roberto de Ciano. It's not impossible but it is unlikely. Robert thought it might be Franco's deputy, Marco Antinori, who was desperate for Franco's job but there was no evidence pointing in that direction.

The police needed to hang it on something or somebody and they spent several days interviewing everyone in the bank. They really wanted to pin it on Robert Schaffer, and may have been incentivized to do so by Rinaldi and Ciano, but even the inventive coroner just couldn't figure a way to do it. Poor Annarosa was next in the police lineup but, Marco Antinori, who happened to be on his way to Schaffer's office, swore that she never entered the men's room and that saved her. Marco also testified that he never saw Robert in the loo alone with Franco and Robert did the same for him because it was true, but then with all the chaos who really knows who was doing what to whom. Lots of people were coming from and going into the men's room where Franco died before the police finally arrived, including at least five different firemen. It was one of those situations where a massive heart attack became the most convenient solution to the problem and, in the Italy of the early 1970's, convenience was a top priority. In fact, it seems that the coroner was paid to say it wasn't poisoning, a conclusion he readily reached as to do otherwise would have taken months of investigation.

The best thing that ever happened to the bank in Italy was Marco Antinori's appointment as Country Manager. It became clear in fairly short order that he could make money out of old rope, as the English say, and his temporary appointment to stand in for Bob Franco was made permanent a few months after the fateful day. Unfortunately, Antinori's appointment after Franco's death did not mark the termination of the foreign exchange insider-dealing ring. It was more complex than that. Nothing in Italy is straightforward.

In the hours following Franco's death, Antinori performed miracles. His first decision, which took place within a few minutes of Franco's death, was to close the switchboard. He did it to keep the staff from giving the press, family and friends a running account of the chaos within, an act which enraged the staff but which saved the bank about $10,000 in phone bills just in one day. Following a painstaking examination of telephone bills during the next few months, Antinori eliminated about a hundred superfluous lines, a dictum which not only conserved hundreds of thousands of dollars per year, as Italians tend to have family in the US through Brazil and Australia, but also dramatically boosted working efficiency. Productivity advanced so conspicuously, that twenty-five planned additions to staff in the first year alone were avoided.

Schaffer was very upset by Franco's death, mostly because the initial nature of the police enquiry strongly indicated that they wanted to put him away for good. Marco's decision to order Robert to go home and to send the bank doctor to give him a sedative made it futile for the police to question him for more than about ten minutes immediately following Franco's demise. Robert was so distraught during those few minutes that he wasn't able to be very responsive to the police interrogation and by the time they were allowed to see him the next day, Bonnie and the Mancinis and Rudi Cortina had helped him piece together the 'real' story.

Everyone in the bank thought that Roberto de Ciano would cancel his party. Schaffer assumed that he would be uninvited if the party were not cancelled. Ciano rang him up at home one evening just a few days before the event. "Robert, how are you my friend?" he greeted Schaffer's 'pronto' as though he had known Robert for years. "This is Roberto, Roberto di Ciano."

Robert didn't want to seem unfriendly so he called him by his Christian name as well. "Roberto, how..." he paused to search for an appropriate word, "'nice' to hear from you." Schaffer decided not to tell him that he was feeling lousy and hadn't felt particularly healthy ever since Franco's death. Bonnie had told Robert it was trauma and that he needed professional counseling. Robert was open to it, even though most Italians didn't even acknowledge that shrinks existed in the early 1970's, but he was reluctant to be tarred with the stigma attached to it. In Italy people with mental issues either retreated to the mountains to clear their head, and that cure was really for women or, you withdrew to Switzerland for a "break" where authentic psychiatrists could be consulted away from the scrutiny of one's' fellow Italians. Schaffer could not afford either Italian treatment.

"Just wanted to confirm that you and your wife will be joining us this coming weekend?" he asked, switching to his practiced American English. Bonnie had decided they'd go as it would be a "great experience" and Schaffer decided there were more important issues to take a stand on, like starting a family that wasn't at the top of her agenda. "We're definitely coming," Robert said, trying but failing to sound enthusiastic.

"Great," Ciano responded. "Will you need a room for the night?" he enquired and when Schaffer failed to say anything immediately, he said, "I'll save one for you in any case."

Schaffer knew Bonnie wanted to stay for the night, for "the experience", but he hadn't agreed on that yet. "That would be most considerate," he finally said, keeping their options open and wondering why Ciano had really called.

The last bit of their conversation dealt with what they might do the day after. "In case you are able to stay the night," he said in his rather formal, schooled English, please do bring your golf clubs and riding things, if those pastimes amuse you. If not, they'll be bridge to play and pictures for your wife to paint. I really do love her work." Funny thing about that phone call, it rejuvenated Schaffer. The fact that Ciano had done a bit of digging into all aspects of their lives brought out the best and worst in both Robert and Bonnie.

When Schaffer told Bonnie about it, she said: "He's just being the good host, darling. It's important to know that sort of thing about your guests if you're going to have a successful house party." Carlo had told Bonnie that he would be there so Bonnie was determined to go to the party even if Robert did not attend.

Schaffer had been lethargic since Franco's unscheduled departure. He had even set aside plans to uncover the insider dealing ring, feeling life was too short. Rudi Cortina had urged him to be Italian about it and to look the other way, advise which he was tempted to take. Ciano's call and Bonnie's reaction to it changed all that as he suddenly realized that Franco's death had changed absolutely nothing as far as Ciano, Rinaldi and all the others were concerned. They were undoubtedly continuing their merry little ways, ripping off anyone and everyone. Also, Schaffer was a jealous person and Robert was not comfortable with his wife's clear interest in Ciano and the obvious interest he was taking in her.

He spent the next few days in the office doing a minimum of work and a lot of nosing around, including periodic visits to the dealing room, something he hadn't done since that fateful visit less than two weeks previously. He also let off steam by spending a few early evening hours at the driving range, imagining that each ball was Ciano or Rinaldi. He hit some balls so far that the range's owner had complaints from the nearby shopping center claiming he was damaging their patrons' cars.

On the day of Ciano's party Bonnie was in a superb mood early on but became irritable when her hair didn't turn out the way she expected. She had appropriated a good chunk of her household budget and on the advice of Maria Cortina had gone to the Milanese equivalent of Armondo's of Beverly Hills and come back looking like Shirley Temple. "Looks great," Schaffer lied when she reappeared.

"It looks terrible and you know it," she said as she dug the house gift they had agreed on out of her shopping bag and placed it on the kitchen table.

"I wouldn't go that far, Bonnie. It looks fine," Schaffer replied trying to sound approving.

"It doesn't either. I'm going to wash it and redo it."

"OK," he said in a non-committal way.

"If you thought it looked lousy," she said as she turned away from the table where she had placed Ciano's gift to face him straight on, "why did you tell me it looked great?"

"Bonnie, please" Robert said quietly as he moved toward her to try to calm her but she virtually ran out the door toward the bathroom and emerged an hour later looking great.

"I hope you're satisfied," she said petulantly.

A few minutes later Robert and Bonnie were on their way north toward Lake Como in their new deep red Fiat Sports Coupe, an acquisition which Marco Antinori had agreed to finance through a line of credit he decided Schaffer deserved despite what their US based credit card people thought about his credit rating. Robert hadn't had black tie on since the graduation party thrown for their class by the head of the bank's New York Officer Training Program almost a year previously and it seemed strange. On the advice of Paolo and Stephanie he had decided to purchase one rather than rent, an option made possible by the generous Antinori. "Everyone at that sort of party will be able to tell the difference," Stephanie had commented to Bonnie not long after Bonnie told them they had decided to attend. Paolo had agreed and when he said it would be a good investment as formal parties involving bankers were quite common in Italy, Robert took the plunge.

Schaffer glanced over at Bonnie as he accelerated up the Autostrada del Nord and couldn't resist reaching over to give her leg a squeeze in recognition of how lovely she looked and as a little gesture aimed at patching things up. She gave him a smile and said "Sorry I was such a bitch, earlier. It's just nerves," she admitted honestly.

"Me too," he said rather generously as he slipped between two family saloons that were occupying both lanes of the highway, gave them the traditional finger salute as their horns sounded angrily and accelerated rapidly. The saloons quickly faded into the distance.

"You seem so calm, Robert, like a duck taking to water. I wish I could be like that but parties and new people have a way of making me nervous."

"Join the crowd," Robert responded.

"I'm also regretting that we're going at all, Bonnie admitted. This guy, Ciano and his friends would be a lot happier if we were dead." In fact, she had become concerned that her affair with Carlo might somehow be revealed and had no idea what she would say to Robert if that happened much less how her husband would react. She had just about determined to tell Carlo she could no longer see him when he made her squirt the day he penetrated her bum. She had never previously squirted and was amazed at the overwhelming sense of well being that it had brought on. She was simply unable to give up hope of repeating the feeling that she knew could not be accomplished with Robert but wished that she had not placed herself in the position of being around both men in her life at the same time.

Robert heard her muttering about Ciano and his friends wanting them dead but couldn't focus as a guy in a van was trying to force him into the center guardrail and he had to break suddenly to avoid a crash as the van had the angle on him. He could hear Bonnie screaming as the little car swerved from side to side and finally came to a halt on the right side of the road as the van sped off into the distance. "Jesus, that was close," Robert finally managed to say as his hands begin to shake in recognition of the fact that they were very lucky to be alive. "Thank god the road was deserted or we would be dead now."

“My God, Robert,” she replied. “That van,” she paused for a deep breath, “whoever was driving it, tried to kill us.”

“There is no doubt about that,” he stated flatly as he looked in his rear view mirror to survey the road behind them. “Did you see any markings on that van or spot a license number?”

“I can’t recall anything about the license number other than the fact that I don’t remember seeing one. I think the van was dark blue, or some dark color and I don’t think it had any markings at all.”

“Same for me,” he said as he quickly checked the road for traffic and accelerated into the right-hand lane. Schaffer suddenly realized that there may have been another van or car and other people who would want to finish what the first van had failed to accomplish and they were sitting ducks just stopped on the side of the road. “Keep your eyes peeled. That van may be waiting for us up ahead or there may be others behind us,” he added.

They drove in silence for a few miles until they spotted a rest area that was well lighted and populated. This one had restaurants as well as a service area. “Let’s stop here for a few minutes, Bonnie. I want to report what happened back there to the police. I’m pretty sure the Carabinieri have stations at each one of these rest areas, and, we’ll be safe here.”

“Fine by me,” she replied.

Schaffer found the Carabinieri station on the far side of the service area and pulled right in front. There was a young, uniformed officer just inside the door of the small building and three Carabinieri cars parked on the side of the building. “Let’s both go in,” he said to Bonnie. Your Italian is better than mine and these guys are always sympathetic to pretty young women.

Bonnie managed a smile and put on a brave face as they went in the door.

“Good evening,” he said to the young officer in his careful but improving Italian.

The officer looked up from some paper work, stubbed out a half smoked Muratti cigarette and rose to his feet while he put on his uniform hat. “Good evening, madam, sir,” he responded nodding to each of us in turn. “How may I help you?”

“Someone in a small van tried to run us off the road a few miles back,” Bonnie said as she motioned toward the south. “I,” she continued and then corrected herself to say ‘we’, “We think the driver was trying to kill us.”

“Could it possibly have been that the other car, the van,” he said correcting himself just to show that he had heard what Bonnie was saying, “that the van perhaps lost control, regained it and then went on its way as you seemed unhurt?”

Robert only understood a part of his suggestion but got the clear impression that he was trying to find a way for us to retract our accusation. Bonnie had understood every word and was in no mood for an "Italian" solution to the problem. "The van aimed for us," she said as she fixed his eyes with her own.

The officer pretended not to understand. "Maybe the van had a steering problem," he countered. "It was probably of French or British manufacture," he said reasonably.

He was not going to give up easily, Robert thought. Then Robert looked at Bonnie who was mentally planning her next oral assault on Italian bureaucracy and he said to her in English "Ask him if we can just send in a written complaint and see if we can address it to him," Robert suggested.

Bonnie hesitated but decided to pursue Robert's approach when she saw that the young man was already beginning to eye the waiting mound of paper on his desk. His response was not surprising. "Of course, madam, a written complaint is always more efficient. It cannot go away," he said as he pointed to the pile of paper. "You can see that I am only a very junior officer as I am having to be here on a Saturday night. You should address it to the commandante in Como who will surely give it the attention it deserves."

Schaffer understood enough to know that they ought to leave the office and go into the restaurant next door for a good stiff drink. Robert leaned across the counter and took a long look at the officer's identification badge. Once he had it in mind, he extracted a piece of paper from his wallet and a pen from his pocket and made careful note of his name and badge number and said in very slow and precise Italian "You have been very helpful, officer. I must commend you to your superiors in Como and to my friends in the ministry in Rome. You have been most understanding."

The change in the demeanor of the young carabinieri was noticeably improved but in no way panicky. He tipped his hat, went with them to the door and then stopped them before they could go through it, saying "We," with great emphasis on the 'we', "must do something. We cannot simply let this incident become one more unresolved criminal act."

The papers were completed in a matter of minutes. He even put the papers on the top of his pile and promised to begin his investigation that very evening.

The encounter with the young officer and the half hour it took to complete the report had a calming influence on both Robert and Bonnie. They both were more relaxed after the half hour drive from the service area to Ciano's magnificent villa that was set on the side of a small mountain overlooking Lake Como. It was ablaze with lights, and hundreds of gas lanterns, set about fifty feet apart, lined each side of a half mile long winding private entry road, giving the whole scene a roaring twenties film-like atmosphere. Bonnie and Robert had recovered their composure and as they remained convinced that someone had deliberately tried to ram them, they were glad they had filed the report. "Bonnie," Robert began evenly, "when we get back to Milan I'm going to get in touch with my Sicilian Family to arrange a visit to my cousin. I should have done it long ago," he said emphatically.

"They have asked us to visit more than once. Maybe we should take a long weekend to do so," Bonnie suggested.

"Great idea. I've wanted to see Sicily in any case," responded Robert. I'll call my cousin on Monday.

Despite the evening's early winter air, Ciano was on the terrace of his home welcoming his guests as uniformed men opened car doors and placed the arriving vehicles out of sight at the back of the villa. When their turn came, Ciano treated them like royalty. He took Bonnie by the elbow and personally led them into the flower adorned entry hall which was papered with huge oil paintings of what seemed to be Ciano's ancestors judging by the similarities between Ciano and the portrait of a man set in a place of honor at the back of the hall. An enormous chandelier filled with lighted real candles cast a flickering, golden glow over arriving guests, butlers, footmen and maids who were showing guests wishing to spend the night and to freshen up from their journey, to their rooms. Ciano assumed we were staying the night and ordered a footman to retrieve our luggage from our car and to place it in the room next to his own.

The first guests to whom they were introduced were the US Consul General, Mr. John Tremarco, an elegant looking American in his early fifties and his young, film star beautiful, Milanese wife, Anna who immediately attached herself to Robert much to Bonnie's surprise. Ciano sensed Bonnie's fellings and Robert was shocked when a very tall and handsome, southern Italian looking man that Robert estimated to be in late 30's materialized almost out of nowhere, took Bonnie by the arm and Robert thought swept her off her feet. These were magical moments and Schaffer sensed that it would take great self- control from both of them not to be swept up in the glamour of it all.

Schaffer wasn't wrong. An hour later, after too many glasses of champagne and fists full of caviar, he was seated next to the gorgeous Anna at the center of a fifty foot long, ten foot wide dining table set with china, crystal and silver bearing the Ciano family coat of arms. Huge candelabras, which were set on long, slender, silver stems so as not to interrupt the guests' view, graced the table every few meters. Bonnie sat almost opposite him, ensconced between a handsome young man who turned out to be Ciano's son and heir, Alberto, and the southern Italian man who Robert learned later was a famous Roman artist. As Robert searched for familiar faces among Ciano's fifty or so other guests, he felt Anna's delicate hand making its way slowly up the inside of his leg as she chatted effortlessly in German with the man on her right. It turned out that he was from the super rich and powerful Von Lasttenburg family that has and still controls so much of Germany's land and industry.

The much older but, in her own way, even more beautiful wife of Ciano, the Contessa Maria-Teresa, whose family were related to the Austrian Hapsburgs, sat on Robert's left, speaking to him in a soft Parisian accented French that Schaffer could understand without effort. Her own English was nearly perfect but she thought Robert might enjoy practicing his French that was and remains fluent as a result of the time he studied in Paris in the winter of 1968-69. "Don't let Anna's attentions frighten you," she was saying as her eyes searched for Anna's hand, which was now hidden from view by my napkin and the large tablecloth, but which was gently and expertly caressing his leg. "She's a lovely, lively girl who adores her husband but needs occasional diversions from her all too serious responsibilities as wife to the American Counsul General."

"Oh, they don't frighten me, Contessa. I only wish I knew her ... better," Robert stammered as Anna's hand cupped his balls. He felt both the Contessa and Anna's eyes on him.

The Contessa giggled like a little girl when she saw what was happening and after a moment decided to intervene. She leaned forward so that she could see Anna clearly. "Anna, Anna, darling," she called to her. "You are neglecting Mr. Schaffer and me."

"Oh, am I?" Anna said cheerfully as she removed her hand and gave me a little, red-faced smile. "Do forgive me," she pleaded. "I see Eric so infrequently."

"Tell me, Anna," said Ciano's wife. "Will you and John be going to Saint Moritz for Christmas or staying in Milan?"

As the ladies chatted about plans for the winter months Robert had a few moments to survey the room and to watch Bonnie enjoying herself with Ciano's handsome son and the Roman who he had learned was an artist of some standing. She had both men locked in conversation about art and her work at the Milan Academy.

"Robert," a man's voice was calling him from the other side of the table.

He looked across the table and the familiar voice began to awaken memories of the man's face.

"You don't remember me, do you?" asked the familiar, American voice.

Schaffer hated it when people made you play guessing games and felt like saying so. He looked him over carefully and couldn't place him but both the voice and face begin to remind him of a young, much thinner man he had become acquainted with in Paris during his year of studies. Suddenly the face was beginning to resemble that man, an American he had met when he was doing research at the Biblioteque Nationale. He finally made the connection. "Max," Robert asked. "Is that really you?"

"Body and soul, Robert, body and soul."

Robert hadn't heard from him since Paris even though they had both promised to stay in touch. "Did you go into the Foreign Service after all or succumb to your father's pressures?" Robert asked, remembering that Max's family controlled one of Wall Street's smaller but most prestigious investment banks, Feathers & Co., which bore Max's family name, and that his father wanted him to join and eventually take over the firm despite Max's complete lack of interest in anything remotely connected with banking, other than his own bank account.

"Foreign Service, sort of," he said with that now much more familiar smile. "Let's catch up on all tomorrow," he offered. I gather from Roberto that you and your wife are spending the night and so are we."

"Who is we?"

Max pointed toward the far end of the table where Schaffer could see several voluptuous young women, any one of which would have been more than satisfactory in the pure looks department. "Take your pick of that lot down there," he said in an off-hand way, as he nodded again toward them.

"I'll take them all," Robert said diplomatically and, frankly, very honestly, as they were all absolutely stunning.

He mouthed "see you for a brandy".

Robert nodded his agreement and then turned his attention back to the companions on his right and left. He decided now was as good a time as any to heighten his own standing. "Do either of you know the Ritz Hotel in St. Moritz?" Robert asked them both. Their friends, the Mancinis, had forewarned them that, as a little girl Ciano's wife had spent World War II with her parents at that famous hotel and that she adored it and the family that owned it.

The Contessa and Anna looked at each other. Anna bowed her head in deference to the Contessa. "I know it quite well, Mr. Schaffer," she said, "quite well indeed. And I believe Anna and her husband holiday there regularly. Isn't that right, Anna?" she asked. When Anna had nodded her agreement, the Contessa said: "Why do you ask?"

"I gather it is to be put on the market in the next few months," Robert responded. The current owners are rumored to have some temporary financial difficulties," he volunteered, "and I thought you and the Conte might have an interest in purchasing the hotel. If you do, you would need to move quite quickly." The Cianos had begun to make investments in luxury hotels just after Roberto's marriage to Maria-Teresa, whose family had always held investments in this industry, so Schaffer was fairly sure that this news would provoke an animated response and he looked forward to it and to the possibility of creating a deal.

Chapter 5

Sexy and Dangerous People

The look of pure horror on the Contessa's face said it all. She had no idea that St. Moritz's famous Ritz Hotel was to be put on the market or that the established Swiss family that owned it, whose members she had known for over half a century, might have financial difficulties.

Schaffer had no idea whether the owners of the hotel had financial problems either or whether or not the hotel was for sale. He had decided, as a result of his recent experience in New York and even more recently in Milan, that creating deals doesn't depend on these types of facts. Most of the guys that he had worked for in New York had found that knowledge of this type actually inhibited new ideas and approaches. In any case, it was clear to Schaffer at this point in his banking career that deal creation depended on knowing people, knowing which people know which other people and what people want to achieve. All the rest of it seemed to him to be technical stuff and few real deals that he had seen, heard about, or worked on, the ones that people needed or wanted to get done, had been concluded or failed based on such considerations. He knew that economic conditions in Europe at the time were difficult and at best unpredictable so virtually anyone could have had "temporary financial difficulties". He figured if such difficulties did indeed exist, so much the better, as a deal would be more rather than less likely. From his experience to date, he was confident that some of the last people in the world to find out about such problems would be close friends of the owners of the hotel.

"Surely, you are mistaken," said the Contessa, in little more than a whisper.

Robert paused as if he were rethinking what he had just said. "Contessa, I only wish I were mistaken. Most sincerely, Contessa, I wish it were not true," he said clearly, carefully and succinctly, trying his best to replicate what he had seen the senior deal guys in New York do with important clients.

The Contessa's eyes fixed Schaffer's and he felt like she was trying to drill a hole into the center of his brain to check whether he was being truthful. Finally, she asked, "Who has told you this news?"

"I am not at liberty to say," Contessa. "Banking secrecy laws," Schaffer said by way of explanation, a comment that Marco Antinori used as an excuse for virtually everything. "I am, however, prepared to assist you in this matter, if you have an interest."

She looked at him and said very softly "You know that I must have an interest, that our family," she corrected herself, "must have an interest."

Schaffer merely nodded his agreement and waited for her to make the next move. He was really enjoying this and only felt a bit guilty about the discomfort he was creating for the Contessa. Hell, she was probably just as big a crook as her husband, he thought.

"We are boring, Anna, Robert. You are staying the night, I believe?" she asked.

"Yes, yes we are," he replied.

"Good. We'll take this up in the morning, if that is all right with you," she said it as a statement and then turned her attention to her other dinner partner and left Robert to fend for himself with the playful Anna Tremarco who had been sitting quietly and listening very attentively to his exchange with the Contessa.

"John would be interested in what you've been saying," she said matter of factly. "May I tell him?"

"Of course, Anna, by all means, do let him know if you think he would be interested," he said with more calm than he actually felt.

Ciano suddenly stood up, looked up and down the table at his guests from his own position in the middle, and waited for the conversation to die down. Just before he begin speaking, I felt Anna's hand give my leg one last little caress as she leaned toward my ear and whispered "John has to go back to Milan tonight, 'business'," she said by way of explanation, "but I will be staying over. My room is just across from yours. I hope you're able to join me."

Schaffer shouldn't have been surprised. He hadn't exactly discouraged her. But he wasn't used to these sorts of things so he turned to see if she were teasing. She didn't return his gaze as she had already switched her attention to Ciano who was just starting to say a few words but suddenly he was very sure that she wasn't jesting.

When Ciano finished speaking he invited the men to join him for coffee and brandy in the lounge and suggested that the ladies could join the men for dancing in the ballroom after they had freshened up. Robert waved to Bonnie as she joined Anna and the other women and had mixed emotions when he saw how happy she looked. She had clearly had a great time with Alberto Ciano, who had flirted outrageously with her throughout the dinner, and also with the Roman artist who seemed almost too comfortable with her. It was, he thought, as though he already knew her. As Robert watched her leave the dining room, he wondered jealously whether the younger Ciano had been caressing Bonnie's leg during dinner and, if so, what she had done about it. The thought of her doing to Alberto what Anna had done to him seemed unlikely but she had mentioned spicing up their marriage only a few weeks ago so he didn't rule it out and felt the jealousy building-up once again.

Once inside the comfortable, dark wood, paneled lounge, Max Feathers made his way over to Robert. "Well, well, Robert," he greeted him. You're looking well and so is Bonnie. I see you're still together," he said as though he was surprised that they were.

"Very together," Robert responded. "And you're not looking too bad yourself, although you may have put on a few pounds since Paris, which is undoubtedly why I didn't recognize you at first," he said, as he tried to find a lighthearted way of apologizing to him.

You're being generous," he responded, as he put one of his bear-like arms around Robert's shoulders in the way that Americans sometimes do. "I've put on almost fifty pounds since you saw me last and its all muscle!" he boasted.

Schaffer had another look at him. "You're right," he said, somewhat surprised. "It does look like muscle. I didn't know 'bulking up' was a requirement of our State Department," Robert said facetiously.

"I'm not exactly in the State Department. I joined the Department of Defense instead. Less fags in the DoD!" he joked.

Schaffer laughed aloud. "Which of the pretty young things is yours? Robert asked.

"I'll introduce you when we go upstairs. She's the prettiest of the lot, loves sports and music and she hasn't got a brain in her head!" he said laughing. "Never thought I'd marry one like her. You know how I was, always looking for the intellectual type."

Robert laughed aloud again. "Bull shit! All you ever cared about was boobs and bums. Bonnie and I could never figure out why you decided to study in Paris. Naples would have been much more up your alley."

Roberto de Ciano saw them laughing and talking together and left the small group of guests clustered around him to join them. "I didn't know you two knew each other," he said as he put large glasses with huge helpings of what looked like brandy in their hands.

"We met in Paris in 1968. We were both doing research for PhD's in international studies," Max told the elder Ciano. "We're just catching up."

"Then I won't interrupt," he said affably. "As long as you are enjoying yourselves," and moved on to another group of guests before either of them could object.

Bonnie and Robert were among the last of the guests to go to their rooms. Robert had a fabulous time dancing, sipping champagne and chatting with people that he thought were the most interesting he had ever met. He looked at his watch as Bonnie closed the door to their room. "My god, Bonnie," he said with genuine surprise, "its three thirty. Can you believe it?"

"I really can't," she said. "I've never enjoyed a party more."

Robert watched her stroll over to the large French doors that opened onto a terrace that overlooked the front gardens of Ciano's villa and the lake beyond. She drew back the heavy green brocade curtains which the night chamber maid had closed earlier in the evening and gently pulled open the doors, allowing the crisp night air to pore in and clear the room of the stale air which had been warmed by the pre-war heating system. "You look lovely, darling," he said.

She turned and looked at him, started to say something and then turned back to look out at the lights coming from the tiny villages which dotted the mountain on the other side of the lake. "Come and hold me tightly, Robert. Look at the lights," she was saying.

He went across the room, put his arms around her and felt her give off a little shiver as he gave her a squeeze. "Come to bed, Bonnie," he finally said.

She turned, gave him a little kiss and said quickly "You go to sleep, sweet. I need a hot bath, just to relax."

"Why not wait until morning?" he responded, hoping that she would change her mind. He had been looking forward to making love and saw that possibility fading rapidly. "Besides," he added "we don't have our own bathroom and...."

But she interrupted him saying "I asked a maid to run one for me just before we came up. The bathroom is just up the hall. I hope you don't mind, darling."

It was pointless to argue. Once Bonnie made her mind up about something like this, it was best to simply agree. "All right," he said, and gave her a kiss on the cheek.

She turned, picked up her nightgown and robe from where the maid had left them on the bed, waved to me and went to the door. He returned her wave with a smile and begin to undress as she went out the door. As he lay in the dark wishing Bonnie were with him, he wondered whether Anna was still awake lying in the dark, waiting for him. He brushed the thought aside as quickly as it arose but couldn't help returning to it. After several minutes of trying to force himself to put Anna out of his mind he slipped out of bed and went in search of Bonnie. Their room was at the beginning of a long dark and narrow corridor that opened onto at least ten rooms on either side. Robert looked down the hall in search of a room with light coming from under the door. He immediately saw several and quickly realized it would be ridiculous to go along the corridor listening and/or knocking on doors in the middle of the night in search of Bonnie and just as he turned to go back into their room, the door across the hall opened and the completely naked figure of Anna came gradually into view as she saw that it was him. "Hurry inside, darling, before someone sees you," she whispered. He hesitated and she added, "Don't worry about Bonnie. I saw her go into the Roman artist's room when I came out of the bath." Schaffer must have looked more than just surprised because she gave out a little giggle before she left her door fully ajar and walked back to her bed allowing him to see her in all her glory. Her perfect figure was highlighted by the light coming from a small candle set on a table in the center of the room and was only covered by her long blonde her which now fell all the way to the middle of her back. He looked up and down the corridor and, seeing it was clear, moved quickly into Anna's room and closed the door behind him.

"Take off your clothes, Robert. Come to me and make me glow inside and out," she ordered him lustily. "By now Carlo will be inside Bonnie and I need you inside me."

"Carlo?" he asked lamely.

"Forget him for now, my darling. Come to me. I will make you feel wonderful all over."

Schaffer hesitated only a moment for Anna had opened her arms and legs to him and she looked more glorious than any woman he had ever had. He tore off his clothes and got in beside her and when she touched his huge erection and began to stroke him expertly, passion overcame his worries about Carlo and Bonnie. He kissed her all over her face while massaging her full breasts and erect nipples. She moaned as his hand slid between her legs. "You're so wet, Anna, so ready, darling."

"Put it in me, Robert, but gently, darling. You are very big."

Schaffer got between her legs and bent down to lick her open, wet pussy. She moaned and arched her back in response and used her hands to push his face into her. Robert put his tongue inside her and then used it to make her have a little come.

"Robert, please, darling, put your cock in me, angel. I need to feel you inside me and want your come in me."

Schaffer used his knees to spread her legs as far as they would go and then lifted her arse off of the bed and slowly entered her. Anna arched her back and made it easy to penetrate her. "Oh, that's glorious, darling, really lovely. You feel so big inside me."

Robert could not help himself and lost all control as she writhed on the bed and told him "fuck me hard, Robert, give it to me, harder, harder."

"You are such a great fuck, Anna, my God, I really need you, babe. Spread those legs and suck me all the way in you."

When she did just that, he began to come and in response Anna's body began to shudder. "Oh, my God, Robert, I'm coming, darling, coming all over you. Fill me up with your sperm, baby, fill me all up." As he did so, Anna's head began to uncontrollably move wildly back and forth on her pillow as she screamed, "Fuck my brains out, Robert. That's it, angel, that's it, ahhhhhhh."

Robert was back in bed, faking sleep when Bonnie returned. She slide in almost silently and, within what seemed like seconds, was asleep. He wanted to wake her, to confront her but his own jealousy was overcome by guilt for his time with Anna and instead he lay awake long enough to see the first signs of the morning sun wondering in which direction their lives were headed.

It was late morning when a light tapping on their door awakened them. A butler handed him a note and left before Robert had a chance to read it. He opened it quickly and recognized Roberto de Ciano's hand. "Sorry to disturb your well-deserved sleep! A few of us are going for a light lunch and a game of golf in about half an hour. We'd love you to join us. Maria-Teresa has plans for Bonnie. Yours, ever, Roberto." Schaffer's surprise at the intrusion did not last long. His watch said 11:30. Bonnie was still sound asleep and looked as though she would be for hours unless Maria-Teresa ordered a maid to throw cold water on her or Carlo pounced again.

Robert found his casual clothes in the second of the dresser drawers he opened and left the room with his clothes over one arm and his shoes clutched under the other, clad in a robe. As he went in search of the bathroom, a floor maid spotted him from the other end of the corridor and guided him to a suite of rooms which housed a bathroom, separate toilet and a small dressing room where a pot of hot coffee had been left on a hot plate along with what proved to be country fresh cream, homemade croissants, jam, etc. By the time he had dressed it was nearly noon so he only had a sip of coffee and two bites of a croissant before making his way to the main hall downstairs where Roberto and Alberto stood talking with Max Feathers. Alberto saw him first. "Robert, good morning. Hope you slept well!" he said in that good-natured, "your house is my house" way so characteristic of his race.

Robert greeted him and the others warmly. "Morning to you Alberto, Roberto, Max" he said, nodding to them. "Hope I haven't kept you waiting?"

"Not at all," Roberto answered for all of them. "We should apologize to you. Virtually everyone else is asleep but Max thought you'd be upset if we didn't include you in our game," Roberto said as he turned to Max for confirmation.

"Yeah," said Max, "you can blame me, Robert. I have to leave by five-thirty this afternoon and wanted a chance for a good chat before then."

"Right," said Roberto. Let's get moving or we'll miss our tee off time."

They were only five minutes from the very private and very exclusive Lago di Como Golf Club and, after a lobster salad and a glass of Gavi di Gavi were on the first tee by 12:30. On the third hole Robert had the honors following a thirty-foot birdie putt. His golf in those days was praiseworthy, unlike the horrible game he scrapes together now, but he hit a ball into the trees on the right after Alberto complimented him on how charming and 'yes'-pretty Bonnie was as they walked from the second green to the third tee. God, he thought, maybe Bonnie screwed Alberto and not the Roman as Anna had suggested. As he thought about the possibility of Alberto putting his cock inside Bonnie, Robert wanted to finish him right there but, in the hours of sleeplessness following Bonnie's return to bed, he had resolved to torture the interloper both mentally and physically before dispatching him. He had also resolved to sort out his life!

Both Cianos hit long and down the left-hand side of the fairway, undoubtedly the place to be, Robert thought at the time, and Max followed Robert into the trees on the right. Roberto's ball had finished in heavy rough on the left so they went in search of his ball and left Robert and Max on our own. "You were a scratch golfer in Paris, if I remember correctly, Max," Robert said, remembering how frustrating he had found it when they played there together. "You hit that drive like you wanted to be in here," Robert added as they made their way into the woods.

"I did," he said.

"Did what?" Robert asked without really thinking, as he lifted a branch out of the way and uncovered what proved to be his ball.

"Hit my drive in here, deliberately," he answered.

Robert turned around and saw a new, different Max, one he had not really seen before. He looked very serious and very confident and business like, and he had a message. "Robert, you need to know that these people, the Cianos," he said their name with distaste, "are ... dangerous," he finally selected a word.

Schaffer studied him and understood. "You're not speculating are you, Max?"

He looked at Schaffer and paused, giving very careful thought to what he was going to say next. Robert couldn't see even a trace of uncertainty or nervousness. "No, Robert, I'm not speculating," he finally said.

Robert supposed he should have gone "all weak at the knees" as the English would say but the confirmation of his own suspicions about this powerful Italian family had the exact opposite effect. Schaffer had been uncertain as to how to play his next shot. At first glance it looked hopeless but further study told him he could put it on the green with a good, crisp, accurate swing at and through the ball. "Thanks, Max," he said, as he slowly took his backswing and then came through the ball flawlessly. "I think their bark is worse than their bite but, if you're right, I guess I'll just have to help you cut their balls off." They both watched Robert's ball sail almost impossibly between two trees that were between them and the green, land just over the sand trap guarding the front of the green and roll to what looked from where they were standing very close to the pin.

"Don't underestimate Maria-Teresa Ciano," Max said without even commenting on his shot. "Or her step-daughter for that matter."

"Step daughter?" Robert asked.

"Yea," said Max. "Anna Tremarco is the Contessa's step daughter. Roberto is Anna's father by his first marriage."

"What are you saying Max? What are you implying?" Schaffer asked as he turned to see and hear his response.

"Robert," he addressed him very seriously. "Look beneath the surface. Don't accept anything you see in Italy at face value. And," he paused briefly as he looked away from him and began walking to where his own errant shot lay, "make sure Bonnie does the same thing, especially where Alberto Ciano and her Roman artist friend are concerned."

Even now when Schaffer remembers this chapter of their lives, he feels the same pain and humiliation he felt then. Max knew what had gone on the night before between him and Anna and Bonnie and it would seem now, "her Roman friend," or he at least suspected what had gone on and what might occur in the future. That alone was bad enough. The possibility that the Roman artist's and Anna Ciano's attentions to him and Bonnie were directed by Roberto de Ciano was more than just a shock. Schaffer had only been in Italy at this point in his life for months, not years, and he had not yet understood that Machiavelli was not just philosophizing, that he was telling it as it was.

When he returned to Ciano's villa a few hours later Robert found Bonnie, surrounded by Maria-Teresa, Anna and a small group of other people who had spent the night, near the large windows looking over the lake in the main living room. Most of the guests who had availed themselves of Roberto de Ciano's hospitality seemed to have departed. The few that remained were listening to and watching Bonnie as she sketched. Robert walked over to where they were standing and came up behind Bonnie to see what she was drawing and forced himself to relax and to put the painful thoughts of Bonnie and her Roman friend and of Alberto out of his mind. "I hope you're charging for the lesson, Bonnie," he quipped.

Everyone but Bonnie laughed. She continued with her work and finally said "I suppose I really should, shouldn't I?" and then she laughed as well, turned to Robert, stood on her tip toes and gave him a kiss. "Play well?" she asked.

For some reason he was surprised by the question. He felt like telling her and the others exactly what had happened. He and Max had trounced the Cianos. Instead he simply said "Very."

"Good," she said. And then she turned back to her little group of admirers, who had refocused their own attentions on the easel that held Bonnie's work, and said to them "if you want to see the completed version, you'll just have to come to my studio in Milan."

There was a sort of communal groan to which Bonnie responded: "Robert and I need to be on our way. We have a dinner tonight in Milan, don't we darling?"

Robert knew of no dinner but certainly was more than ready to see the last of the Cianos, especially Alberto. The thought of the tall, handsome and 'yes' young Ciano with Bonnie was beginning to sink in all too completely. The older man, the Roman artist seemed less of a threat to their relationship than the handsome young aristocrat. As far as he knew Bonnie had only one other lover in her life and that was before they were married and during an interval when they had briefly gone their own separate ways. He had several women before they were married but no one other than Anna since then. "Unfortunately, yes," he said.

Less than an hour later they were on their way back to Milan. Neither of them said very much and, as the mountains faded into the evening mist that rapidly became a thick fog, Bonnie curled up and fell sound asleep. His own unpleasant thoughts also faded away as the fog caused him to focus all his attentions on survival. The lights of Milan were a welcome sight, as was their apartment building that was located on a little street not far from the bank. Bonnie awakened the moment he slipped the car into its assigned spot in the underground garage located below their building. As she sat upright rubbing her eyes, Robert got out, retrieved the luggage from the boot and met Bonnie at the elevator. "You, OK, Bonnie?" He asked as he held open the door for her.

"Fine," she said with more than a trace of melancholy in her voice, "just a bit sleepy. I'll be great after a good night's sleep."

Chapter 6

The Elephant Hunter

The week before Christmas and the Christmas holidays themselves passed quietly and all too quickly as far as Robert was concerned and everything seemed to return to normal. Bonnie had been calm and just seemed to enjoy being around him and their lovely apartment and a Milan covered by fresh, almost daily snow showers. They had made an overnight trip to Monte Carlo between Christmas and the New Year that was great fun especially as they won a little over $1000 at the famous Casino. Their winnings had paid for three great dinners in Milan's finest restaurants and they had spent a few lovely afternoons with their great friends the Mancinis and their family. Bonnie had never once mentioned the Ciano's or the weekend with them and Robert had been lulled into a false sense of complacency.

The wonderful holiday season was stood on its head when he arrived on the mezzanine floor of the bank on the morning of 7 January, Robert's first day back in the office since the Christmas-New Year break. Antinori's secretary motioned for him to go into Marco's office. Robert knocked and opened the door without waiting for an answer and found Antinori pacing back and forth in what had been Franco's office until just a few weeks ago. "Robert," he greeted him as though he were in another world when he saw him come in. "I'm glad you're here, he whispered."

Any idiot could see he was extremely upset and he looked terrified. "What is wrong, Marco?" I asked him. "You look awful," Robert added, as he saw Antinori's hands begin to shake.

He went behind his desk and stood momentarily behind his chair which was pushed almost completely under it, bent his tall, stork-like frame forward and put his palms face down on either side of the leather blotter which lay in the middle of his desk. A thin layer of many pieces of paper covered all but the silvery edges of the blotter and seemed to have been placed there to hide something from view. "He's here," was all he said as he begin to slowly remove each piece of paper from its place on the blotter and, in what amounted to slow motion, put it in a neat little pile off to the right, next to his telephone. Eventually, very tidy little rows of red, white, and green pills were revealed. They were assembled in a formation reminiscent of an impressionist Italian flag.

Robert was nearly speechless. A year in New York City had not overcome his formative years in the then relatively drug free society of a small mid-west American town and the sight of row upon row of various sized and colored pills gave pause for more than a little thought. He finally asked, "Who's here, Marco?"

"The elephant hunter," Antinori said in Italian.

"The elephant hunter..." and then Schaffer remembered a story Rudi Cortina had told him on his second or third night in Milan about a very clever but frail little South African called Ross who had been sent to Milan by the supermen in authority in New York to teach Marco Antinori how to build the lending side of the business. Antinori was not only insulted but he saw the man as a threat and had made his life a complete misery. He had humiliated him publicly on more than one occasion and did little things solely for the purpose of annoying him. The last straw for Ross was when Antinori used the exhibits from a presentation Ross was making to officers from all over Europe to blow his nose loudly. Ross had finally asked for and received a transfer but, on the day he left, he vowed to return with his elephant guns to blow Antinori away. He had departed Milan just before Robert arrived but since that time he had periodically sent Antinori postcards of professional hunters carrying their guns or exhibiting tusks or whatever. Each card, according to the people in the post room, had some kind of threat written on it. The last card had been rumored to say something like "I'll be there shortly and I'm going to blow you from Milan to Cape-Town". "You mean Alec Ross, Marco?"

Antinori looked up from the little rows of pills, eyed Schaffer for a moment and then looked down again and begin to select one pill after another. Once he had a multi-colored hand full, he popped them into his month, picked up his ever-present bottle of San Pellegrino and washed them down. "Yeah," he eventually responded, this time in English. "Alec Ross, the guy with the big guns, the elephant guns!"

Schaffer couldn't think of anything to say or do but he was saved from his predicament by uncontrolled screaming from outside Antinori's door which burst open and there was Ross in hunter's garb with two of the most enormous guns Robert had ever seen in his entire life. "Holy shit," Schaffer said in great alarm.

Ross looked at Robert and said in English laced with a South African background: "So you're the cretin that has taken my place" and then he leveled the gun my way.

Out of the corner of his eye Robert saw Antinori throwing up his pills and whatever it was he had for breakfast all over himself and his desk but now was no time to worry about him. "I didn't take anybody's place" Robert shouted at him. "I'm Robert Schaffer, the Head of the Credit Department."

Ross said "OK. Outta here Schaffer and close the door after you."

Robert did as he was told and, as he carefully made his way out of the office, he saw Antinori, his shirt dripping with throw up, trying to back away from the guns which were now leveled unmistakably in his direction. There was an enormous explosion from one of the guns and Antinori cried out as a huge hole opened in the wall about two feet away from where he was now kneeling. "Close the fucken door," Ross told Robert.

When Schaffer was safely outside he managed to find the little button under the desk of Antinori's secretary and he pushed it all the way in which caused every alarm in the building and the one at the police station on the backside of Piazza Cordusio to go off. And then there were three more explosions, which were only slightly muffled by the closed door, at about two or three second intervals. Suddenly Antinori's door crashed open and Ross came running through it with his guns held high and with a wild, animal like expression on his face. For the first time Schaffer saw that he had grenades attached to a leather strap that hung down from his neck. Having worked in the building for a number of years he knew his way around and made for a recessed door that lead directly to the underground parking garage.

Robert thought he was gone but, just as he turned to go in and see what was left of Antinori, Ross called out to Robert: "Schaffer." When Robert turned to face him he said in a very cool and calm voice that was laced with hatred and menace, "Unfortunately, he'll probably be fine. This time I deliberately missed him. I'd hoped he'd have a heart attack but I think the jerk just plain fainted. When he wakes up tell him that I'll be back and that when I do come back I'm going to blow his balls off, literally. And, if you've got any brains at all you'll get out of this insane asylum like yesterday!" And then he was gone.

Robert found Antinori out cold behind his desk lying in his own filth. He was just bending down when the first police begin to pour through the door with guns held high. They motioned for him to move away and it all became too familiar as Schaffer was marched down a corridor and left on his own in a little room with a guard at the door. This time, however, there was no Marco Antinori to whisk him away, to save him from what became a lengthy and more than just a little stressful interview. The enquiries over Bob Franco's death took place only a few weeks previously and now, here he was again, at the center of what looked like another death and this time there was a smoking gun. After several hours Schaffer's interviewer was called away. Robert sat back and wished he hadn't quit smoking just before he was assigned to Milan. God, he thought, a cigarette would be wonderful! As he sat contemplating buying a pack as soon as they let him out of his imprisonment, the door opened and a new, smiling face appeared.

"Dottore Schaffer," he begin. "I am so sorry we have had to detain you. Dottore Antinori has recovered and has insisted that you saved his life. Please accept my apologies for your temporary confinement."

"No problem," Robert said simply. He looked at his watch and seeing it was only noon made his way back to his office where he found Mrs. Gavi arranging some papers for his review.

"Dottore Schaffer, are you all right?" she asked him sincerely.

"Could be a lot better, Annarosa," he answered honestly.

"They say you were there when Mr. Ross shot his guns in Dottore Antinori's office. Was it horrible, Dottore Schaffer?" she asked solicitously.

Robert thought for a moment and knew he should put a brave face on it but he was fed up. Ross may have been right. Maybe he should get out of the insane asylum, as he had put it. "Yes,

Annarosa," he said. "It was horrible, to say the very least," he concluded with more than just a little emphasis.

"I knew he would come back, Dottore Schaffer. I should have warned you about him."

Schaffer looked at her carefully and could see that she was serious. "You couldn't have known that he would do what he did today, Annarosa. Please, don't blame yourself," he told her sincerely.

"Thank you. You are a very kind man," she said to him.

Schaffer knew she meant what she was saying and what pained him was that she was basically right or would have been right had she said it just a few weeks before. He was beginning to feel more guilt about his own weakness with Anna and, as he sat there he begin to think that it was just possible that Bonnie had simply taken a long bath and had not gone to Alberto's or the Roman's room. But that thought was dashed almost immediately as his phone buzzed and Annarosa put Bonnie on the line. "Robert, I heard from Annarosa what happened. Are you all right?"

"I'm fine, Bonnie, absolutely fine."

"Oh, that is great news. Annarosa really had me worried for a moment but I can hear in your voice that you're OK."

"Yes, darling," Robert forced himself to say as the naked body of Anna Ciano forced its way back into his mind. Being back in the office had wiped out almost two weeks of holiday bliss. It was as though Christmas and New Year had not even occurred.

"Would it be all right, then," she went on, "if I took a few days away, with Maria-Teresa. She rang this morning and asked if I'd like a little break. She's going to St. Moritz this evening to check on her friends, the ones that you told her may be having financial difficulty and may want to sell their hotel and wants me to come with her."

Robert felt his pulse quicken. He just couldn't believe that she'd be talking about going away with what he had just been through but he wasn't going to change anything by asking her to stay behind. "If you'd like to, Bonnie, yes, please agree to go. It will do you good." He had almost said "us" but decided against annoying her. He was finding it difficult to think.

"Is there anything I can do on your deal, Robert?" he heard her ask. She took his silence as a 'no' and went on to try to convince him. "I mean I'll be with her for four or five days...."

She continued to speak but four or five days in the circumstances were eternity as far as he was concerned and he wasn't really listening to what she was saying now.

"Robert, are you listening to me?"

"Of course, I am" he lied as he tried to refocus.

"Well is it OK?"

"Is what OK?"

"You weren't listening. It drives me crazy when you don't listen to me," she said angrily.

"Sorry," he said. "Maybe it's just the incident here this morning."

"Oh, God, Robert, I'm sorry. I," and then she paused and fought for what she wanted to say, "I had forgotten. I'm not myself. That weekend with the Ciano's before Christmas, it's confused me."

Schaffer remembered thinking that he needed to get off the phone or he was going to go crazy! Forgotten the incident! Jesus, what had happened between them, he thought. Alberto or the Roman artist or both had happened! That was for sure.

"Maybe I shouldn't go," she was saying now. "But being with Maria-Teresa could help to influence her and," and then she paused and said "Alberto to use you to help them buy the Ritz."

Robert was listening very carefully now and interrupted her. "What has Alberto got to do with it?" he asked sternly.

"He runs the family hotel business. He wants me to co-ordinate their art purchases. That is what I wanted to ask you before. Is it OK if I take on the appointment? Maria Cortina told me a few minutes that it's a great honor and that it would be rude to refuse it."

Robert knew that Maria would support Bonnie in almost anything she wanted to do as Bonnie had stood up for her when she was so worried about going to New York. All he said was "Why are you asking me, Bonnie? You know I've never stood in the way of your work and never would."

"I know. It's just that there will be some travel and I thought I should ask, that's all."

Travel. Alberto. Jesus Christ, he thought, what was happening to my life? How much travel he wanted to ask but decided against it because he knew he wouldn't like the answer. Whether she was going to be around what Robert now thought of as a slimy creep for five or ten days and nights made little difference to him at this stage. One night had already changed his whole, well organized, planned and thoughtout existence. "Bonnie, you need to do what you have to do. I'll be here, God willing, unless of course that lunatic with the guns comes back with those firearms and this time decides to use them on Marco and me and not on the walls."

Rather than having lunch, Robert decided to take a long walk. Piazza Cordusio is situated between the central, birthday cake like Milan Cathedral, the city's most important symbol of its Catholic heritage, and the large and imposing Swartzenburg Castle, which reminds northern Italians of the important role that all things German have played in their history. He decided to walk the distance, which takes about a full hour in good weather, and, if nothing else, today was a beautiful day. The early morning fog had been burnt off quickly by an unseasonably warm January sun and the normal smog generated by the thousands of cars that jammed Milan's streets had been blown up toward the Alps by a stiff, warm breeze coming from the south off the Sahara desert.

He was about ten minutes into his stroll when his previously safe, reasonably well-known and understood, little world was pierced again. A trolley car clanged its bell and caused him to jump back onto a curb from which he had just departed and, when he did, he backed straight into Max Feathers who had obviously been following him. "Hello, Robert," he said cheerfully. "Glad to see you survived old Ross, and his guns, unscathed! How were your holidays?"

"Why are you following me around the streets of Milan, Max?" Robert shouted at him, raising his voice above the din of the trollies, cars, trucks and buses that filled the streets. The very sight of Max brought back all the bad pre-Christmas memories and Robert could not contain his annoyance with the man.

"Why don't we continue our little stroll and I'll tell you what I can," Feathers said it as a statement.

For some reason Robert felt comfortable tagging along. Maybe it was the fact that Feathers exuded confidence and, after what Robert had been through before Christmas, that initially at least was more than welcome. "OK, Max," he agreed.

As they walked toward the Cathedral, Max begin to fill him in. "When I came to Italy late in 1970, one of my tasks was to identify and enlist prominent Italians who could play a role in keeping the communists out of power. Ciano obviously fit the bill perfectly. He helps us and we," Max hesitated, "help him."

As they continued to walk toward the Cathedral, he let his words run around his internal quality control track and they ended in the slow lane. They had just reached the square fronting the Cathedral and he thought it was as good a place as any to tell his friend and johnny come lately spy, Max Feathers, exactly what he thought of that. "Here I am trying to expose a foreign exchange insider dealing ring which is costing innocent people millions and winding up in the back pockets of crooks like Ciano and you're telling me that you, that the US government is helping him!"

"We need him, Robert, we need his support and the support of people like him, at least until we can be sure that the Italian Communist Party won't take power."

"And when you don't need him anymore. What are you going to do then? Send Ross in with his elephant guns?"

"It's a thought," Feathers said laughing. "Come on, Robert. Lighten up. Ciano and the insider-dealing ring aren't your problem. Just do your job, enjoy yourself and stay out of it."

Robert wanted to take Max's statement as advice but it was really like an order. The only thing that hadn't surfaced yet was the "or else". Robert figured he might as well find out the worst so he said "And if I don't or if I can't?"

To his credit Feathers looked Schaffer straight in the eye when he answered. "I won't be able to help you, Robert," and after another one of his pauses, he added, "or Bonnie."

A few months or even weeks earlier, the implication that Bonnie could be harmed, at the bear minimum, would have caused him to kick Feathers right between the legs. It bothered him, all right, but it would be less than honest to say that Schaffer suddenly felt an urge to see old Feather's doubled up on the sidewalk. Maybe I am still in shock, Robert thought. He honestly didn't know but he supposed his reaction, as far as Feathers' was concerned, was pretty unpredictable, given his straight arrow approach to business, his up until now square marriage and sexual habits, and his general overall "tank commander" attitude. So he was not all that surprised when Feathers reacted the way he did when he said "What's in it for me, Max?"

The knowing look, the smile of self-satisfaction, the "everybody has their price" acknowledgement wasn't there. Instead Robert got a harshly stated "what do you mean, what is in it for me?" accompanied by a look of astonishment.

He guessed Max's view of him and whatever book existed on him in government files said he would roll over and wait for his tummy to be scratched or that he would just go back into his little house and wait for the next bone from the table. Rudi Cortina had been urging Robert to become more Italian or to leave Italy. Robert's gut told him that Rudi was right. "You heard me, Max," he said, beginning a speech which he must have rehearsed more than a few times after doing something the hard way, the right way, without any immediate reward only to watch virtually everybody else take the shortcut. "If I'm to get out of your way, if I'm to expose myself to conspiracy charges," Robert almost yelled as a huge truck gunned its engine on the turn just before the entrance to Piazza del Duomo, "if I'm to risk my career by doing nothing about an activity which is not only grossly illegal but is costing my bank millions of dollars every year, what is in it for me?"

He still remembers Max Feathers looking up at the top of the Cathedral and then, slowly, very slowly, turning his gaze back down to him. He said "Robert, if you're a good boy and you mind your own business, you and Bonnie might just make it back to the heartland of America with a few dollars in your pocket and some semblance of a life together, or apart. If you behave like the idiot that you are today, you'll be lucky to be reported missing after a freak avalanche the next time you go skiing."

The mid-west of America was and, in most places more or less still is, a funny old place. People are generally good-natured and they try to be helpful and understanding. There are one or two things most people try to avoid. First, you try your best not to threaten anybody. What is the point of unnecessarily threatening people? Second, you try not to talk down to folks, especially if you come from say, east of Cleveland's Cuyahoga River, or west of the Appalachian Mountains. Old Feathers had the misfortune of not only coming from east of the Appalachian Mountains but the sucker was clearly threatening Schaffer.

"Max," Robert begin pretty unemotionally, remembering what his own Italo-Americano uncle by marriage had told him about how a foreigner should behave in Italy, "I have relatives in this country who can and will protect me or, if that proves to be impossible, they will make anybody pay, and I mean anybody, who hurts me or my family." Schaffer could see from the expression on his face that the mention of relatives in Italy had taken Feathers by surprise. He now looked less sure of himself and so Robert decided to put the knife in. "If Ciano or for that matter anybody else gives me a serious problem, or if Bonnie or I encounter a strange or mysterious health problem or die unaccountably, I doubt anyone will ever even read how he or they perished. I've given my uncle a list of people who might not have the best interests of our family at heart, Max, and unless you plan to do something about me in the next hour or two, I'm gonna put your name right near the top, just for old times sake! By the way, Max, my uncle tends to use people like the elephant hunter to do his dirty work. Crazy people like Ross do crazy, unpredictable things."

Chapter 7

The Road to St. Moritz

Schaffer left Feathers contemplating his navel in front of the Cathedral. Max had tried to turn things around by telling Robert that he was over-reacting, that he had misunderstood him, that he had not intended to threaten him but Feathers had truly infuriated him and Robert was determined not to let him off lightly. He was also more determined than ever to do something, anything about the crooks that were suddenly standing his entire life on its head.

As a first step he abandoned the stroll to the Castle and went instead toward the Old City and his apartment thinking he might catch Bonnie before she left with the Contessa for St. Moritz. He had decided to tell her about his confrontation with Feathers and his revelations about the Cianos and to use that as grounds for severing any ties with them, including Bonnie's acting as an art consultant for the hotel company. As he rounded the corner which opened onto the small tree lined court-yard which fronted his building, he saw Bonnie come out the front entrance dressed in a tight fitting dark brown sweater and skirt with her white mink coat draped over her arm. The outfit showed off her glorious figure and she looked as happy and carefree as he had seen her in a long time. He could not see the Contessa anywhere and was puzzled as to why Bonnie was dressed the way she was. He was just about to call out to her when he saw where she was headed, toward a deep blue Mazzarotti bearing Alberto Ciano and no one else. He literally froze when Bonnie climbed in and leaned across to give him a kiss on the lips just before he reversed the car and headed in the opposite direction so that he could take the exit which lead to the Autostrada del Nord.

Schaffer felt his knees buckle and he dropped to the sidewalk. For a moment he thought he was going to pass out but several passersby rushed over to him and, once satisfied that he was not having a heart attack, helped him to the neighborhood cafe where Pietro, the owner, gave him a large brandy and some strong black coffee. Robert tried to object, as he was feeling sick to his stomach, but it was no use. Pietro was insistent as were his rescuers and Schaffer surrendered to their ministrations. They left him in the care of Pietro and, after another brandy, he made his way to his apartment. Once inside he begin to shake and then to sob like a baby. He managed to get to the bedroom, where, a few hours later, after he had cried his heart out, he fell into a deep and welcome sleep.

When Schaffer awakened, it was dark inside and out. He looked at the illuminated bedside clock and it said 1 AM. He had slept for almost eight hours and he was ravenously hungry. He went into the bathroom, threw some cold water on his face, ran a comb through his hair and quickly put on a clean blue, button down dress shirt and a pair of grey woolen slacks. He found his blazer and put his wallet, passport, some extra cash and the keys to the car and the apartment in the pockets and then had a quick look around the apartment to see if Bonnie had left a note. He wasn't surprised that his search revealed nothing.

A few minutes later he made his way into the quiet streets of the Old City. A freezing fog hung between the buildings and submerged the old gas lamps that still graced this section of Milan, creating an eerie glow. Robert passed a few young and old ladies offering their favors and made his way to a rustic Roman style restaurant that he knew would be open. Three small, connected rooms at the front of the restaurant housed a piano bar which had been founded between the two great wars and the owner's son sat easily behind the keyboard playing a soulful Milanese love song. Robert nodded to him as he passed and took a table just inside the dining area and as close to the piano as possible, a position which commanded a view of the entrance, the bar and the restaurant. He ordered his favorite pasta dish, a simple mixture of oil, garlic and mild red pepper seeds along with a mixed green salad and a half bottle of Amarone, an outstanding north Italian red wine that he relishes to this day. He was not totally surprised to see two men come in within minutes of him being seated. He had wondered if he would be placed under surveillance following his confrontation with Max Feathers earlier in the day and the possibility that these men had been sent to watch him was more than slightly unnerving. They certainly looked the part of a couple of CIA heavies.

His pasta arrived within just a few minutes and, as he devoured it, he washed it down with liberal doses of red wine, as thoughts of Bonnie and Alberto would not stay out of his mind. What in the name of god had happened to us? He wondered. The thought of Bonnie with another man even now seemed completely ridiculous. They were not just in love and good lovers to boot but they were friends, almost soul mates. And God knew that he had compromised on his own career ambitions in choosing to come to Europe rather than making a name for himself at head office as almost everyone he knew had advised, a decision he had taken in order to satisfy Bonnie's lust for all things European. When he had finished his salad and drained the last dregs from his half bottle of wine, he ordered another half of Amorone, this time, an even better vintage together with an excellent selection of cheese including his favourite, Gargonzola. The facts that the younger Ciano was three or four years his junior, that he was handsome and rich and that Robert and Bonnie had been together for over a decade begin to cause the inevitable self-doubt.

As his waiter poured wine from the new bottle into his glass, Robert begin to study the CIA types who were just beginning their own pasta dish accompanied not by wine but by mineral water. Odd, he thought, unless my suspicions are indeed correct. And then his concerns took on a new dimension when he looked up and saw Alec Ross appear in the entrance, glance quickly around and go to the table with the heavies. If he recognized Schaffer, he hid it well. The heavies acknowledged his presence but went on eating as colleagues who had been together earlier would do. Ross threw his coat over a chair at a table near to them, undid his tie and helped himself to some of their mineral water. Within minutes of being settled a waiter appeared and he could hear Ross ordering veal to be done in the Milanese style and a carafe of house red wine. He was about twenty feet away with his back to Schaffer. The three men immediately became immersed in a low volume, English language discussion that soon became intense and then heated. They were arguing about something and Ross seemed to be on the defensive.

Suddenly, just as Robert became convinced that their presence had nothing to do with him, Ross pushed his chair back, turned to face Robert and walked straight over to his table. "Sorry about the unpleasant way we met this morning, Mr. Schaffer. I'm Alec Ross, and I think you could use our help," he said as he motioned toward his colleagues at the other table. "I suggest you come and join us."

The animal hunter attitude was gone and Robert was face to face with a man about his own size and weight but about five years older who seemed as calm, cool, self-assured and collected as the captain of a ship welcoming you on board. It was difficult to resist his approach, particularly in his current state of mind. "OK, Ross," Robert said as he returned his steady gaze and for the first time noticed a light but unmistakable scar running from the corner of his right eye down to his cheek bone. "Maybe you can be helpful to me."

He stood by the side of his table looking down at Robert, a slight smile rising from his lips. "Come on, he said again," and waited until Robert stood up before leading the way back to his colleagues. "Robert Schaffer, meet my friends," he said nodding to the two heavies.

The short, stocky one pushed himself to his feet. "George Kleftis," he said as he grasped Robert's hand firmly.

Robert nodded to Kleftis and turned to shake the other man's hand. "Mario Salerno, at your service," he greeted Robert cheerfully. "Take a seat, Mr. Schaffer."

For some reason Robert felt he was among friends. "I'm pleased to meet you," Robert said and sat in the chair being offered by Salerno.

Salerno turned to Ross and said "Thanks, Alec. It's best if you go now."

Ross nodded and said, "Good luck, Schaffer, you'll need it but at least these guys will help you to level the playing field."

Robert wasn't sure what to say. Hell, he didn't even really know who he was talking to although he was pretty sure that his original feelings about Kleftis and Salerno being part of the CIA weren't all that far off. When Ross had gone, Robert decided to plunge in. "You guys know who I am, where I work and, it seems, where I live. All I know about you are your names, if Kleftis and Salerno are your names, and that you have some connection to what I thought until a few minutes ago was a madman I last saw at the bank terrifying our country manager with his elephant guns."

The two men looked at each other and then back at me. Salerno turned to the next table, grabbed a glass, put it down in front of Robert and filled it with the wine that Ross had left behind. He poured some for himself and Kleftis and then offered Robert a cigarette that he gratefully accepted. "I gather you don't like crooks, Mr. Schaffer," he finally begin.

Seeing that both men expected some sort of response, Robert obliged. "If you know anything more than my working and sleeping habits about me, you know damn well I don't like crooks. Why do you ask?"

Salerno looked down at the table and the stocky Greek American took over. "We don't like them either, Mr. Schaffer, especially if they're ripping off the American banking system. My friend and I work for a division of the US Department of the Treasury, one that takes an interest in things like international bank fraud. For some time now we've been, shall I say, more than just a little interested in the foreign exchange dealing activities of banks like your own."

Robert wasn't sure what to believe but, one thing was for sure, he was going to take some convincing before he accepted what these strangers of the night had to say at face value. Salerno seemed to have read his mind. "Look Schaffer, I know you've been through a lot, today especially. We don't expect you to jump into bed with us tonight. For the moment just listen to what we have to say and we'll find a way to persuade you that we are who we say we are and that we can be helpful to you."

"Fair enough," Robert said. Hell, all he was being asked to do was to drink some decent wine and to listen.

Kleftis took charge again. "We use guys like Ross to keep us informed and to help convince crooks like Antinori to stay on the straight and narrow. Ross went a little overboard today but, hell, the guy tortured Ross for almost three years of his life. He hates Antinori and we can't control everything our informants do. Sometimes it’s actually best for us to just stay out of their way and let nature take its course," he said defensively.

"Ross works for you?" Robert asked incredulously.

"He doesn't work for us in the way you think," answered Salerno. He's an informant. He works for your bank and keeps us informed on what the bank is up to. We help him every now and then with a bit of cash or with getting his guns through customs, that sort of thing."

"Why are you telling me all this?" Robert asked suspiciously.

"We need your help, Mr. Schaffer and we know that you need ours, that is," Kleftis said slowly, "if you intend to stay alive long enough to have a family."

Robert could see he was dead serious and sensed that, unlike Max Feathers, he was not threatening him in any way. "I believe you," he heard himself saying. "I can and will help you if you'll help me and if you can prove that you are who you say you are."

Salerno took out a pack of Winstons, offered Robert one and lit one himself as Kleftis sipped at his wine. Finally, Kleftis asked, "What kind of proof do you want about who we are?"

Robert really didn't know what to ask for. He thought about various types of identification and realized that anything they had with them could be fake. Then he had an idea. "I have a few friends in Washington including a Congressman I worked for during graduate school. Why don't you contact whomever it is you work for and tell them to get in touch with Congressman Mike Rollins. I'll call Rollins tomorrow afternoon Washington time, and if Rollins tells me I can trust you that will be good enough for me."

Kleftis and Salerno exchanged a quick look and then Kleftis said, "OK by us. Assume you hear what you want to hear. Can we get together tomorrow, say late afternoon or early evening, so we can decide next steps?"

"Sure," Robert said. "My wife will be away for a few days so why don't we have an early dinner and then go back to my place."

"Time and place?" asked Kleftis.

"Say seven pm at the Lungarno. You know it?"

"Heard of it. Its near La Scala isn't it?" asked Salerno.

"Yeah, just behind it," Robert said as he took a last gulp of wine, stubbed out his cigarette and called to the waiter for his bill which he quickly settled in cash. "Hope to see you there."

"You will, Mr. Schaffer, you will," said Salerno as Robert got up and left.

Once out in the cold night air Robert decided to take a walk before returning to the apartment, the mere thought of which made it easy to shiver as Bonnie's presence was everywhere. The encounter with Ross and the heavies had blocked her from his senses but now that he was on his own, the sight of Bonnie climbing into Alberto Ciano's Mazzarotti and kissing the Italian on the lips pushed its way back into his mind's eye. He hadn't really allowed himself to think about what it all might mean to the years ahead but he realized that he would have to face the possibility of losing her eventually. Doing so would be easier in the streets of Milan than in the confines of their apartment. The fog had thickened during the last two hours and the eerie glows from the gas lamps had turned from a bright yellow to a golden brown. Robert wasn't tired despite the hour and the stressful day so he decided to finish the walk he had started early the previous afternoon to the Schwartzenburg Castle.

When he came out of Piazza Cordusio and looked north toward the castle, only its watchtowers could be seen through the increasingly dense haze. The single, center headlight of a pre-war tram was becoming larger as it approached from the direction of the fortress and he could hear the melody of its bell toll the warning of its passing. Two men emerged from a small alley and begin to make their way carelessly across the Piazza and Robert was surprised to see that they seemed to be similar in size and appearance to Salerno and Kleftis. He could hear the screech of tires in the distance and seconds later a non-descript, dark car materialized from a side street and gunned its engine in an effort to cross the Piazza before the tram. The men didn't have a chance. He saw them silhouetted against the castle's front entrance by the tram's center light just before the dark car hit them full force from behind and literally threw their tangled bodies into the advancing tram. The tram screeched to a halt but the car didn't even check its progress. By the time Robert reached the scene of the accident and joined the tram driver and his handful of passengers, the car had vanished. There was blood splattered on the tram's front windows and while one man's face had been crushed into an unrecognizable mass of flesh, his stockiness and dress betrayed him as the man he had come to know as Kleftis. Salerno lay unmoving on his side but Robert could see that he was still breathing and bent down to him. "Salerno," he hissed at him, "it's Schaffer. Help is on the way. Hang-on man, an ambulance will be here any second," Robert said in the hope that someone had called one.

Robert could see his lips barely moving and leaned close to try to hear what he was saying. Finally, he managed a barely audible whisper that made the hairs on the back of Schaffer's neck stand on end. "It's worse than anyone thought. Don't go back to your apartment, get to Switzerland and call your friend in Washington. Tell him what happened. He'll help you." And then he was silent and Robert knew he would never speak again.

Schaffer started to get up but there were people all around them and it was difficult to regain his feet. He could hear an ambulance siren approaching rapidly and finally managed to edge his way through the gathering crowd of people that always seems to materialize whenever some tragedy befalls a fellow human being. Once on the edge of the little circle surrounding the car's victims, Robert walked slowly toward the bank's entrance and then made his way around the back to the safety of the courtyard he had come to know so well. It was empty save for Robert's car that he had left there early in the morning and had not retrieved. He searched in his blazer pockets for the keys and was relieved to find they had not fallen out in all the commotion. He momentarily panicked when he realized he would need his passport but he quickly relaxed when he found it and his wallet tucked in his inside pocket. Thank god Bonnie got me into the habit of carrying my passport, he thought. And then his pulse quickened. What in the name of the lord had happened to her? If all this was the work of the Cianos and their accomplices, Bonnie could easily be dead by now.

The old adrenalin was flowing full force by the time he got into the car. He had a fleeting concern about a bomb but forced that anxiety out of his mind, turned the key in the ignition and gunned the engine. So far so good. He eased the car into reverse and carefully edged the sport coupe Fiat out of the courtyard and into the little side street that leads into Piazza Cordusio that, by this time, was ablaze with flashing blue lights. The side street was a one-way road into the Piazza but at this time of night it was deserted. Given the mayhem going on in the square, he decided to go down the little street the wrong way. He negotiated the initial few hundred yards without incident. However, when he arrived at the first intersection, he spotted a large truck parked about fifty feet down the boulevard he had hoped to use to extricate himself from the maze of small one way roads. Men were loading boxes from a nearby garage into the side of the truck and seemed startled by his arrival from the wrong direction. Robert saw one of them reach inside a coat pocket and pull out what looked like a gun so he floored the car and continued his journey down the one-way system. As he neared Piazza della Scala, he slowed to a snail's pace and entered the main road that passes between the Scala and the Galleria. One taxi stood in a rank just across from the Opera House but otherwise the square that fronts on the City Hall was deserted. From this position the drive to the autostrada and on to Switzerland was relatively straightforward.

He debated momentarily whether to take an alternate route and this internal argument led him to reconsider his natural anxiousness to get to Switzerland as quickly as possible that was by taking the autostrada to Como and then into Chiasso, Switzerland. If there were people following him or waiting for him it would be on that precise route. He doubled checked the square in front of him to be sure he was still secure and then took out a road map and the miniature flash light that Bonnie had placed there just a few weeks before. After a few moments Robert found what was called the "Old Road to St. Moritz" and knew instinctively that was the way to go. It would mean being in Italy for almost two hours instead of forty-five minutes but it would be far less likely that he would be followed or seen. He would also be in St. Moritz for breakfast with the possibility of seeing Bonnie, with or without Alberto Ciano, rather than fighting for sleep in some hotel in Chiasso or Lugano. It was a no brainer.

He saw a dark, unlit car, not unlike the one that had crushed Kleftis and Salerno, move into the square. Robert literally froze. He had been through so much in the last twenty-four hours that he knew that anything else at all might put him over the edge and into the abyss. He quickly pulled off to the side of the road, put out the lights and left the car. He tried to walk slowly toward the apartment building just behind and to the right of him but found his legs locked in first gear. When he reached the relative safety of the building's entrance, he turned and saw three men making their way toward him from across the square. He made a split second decision. If he ran through the streets of Milan he had a decent chance. If he ran back to his car, he had an even better chance. He might even be able to run one of them over; a thought that he admitted didn't bother him in the least.

He took a deep breath and used his football player’s speed to make a successful dash to the Fiat. He had left the doors unlocked and, as luck would have it, almost immediately found the ignition with his keys. The engine caught just as the three men raced across the street and narrowed the distance to about fifty feet. He double shifted and let the little Fiat fly forward and smacked at least one of them with the right rear wing as he turned the sport coupe in a tight semi-circle and accelerated toward the north end of the square and the road to St. Moritz.

Chapter 8

He'll Go to Rome

As Schaffer neared the Italian-Swiss border and the first light of the day begin to display its early morning radiance, he slowed to a near crawl. The clock on the dashboard read 6:45 am. The drive from Milan had taken just about two and a half hours and had been uneventful. A large semi was in one open lane and a line of what looked like about five cars waited to be cleared in the other. While everything appeared normal, Robert prepared himself for another crisis. The drive had refreshed him both mentally and physically and while he hoped for an uneventful entry into Switzerland, he was ready for a challenge. The cars were inching forward when a uniformed Italian guard appeared from nowhere and begin to walk toward him. In his frame of mind, if he had a gun, he probably would have used it and spent the rest of his life in a dank Italian jail cell at the tip of the boot of the country.

His turn came and went uneventfully and less than an hour later he arrived at the entrance to the Ritz Hotel where the doorman greeted him warmly, took his luggage inside and promised to look after his car all in one smooth move. It was the sort of attention that made you want to open your wallet and give him whatever you had immediately at hand. He was shown to reception and was lucky to arrive just as the night clerk was going off duty. "I'm Robert Schaffer, my wife should have checked in yesterday."

The newly arrived receptionist did not react one-way or the other to the name. Instead she logged onto their computer, checked and double-checked the data he had given her and finally responded, "I'm terribly sorry, Mr. Schaffer, but your wife has not yet arrived."

He thought for a moment and then asked "You do have a reservation for her, don't you?" When she looked embarrassed, he added, "She may be registered in her maiden name, 'Ciano'."

Another flurry at the computer revealed nothing. "I'm very sorry, Mr. Schaffer. Perhaps her travel arrangements have been altered," she offered as an explanation.

"Yes," I said without any conviction. "You do have a room available, don't you?"

"Of course. We have several good rooms. It's really not too much of a problem at this time of year. Do you have anything in particular in mind?"

"Not really. Just something very quiet, ... with a view," he added absently.

When he was settled in his room with a cup full of steaming Swiss coffee in hand and a brimming pot to back up the one he had just depleted, he gazed out of his broad bay window and inspected the pastoral scene. The valleys of St. Moritz were full of fading autumn colors and even the lower mountaintops were already laden with the first snows that signaled the beginning of winter. The peaceful setting helped him to think. After a few moments he picked up the phone, got an outside line and dialed the Milan number of his friends, the Mancinis. It was Paolo who answered the phone in his deep, resonant Milanese tones. "Pronto!"

"Paolo, it's me, Robert."

"My God, Robert, Stephanie and I have been so worried about you and Bonnie. Thank the Lord you're safe."

"I'm fine, Paolo but I'm worried about Bonnie..."

Paolo cut him off before he could say anything more. "Robert, listen to me. Some terrible things have been happening. Don't tell me where you are," he said and paused before saying, "we know you're not in your apartment in Milan. Go to a pay phone but don't use a credit card. Get plenty of change and then call me at Pietro's."

Damn, thought Robert, somehow Paolo and Stephanie have been dragged into this. That is the last thing they need. And then he suddenly panicked when he didn't understand what he was telling him. "Pietro's? He asked him.

"You need to think carefully, Robert," he was saying. "I think he helped you when you collapsed yesterday."

And it hit him; the little cafe near his apartment building was what he was trying to tell me. "Give me ten minutes and I'll ring you there," he said.

"You do understand?" He was asking. "I know you've been under enormous pressure during the last twenty-four hours."

"I'll ring you," is all Robert said and put the phone down.

He put on his blazer, made sure he had money and stopped at the cashier's desk to change some notes into Swiss Franc coins before he went outside to find a pay phone. There was one directly across from the hotel but he decided to be ultra cautious and find one in the center of the town that was literally a five-minute walk from the Ritz's front door. He selected one near the church in the main square, inserted some coins and quickly got the number of Pietro's through the Swiss operator. A few moments later the ringing tone began to sound and then Paolo's voice came on the line. Once they had identified each other he took the lead in the manner of a professional. "Speak softly and don't say anything more than the bare minimum," he ordered Schaffer and then asked, "Where are you?"

"In the main square in St. Moritz," Robert told him. “I'm staying at the Ritz Hotel."

"Good," he said with obvious relief in his voice.

"Do you know where Bonnie is, Paolo? I was hoping you or Stephanie might know."

"Don't worry, we'll find her and she'll be fine. I promise you that, Robert. If they even seriously frighten her, Ciano and his family will end up at the bottom of a north Italian lake and I think they know that."

He had only known Paolo for a little less than a year but, until now, he thought he knew him well. This was a different, much more authoritative and decisive man and, given the circumstances that was reassuring. However, he needed more reassurance than he had just been given. No matter what had happened between Bonnie and the younger Ciano, he loved her dearly. "How can you be so sure?" he asked him.

"Just trust me, Robert," was all he said and when he thought about it later he really had no other practical choice at that point in time.

"OK, Paolo," Robert responded.

"Now listen to me carefully, Robert. Max Feathers called me about an hour and a half ago and asked to meet me urgently. I told him to come to my flat but he said it wasn't secure and insisted on meeting me in front of my building and taking a stroll."

"Christ, Paolo," Robert interrupted him. "I'm sorry you've been dragged into all of this."

"Save that for later, Robert. For the moment, just listen."

"OK."

"Right. Feathers has offered a deal."

"He's done what?" Schaffer shouted, unable to conceal his shock, which in retrospect was silly. He was the obvious choice for a deal.

"He's offered a deal," Paolo repeated himself. "They figured you'd contact me. They have reason to know that I am a man of my word and have decided to use me as the intermediary. They have also offered to clean out the insider-dealing ring in your bank. As a sign of good faith, you will learn when you call your secretary that your chief dealer, a guy called Rinaldi, has handed in his notice this morning in order to take up a post at another bank. All the others who have been involved will gradually be placed in other financial institutions. I gather that means that your entire FX Department and a good chunk of their administrative backup will be departing."

"Paolo, this is incredible."

"You haven't heard anything yet," he said, and when he had finished, Robert couldn't have agreed with him more.

When Robert got back to the hotel, he checked out and headed north for the tunnel that leads from Switzerland into a tiny, autonomous province of Italy called Lovigno, an enclave surrounded by some of the highest mountains in the Alps. This little area has maintained some political ties to modern day Italy but it is economically independent and is virtually free of any meaningful taxes. It is also free of border guards and customs agents and was and still is a good place to conclude the sort of deal being offered by Max Feathers. As long as you didn't use a credit card, it was difficult to establish that you had ever been there.

The tunnel leading into the miniature country is impressive not so much for its length or dimensions but rather because it just sort of comes out of nowhere. One minute you're driving on a decent sized, but winding road, and the next, you make a slightly more pronounced turn and you approach what initially looks like a mineshaft. Five minutes after entering the tunnel you materialize in a captivating valley and the small but charming town.

In those days the center of the town was marked by a handful of contemporary hotels and two small, characteristic pensione plus a smattering of shops selling duty free goods, especially alcohol and tobacco, and by St. Mary's Church. Robert drove in front of the little pensione where Paolo said he could conclude the arrangements, parked his car in an open space and went inside. A friendly young woman in her early twenties greeted him instantly. "Mr. Schaffer," she said more as a statement than as a question.

"Yes," he answered, failing to keep the surprise that she knew him, out of his voice.

"I was told to expect a man of your description, Mr. Schaffer. Your red Fiat 850 made it easy to identify you," she offered by way of further explanation and, it seemed to Robert, to make him feel comfortable.

If the Cianos were trying to put me in a receptive frame of mind to do a deal, they were making a lot of progress. Bonnie's warning only a few days before that we needed professional help was suddenly ringing in his ears. Robert nodded and said "Lovely hotel. Are you normally busy at this time of year?" he asked to give the impression that he wasn't flustered.

"No, not usually," she replied while giving him a disarming smile. "We're quite surprised by all the activity. It's usually fairly quiet until just before Christmas and then after that until February."

Robert smiled back at her, which was easy given her good looks and genuine friendliness and then just waited for her to make the next move.

"Mr. Feathers is waiting for you in the breakfast room, Mr. Schaffer. I'll bring a fresh pot of coffee through immediately or would you prefer tea?"

Robert took a quick look at his watch and seeing that it was nearly 11:30 am he asked "Any chance of a bloody mary?"

"Of course, that is no problem at all." And then she turned and said "This way, Mr. Schaffer. The breakfast room is at the back of the hotel so the guests can have the best views of the valley and the mountains while they are dining."

He followed her down a narrow passageway that lead past the reception area and the ground floor guest rooms and opened onto a pleasant reading room that seemed like it might double as a bar. The decor throughout was mountain style, deep brown-beamed ceilings, mounted on wooden walls of the same color. The carpets were deep red, heavy-duty wool and the curtains were white lace. It was the sort of place you dream about but never find. When he entered the dining area, Feathers was staring out the windows while he absently puffed on a cigarette and drank coffee. He heard me come in and gave me a nod of acknowledgement before he stubbed out his cigarette and pushed himself to his feet to greet me. "Come, sit down. I know you've been through a lot," Feathers said, but he said it in a way that conveyed the impression he was the one who needed to sit down. He looked completely exhausted.

Robert had tried to rehearse first his opening remarks and then the whole conversation but finally concluded that the best thing to do was to be as silent as possible.

"Let's get this over as quickly as possible," was what he finally said.

Feathers thought for a moment and said, "I suppose that is best."

"Let's deal with Bonnie first," Robert demanded.

He didn't react one way or the other for what seemed like days. "OK," he agreed at last. "She's not far from here. I told her to join us at about one o'clock. I've no doubt she'll turn up. If we've done a deal, she goes with you. If not, she stays behind." Seeing my look of bewilderment he added "All she knows is that the Cianos have had second thoughts about retaining her as an art consultant. They've asked her to bear with them for a few days while they sort out certain internal issues. In the meantime, they've given her the use of their chalet which is about a five minute drive from here."

Well at least his suspicions about the Ciano's real motives for retaining Bonnie as an art consultant were confirmed. "If we do a deal, she loses the job and if we don't do a deal..."

He interrupted me saying "She not only gets the job but gets a six-month assignment to the Group's

Paris based headquarters."

"And if I explain all this to her?" Robert asked stupidly.

"I think you know the answer to that better than I."

He looked down at the table in silent admission that he knew all too well that she would never believe him, at least not now.

"Did you call your bank and get confirmation about Rinaldi leaving?" he carried on.

I shook my head that I did.

"Fine. Lets discuss the dossier," he said it as an order.

"Dossier?" I asked in astonishment. How could Feathers know anything about that, he thought to myself.

"We know you told Franco you sent a dossier to your family lawyer in the States. What's in it and where is it now?"

His mind raced. Robert suddenly understood that if he knew the truth about the dossier his position and Bonnie's would be altered completely. He knew what he said next was critical. "There is more than one dossier," Robert informed him.

"More than one?" he asked incredulously.

"Yea," Robert said evenly. "I made three copies all together."

"Three copies?" he inquired helplessly, as his shoulders sort of drooped forward along with his head.

"Yeah," Schaffer stated, reasonably, as he watched him take out another cigarette and light it quickly with his aging Zippo. "I was going to make a fourth and keep a copy in our apartment in Milan but decided that was too risky."

"You're playing with fire, Robert," said Feathers as he nervously picked at the tip of his nose.

"Yeah," Schaffer said. "I know I am, but I'd hate to think where I'd be now if I didn't have any."

"So where are they? Your family's lawyer in Michigan told us he hasn't heard from you in almost two years."

"You CIA, FBI, or what, Max?"

"What difference does it make, Robert?"

"Just curious, Max. I thought the CIA couldn't work in the US and that the FBI couldn't work abroad."

"Sometimes we work together," he declared honestly.

"Tell your buddies that there is one copy in a bank vault in Campione d'Italia, another in a bank vault in New York and a third with a family lawyer which he is keeping in yet another bank vault. There are two keys to each safety deposit box and two signatures are required to get into any one of them, unless I die, of course."

"What is in the dossier, Robert?" was all he said.

"Transcripts of tape recordings, pictures of people doing various things plus a road map that I drew up setting out as clearly as I could who I think is involved, how it all works and where the money goes." Old Bob Franco's colorless face seemed to rise from the grave right before his eyes. The only difference was that it had the unmistakable features of Max Feathers.

"How did you compile all this stuff, Robert?" Feathers asked miserably.

Robert looked up at the ceiling as if searching for some kind of heavenly inspiration.
"We'll, when I got wind of it...."

"When was that?" he interrupted me.

"A few weeks after I got here, I guess."

"That's not possible," he insisted.

"Why not? Everyone in the bank, even the secretaries have known about it for as long as they can remember. Anybody who wants to know about it, can, with just a bit of effort."

He appeared to be genuinely astonished. "Don't bull shit me, Schaffer!" he said.

I surveyed him very carefully and then stated "Feathers, if the western world is depending on guys like you to defeat the bad guys from the other side of the iron curtain, it won't be the easiest victory in history."

Robert's outburst seemed to bring back a semblance of professionalism. He paused for a few moments and then said sensibly "I don't like this anymore than you do. Let's just get it over as soon as possible." Robert nodded his agreement and so he continued. "If the dossier or any of the copies gets into the public domain, I won't be able to help you. No one will," he declared seriously. "Be sure you have ultimate control over its release," he advised me.

"That won't be a problem."

"OK. Let's discuss your next assignment."

"What are you talking about?"

"There is no way you can stay in Milan." He saw my look of protest and cut it off decisively. "There is no negotiating on this point. You can go back to New York or to another posting abroad, Paris, for example, but you can't stay in Milan."

Schaffer was astounded. "How can you organize that?" he asked.

He smiled for the first time since my arrival. "We have one or two friends in positions of influence in your bank," he responded. "Everyone would be happier to get that aspect of all this moving like yesterday."

Not long ago Schaffer discovered what an understatement that was. Hell, the FBI and CIA had people at virtually all levels of the bank. Some of the most senior officers, especially those responsible for the international side, were long standing US intelligence officers or were periodically used for the odd crumb of intelligence gathering. At the time Robert's mind was racing. He thought, if I were to request to be assigned back to New York at this stage, it would be seen by the bank's careers department as a sign that Robert was not cut out for the international way of life and, more importantly, his fellow officers would see Robert as a loser. You needed to be abroad for at least two full years and preferably three before going back to head office. It was kind of like the State Department in that respect. Robert also knew that if he were assigned to another European country, people throughout the international division would think that he couldn't cut it in Italy. Finally, he said, "I'll go to Rome."

"You'll go to Rome?" he mimicked me.

"You heard me, Feathers, I'll go to Rome. I hear that the number two guy is due for reassignment. It would be a good promotion for me and I know I can do the job. Tell them I'll go to Rome."

When Feathers left, Roberto found a pay phone and called Rudi Cortina. "Rudi, " he begin, "you and Maria could be in danger because of my relationship with you. The best way for me to help you and Maria is for Bonnie and I to leave Milan. I," he paused and then said "Bonnie and I just want you and Maria to know that we want you and Maria to distance yourselves from us."

Rudi Cortina had not expected the call but had intended to do exactly as Robert advised. Even though he was a young man, he knew Italy and realized that being close to Robert and Bonnie could only hurt him and his wife in the long term. "I understand, Robert. Thank you," was all he said.

Chapter 9

Renoir and Matra

The Schaffer reunion in the little pensione in Lovigno was strained but, in the end, not momentous. Before Bonnie arrived, Feathers and Robert had assented to the bare bones of an accord. As Paolo Mancini had counseled him, Robert told Feathers to confer with Paolo to iron out the details. Until Robert was able to explain everything to Bonnie, she was baffled by the loss of her commission from the Cianos and by their transfer to Rome. She adjusted quickly, however, as her greatest anxiety, having to leave Europe, was now safely laid to rest and Paolo had persuaded Feathers to obtain a teaching position for Bonnie at Rome's most distinguished art institute. Equally, the knowledge Robert acquired in those days that one doesn't always get where one gets to by merit and that there aren't too many angels in a world pretty much controlled by felons of one type or another proved to be invaluable assets for his future advancement.

Three days later Bonnie and Robert were on an early morning Alitalia plane for Rome to meet the people in the branch and to search for an apartment. The subject of their infidelity had not been addressed in any specificity and Robert thought now was as good a time as any to get it out of the way. The bank had paid for them to fly first class, as was the custom for the first and second officers of all overseas branches. As soon as they were in the air, a young steward who resembled the younger Ciano served them champagne and Robert used his similar looks to bring up Alberto. "Resembles Alberto, doesn't he," Robert said as he pointed his glass at the steward.

Bonnie looked up from a map of Rome that she had just begun to inspect and quickly surveyed the young man. "The face does a little," she commented and then instantly turned her attentions back to her map and centered her mind on it.

Robert wanted to say, "I saw you go into his room and get into his car" but instead said: "I don't think any of the Cianos would enjoy Rome, do you?"

She didn't say anything for a moment but he could tell she was considering an appropriate reply. "Doubt that Roberto or Alberto would for any length of time, but I gather that Anna comes down occasionally, for parties with her husband at the US Embassy."

Their plane lurched as they hit some turbulent air and the "fasten your seat belt" sign flashed on followed by the normal instructions over the intercom. Robert turned quickly to look out of the window just to be sure that things looked normal and Bonnie mistook his movement for an attempt to give her a kiss which she then did to Robert and said "If you see her again, Robert, it will give me the excuse I need to take a handsome, sexy, young man with a cock even bigger than Alberto's as my lover." Robert looked into her eyes, forced a laugh and decided he didn't want to know about Alberto's dick. He gave her a kiss and felt that the younger Cianos were pretty much behind them.

They landed at 9:15 and, as they only had hand luggage, were out of the airport within fifteen minutes. The branch manager, Jean Pierre Matra, a Frenchmen had sent his dark blue, chauffeur driven Renault to meet them and an hour later they were settled in the five star Hassler Hotel which is situated at the top of the Spanish steps.

While they had lived and studied for six months in Rome four years earlier, they had visited Rome only once since coming to Italy with the bank. This was a thanks largely to Bob Franco who refused to give Robert any holiday until he had served in Italy for a year.

Bonnie was eager to get on with the apartment hunting so they could be settled as soon as possible and Robert was keen to see the Rome Branch and to meet its staff so that he could get a feeling for his new working life. They had an espresso together in a small cafe at the foot of the Spanish Steps and agreed to reconvene around six pm for an early evening drink on the roof of the Hassler. There is a delightful garden and bar there and one of the most spectacular views of Rome imaginable. As soon as Bonnie had gone off with map in hand to see a couple of apartments not far from the hotel, Robert hailed a passing taxi and asked him to take him to his new office which was located not far the Presidential Palace on one of Rome's seven hills.

He had plenty of advance warning from colleagues on what to expect but when the taxi slowed about fifteen minutes later at the ornate gates to a court-yard bearing an exquisite Bernini fountain behind which sat a palace dating back to the fifteenth or early sixteenth century, he told the driver in Italian "This can't be it, you must have the wrong address."

The driver pointed at one of the imposing pillars that held the gates in place and asked, "Is that the name of your bank?"

"Where," Robert demanded.

"On that tiny bronze plaque set in the wall," he said angrily. "Can't you see it?" he shouted. He then pointed to a man with a suitcase that was hailing him from across the road. "If you don't pay quickly, I'll lose that fare!"

Robert paid him off without a tip and yelled, "I hope he's going to the train station in downtown Rome," and then handed him the money.

"Screw you," the taxi man said once he had the money tucked away, and then he gave Schaffer the universal finger salute as he turned sharply in front of another taxi that was approaching from the opposite direction in order to get the fare.

As Robert walked through the gates, he noticed that his driver was having a heated discussion with the suitcase man and he couldn't help laughing aloud when the taxi refused to take him as the words "crook, rogue, charlatan, cretin" spewed out of the driver's windows and the taxi left the man standing as the driver laid a black strip of rubber and another finger in his track.

There was a voluptuous, fawn eyed, dark haired receptionist just inside the palace's front doors with a pleasant expression on her face. Her desk was situated on a tiny landing two short sets of marble stairs below the main banking floor which Robert could see was adorned with four massive pillars of the same deep aquamarine colored marble. "Good morning," Robert greeted her in English as much to test her capabilities with the language as to set the tone for his arrival. The branch was notorious throughout the international division for dealing solely with Italian companies and not even bothering marketing the US client base and that had to change if the branch was ever going to make a profit.

"Boun juorno, signore," she replied as her pleasant, disarming countenance was replaced with a look of sheer terror.

"Is the branch manager here?" Robert asked continuing on in English as much as anything because she had decided to call me "Mister" and not "Doctor".

"Escusi, signore. Non parlo Inglese. Un attimo solo."

Robert stopped her from running away to find someone who could translate for her by saying in Italian "Don't worry I speak a little Italian. I'm Mr. Schaffer..."

But she interrupted him before he could utter another word and, speaking Italian, said, "Your Italian is perfect, dottore. Dottore Matra is expecting you, as is everyone else. I'm sorry but I have never learned English. Perhaps you would let me try?" she asked as her eyes turned into virtual flying saucers.

If Robert had seen those eyes and everything else that went with them just a month before, he probably would have commenced English lessons right there and then and, he would undoubtedly have offered a special evening tutorial as well. But time was experience and his recent education told him that he ought to at least give it some thought. "Perhaps," he responded.

She smiled and led Schaffer up the stairs to the main banking hall where she immediately took him to a second set of stairs which were done in a light brown marble trimmed with what looked like chrome but turned out to be silver. Matra stood at the top of the staircase with his well known forced smile on his face and his hands clasped tightly together in front of him. He was about six feet one, with a large Gallic nose and immaculate white teeth. His ears were a bit too obvious, especially from the front, and the top of his head was bald from stem to stern. "Robert, welcome to our humble abode!"

"Jean Pierre," Robert responded, as he extended his hand and allowed him to squeeze it with both of his. "What a beautiful building you have here and," Robert leaned forward and begin to whisper "what a magnificent receptionist."

His silly grim broadened and he said, "You like her, huh, you do like her, don't you? Ha, ha, ha."

Robert tried to respond but he wasn't expecting one. Jean-Pierre took Schaffer by the elbow and guided him to his office where he offered him the little, uncomfortable chair that was pushed up against the wall in front of his desk. Once Robert was seated, he found he had to keep his head bowed forward in a respectful position in order to avoid having the top of it tickled by the tentacles of a hanging plant that was positioned just over the top of the chair.

As they sat there grinning at each other he begin to wonder whether losing Bonnie to Alberto Ciano wouldn't have been a better fate. Finally he needed to break the silence. "Thanks for sending your car. We really appreciated it."

Matra's grin quadrupled and he begin to bounce up and down in his chair as he did a tap dance with his fists on his Guicci leather blotter. "That was Jane's idea. She even had Guido, the driver, vacuum the inside of the car."

"Oh, you shouldn't have gone to the trouble," Robert volunteered.

"It wasn't any trouble. Guido, the driver, did it," he said inanely. When Robert didn't say anything, he asked, "When can you move down here? We're under real pressure to turn the red into black." He wasn't sure Robert understood what he meant so he added, "You know, red ink into black ink, losses into profits."

Over the last several days Robert had wondered why an American bank put a Frenchmen in charge of a branch in Rome that dealt solely with Italian companies. He knew the answer wasn't going to be straightforward because the bank never assigned anyone anywhere for obvious reasons. Take his assignment to Rome, for example. Who would have thought that he was coming to Rome among other reasons because he had discovered old Resca in a cupboard with his secretary and to stop his wife from running off with the son of the head of a foreign exchange insider dealing ring which was protected by the CIA? "I can be here this coming week if the bank will put us up at the Hassler until we find a place to live," he eventually told him.

"The Hassler? You're staying at the Hassler?" he asked in a squeaky, high-pitched voice that had suddenly materialized from nowhere.

Robert wanted to look under his desk to see if someone was squeezing his balls. "Yeah, Bonnie, my wife, has always wanted to stay there but until now we couldn't afford it."

A look of complete astonishment crossed his face. "But you can afford it now?" he squeaked some more.

"Well sure," Robert responded reasonably. Antinori said you wouldn't want me to stay anywhere else. 'Only the best in Rome' I remember him telling me."

"Well, if Antinori wants you to stay there, I guess it's OK."

"That is terrific. Bonnie will be thrilled. I'm sure we can be down here this coming Monday in that case."

He looked down at his desk again and started to roll what looked like tiny paper balls around his Gucci blotter. "You gonna work today? I mean, you wanna see your office? It's just across the corridor."

"Sure, I'd love to see my office, meet my secretary and some of the people in the branch, if that is OK with you?"

His face brightened until he tried to jump out of his chair without moving it away from his desk. He was lucky, his stomach had intervened. This time he got up carefully, walked around and led the way across a wide-open space which was flooded by the early morning sun streaming in through a magnificent bay window. The floor was covered in inch deep, light brown carpet and there were two empty desks set in the middle of the open space, one in front of the other. "Who sits here?" Schaffer asked him.

"What? Oh," he said looking embarrassed. "Our secretaries, usually, but they won't be in until lunchtime today," he explained.

"Lunch time?" Robert asked as he watched him rock from side to side and scratch the top of his baldhead with his watchband.

"It's just today," he explained. "I assured them you wouldn't be in until lunch time, so it's really my fault. Anyway, let me show you your office. I hope you like it." He opened the door on the other side of the open space, stood aside and beckoned for Robert to go in. As Schaffer went past him he whispered "It used to be mine until I took over the branch."

There was no way to be neutral about that office. It was nothing short of magnificent. Schaffer had never seen an office like it anywhere in the world. It looked about 300-400 feet square and had bay windows on three walls, all of which looked out over the palace gardens and, beyond that, Rome itself. Each window was surrounded by tasteful floor to ceiling crushed blue velvet drapes. An antique Napoleon writing desk stood at the far end of the room and an Italian antique conference table, dating from Louis Napoleon's time stood off to the left as you entered surrounded by 12 matching chairs. To the right was a comfortable seating arrangement done in dark leather with modern glass topped tables edged in gold. The ceilings were high, Schaffer estimated about 14 feet, and from the center hung a splendid crystal chandelier. The art was original and he immediately noticed what proved to be a good quality Matice behind the writing desk. Robert finally asked, "Why did you give it up?"

"You like it, then, no doubts, no reservations?"

Robert was afraid to give it that kind of rating even though he wanted to. Given what he had been through over the last month, he suspected some kind of ulterior motive. Despite his suspicions, he could not help himself, it was just too overwhelming. "It's unbelievable, Jean-Pierre. I've never seen anything quite like it."

"Good, I'm glad you feel that way. I was a little worried that you might think it was too spectacular. You need this sort of thing in Rome to be successful at bringing in new clients."

Robert tried to recollect Matra's office and found he had a kind of neutral feeling about it. "Are you sure you don't want to keep this, Jean, it's much nicer than yours?"

Matra chuckled. "You haven't seen my entertaining center."

"Entertaining center?" Robert asked.

"Come with me," he ordered as he took Robert by the elbow and lead him back into the open area and then to a small elevator which was tucked down a narrow but elegant corridor fronting onto the stairs Schaffer had taken from the main banking level to the mezzanine floor. Jean-Pierre took out a minuscule, silver colored key and inserted into a lock placed to the right of the entrance to the elevator. The door opened immediately. He led the way into a comfortable compartment, whose walls were done in the same blue crushed velvet Robert had seen in both his and Matra's offices, pushed the upper of two buttons and seconds later the doors opened onto the floor above Schaffer's office. Immediately outside the elevator was a reception area that held antique chairs and two formal but comfortable looking sofas. The walls were done in a very light golden-white fabric and the floor in a matching marble. There were three doors leading from the reception area and Matra chose the one in the middle, turned the knob and ushered me through. "My god, Jean," Robert said, this makes my office pale into insignificance."

"When our beloved chairman visits Rome, this becomes his headquarters."

"I see," Robert said absently as his eyes wandered along the room's walls from one masterpiece to another.

"Do you?" he asked seriously.

"Not really," Robert confessed.

"Come over to the windows and have a look at the view. His favorite city in the entire world is Rome. He spent three years of his childhood here with his mother, and occasionally his father, at a time when the family was spending more time in Europe than in America. Then he did a year abroad in Rome during university years and he tries to spend a week or two a year here if at all possible. There is a room through that door where we keep all of his personal things. The insurance coverage on the contents of that room and this is about $15 million."

"What's the real value in the paintings?" Robert asked.

Matra scanned the room and then took him by the elbow again and led him past odd pieces of pottery and various other types of ancient artifacts as well as each of the paintings. Of everything on display his favorite piece was a Renoir that made Schaffer drool. Matra saw Robert's interest. "You like the Renoir?" he quizzed him.

"Adore it," he said honestly.

"I'll have it placed in your office in exchange for the Matice, OK?" he asked with a little grin on his face.

Schaffer couldn't believe it. A Renoir, in my office! "Jean Pierre, are you sure," he forced himself to ask as it was a dream come true for him to have a Renoir, if only temporarily.

"You must have it," he replied. "I can see how it pleases you. I know how much I am influenced by my surroundings. It will make you work better," he concluded.

By the time they returned to the mezzanine level from their tour of Jean Pierre's entertaining area and from meeting the fifty plus staff members who were dotted around the palace, their secretaries had surfaced. It was difficult for Robert to resolve which he would select if left to his own devices, as both were stunning in natural beauty and in attire. They were almost standing at attention beside their desks. "Robert," Matra begin the introductions, "please meet my personal assistant, Miss Vasta," he said, as he moved his left arm toward the taller and younger of the two women.

Robert glanced at his watch quickly to let them both know how he felt about their arrival time. Seeing that it was 12:10, he said "Good afternoon, Miss Vasta."

She eyed him warily, smiled agreeably and said in flawless, American accented English "Good afternoon, Mr. Schaffer. I feel awful that we weren't here to greet you. We were making arrangements for the bank's Valentine's Day party." She hesitated only fleetingly and then added "I've heard so much about you from Mrs. Gavi."

Robert noticed Matra give her a dour look before he pivoted toward Schaffer's secretary. "Robert, this is Miss Gemelli, Louisa Gemelli. She's been my executive assistant and secretary for the last several years and knows our client base well. I know you will find her to be of invaluable assistance and support."

She stepped forward while extending her hand and made a little curtsy that Schaffer imagined would be suitable if you were meeting royalty. "Mr. Schaffer," she pronounced it in a voice and manner that authenticated what his Milanese secretary had told him about her education in England.

She grasped Schaffer's hand longer than required and gazed directly into his eyes with her own that were a murky green color. Her self-confident demeanor was unnerving but, while she had only spoken a few words, it didn't take a person of gifted intelligence to comprehend that this woman was going to be an indispensable asset. Robert wondered why Matra had parted with her. Finally, he pulled himself together and said "Miss Gemelli, I'm delighted to meet you as well" and then Robert turned to both of them and said "you must know that I am thrilled that the bank has assigned me to Rome and that I will be working with both of you."

Paolo and Stephanie Mancini had told Schaffer that modern day Romans were essentially an insecure people and that flattery and praise would definitely get you somewhere. It looked as though they were right because both women beamed with pleasure. Matra grinned and then made an announcement. "I've just decided. In order to mark the occasion, I think the four of us should have lunch together, 'paga la banca.'"

During the next several years, Schaffer learned to adore those three words 'the bank pays.' In fact, they became his favorite words. As the red ink turned into black and the money rolled in, which was mostly Robert's doing, Matra encouraged him to use those words whenever he wanted. Initially, however, Robert had difficulty knowing what Matra felt the bank should pay for. He had strange ideas about it until he got a bonus for their first month of profitability. After that, as long as profits went up each month, Robert could charge fundamentally anything he wished to the bank.

The first time he got to utilize "paga la banca" was in March, only a few months after he and Bonnie were settled. Bonnie had found a fantastic apartment in Piazza Maria in Trastevere, a marvelous square in the heart of one of the oldest parts of residential Rome. The flat was located on the top floor of a five-storied edifice on the south side of the square. It had a roof terrace that you could reach via a circular staircase from a covered balcony that ran full length along the front of the apartment. It was ideal for entertaining and they decided to throw a party, "paga la banca!"

Bonnie and Louisa had become soul mates almost at once. Bonnie's blonde, northern European looks complimented Louisa's dark Mediterranean appearance and their blue-green cat eyes were virtually indistinguishable. They were both shapely, although Louisa was somewhat more buxom and, in their bare feet, only Bonnie's hairstyle made her seem taller. The greatest contrast in appearance between the two was their nose. Bonnie's was a classic ski jump, whereas Louisa's was unmistakably Roman. Two days before the event Bonnie had asked if Louisa could help her get things ready and, much to the pleasure of Louisa, Robert consented. When he reappeared in the evening, the two of them greeted him with an enormous pitcher of chilled gin martinis, which in those days was his preferred cocktail. They lead him out onto their balcony and then to the roof terrace where they had placed some foldaway chairs and a table that held three glasses and a selection of snacks on it. After they were all seated, Robert reached over, grabbed a hand full of nuts, filled their glasses and sat back to take in the extraordinary allure of an early spring, Roman evening. The clock on the exquisite church at the east end of the square read 7:15 and waiters were beginning to welcome guests to Sabatini's, one of Rome's finest restaurants which was located at the west end of the square, directly opposite the church. People of all ages were milling about the small fountain which occupied the center of the piazza and motor scooters and cars had to dodge them as they tried to make their way from one side to another. They had been making small talk about preparations for the party when Bonnie suddenly took a healthy sip of her drink and then said to Robert seriously "A man saying he was from the U. S. Embassy came by today. I had gone out to collect a few things for the party and he mistook Louisa for me. Louisa," Bonnie said as she turned to her, "please tell Robert exactly what took place."

From Bonnie's initial remarks and bearing in mind the look on Louisa's face, Robert could see that the two of them had not agreed about what he should be told. "Are you sure, Bonnie?" she asked her.

"I'm sure, Louisa."

Louisa looked dubious but went ahead. "Well," she begin, "about mid-day I heard someone messing with the front door. I thought perhaps Bonnie had forgotten her key and begin to go over to open the door, when the fiddling turned into a soft knocking. Before I could ask who it was, the sounds begin again. This time I was frightened as I thought someone was trying to break in." She hesitated and took a deep breath as the recollection of what had transpired was disturbing her.

"Go ahead, Louisa," Robert encouraged her, and took a healthy sip of his own martini, as it was apparent that this could only be trouble.

"I shouted out, in Italian, asking who was there, as much to scare the person away as anything. It turned out to be a man and he replied in English saying that he was from the U.S. Embassy and that he had an important message for you and Bonnie. I opened the door but left the catch chain on and asked for some identification. He looked very American, you know, large shoes, short hair and big and tall. He was surprised by my request but, after a minute or so, he exhibited a highly official looking card with his picture on it. It gave his name as John Foster and identified him as being in the U. S. Embassy's Commercial Department." She paused briefly and looked over to Bonnie as if soliciting confirmation that she was to continue. He saw Bonnie nod to her.

"He asked to come in and, given his credentials, I unlatched the door and invited him to sit down."

"If that bastard hurt you...."

Bonnie broke in before he could finish, saying, "He didn't harm her, Robert. Just let Louisa finish."

Louisa bent forward, lit one of her extremely occasional cigarettes, took a long, deep drag and savored the smoke before she exhaled. "He thought I was Bonnie and, before I could explain that I wasn't, he said 'we want your husband to do a little job for us, Mrs. Schaffer. We want some information and we figure he can get it for us.' I was afraid to tell him that I wasn't Bonnie, so I just suggested that he ring you at the office. He refused and told me to tell you that he would come back tomorrow, before you went to work."

"And that was it? He left?" Robert asked.

"Not exactly," responded Louisa as she became silent and stared down at the floor.

Boinnie got up and went around to Louisa's chair and put her arm around her. "Don't worry, Louisa," she said, "I'm sure its all a big mistake. Just finish quickly and we'll get you a taxi to take you home."

Louisa looked up at Robert and said "As he was going out the door, he stopped and pointed a finger at me and said very slowly and quietly, in a way that really frightened me 'Tell him if he isn't here tomorrow when I come back, you'll both be sorry.'"

By the time Louisa had finished, Schaffer was seriously scared. Bonnie could see that he was and that disturbed her as well. Until now she had evidently thought it was some kind of error. Seeing Robert's face told her it wasn't. Schaffer resisted lighting a cigarette or pouring himself another drink. He knew Louisa was scrutinizing him alertly for any evidence that there was no mistake. "Bonnie's right, it was an error. I'm sure it was," he told Louisa. "I'm just so sorry that you had to go through all of this. I'll have a word with a good friend of mine in the Embassy and sort it all out and get you a formal apology. What a horrible thing for you to go through."

"Don't worry about me," she said sincerely. "I'm just so terrified for you and Bonnie." She paused before she said what she was thinking and then concluded, "He was extremely serious. I'm really not sure it was a mistake."

"Nonsense," Schaffer heard himself saying. "You know what governments are like. They're always making mistakes. I'll call a taxi for you, Louisa. It will take at least 15 minutes for it to appear so while I'm away, pour yourselves another drink and one for me as well. I'll be right back."

Bonnie looked up at Robert as he squeezed between her and the table and her eyes and expression said "Nice try."

Once Louisa had departed, Bonnie and Robert went back to the roof terrace and their pitcher of martinis. They each downed two drinks in rapid succession as they debated what was going on. "Robert, you and I both know that we were way over our heads in Milan. We were playing with fire and that has to have something to do with this."

"Thanks for saying 'we'. I'm the one who got us into this mess with my crusade against the foreign exchange insider dealing ring."

"I did my bit," she insisted on taking part of the responsibility. "If I wouldn't have insisted on going to the party at the Cianos', a lot of mistakes could have been avoided."

Schaffer leaned forward and refilled both of their glasses, looked into her now sad and frightened eyes and said "Bonnie, darling, going to that party or a party like it was something we were going to do somewhere, sometime the moment we decided to come to Europe. That experience is behind us but we'll have others to deal with in the years ahead. Hopefully, we'll be better prepared for whatever awaits us than we were this time around."

"Maybe we should just chuck it and go home to Michigan. We'd be happy there and safe," she added, and he saw her shiver from the rapidly declining temperature and, he was sure, from Foster's threat and the prospect of seeing him in the morning not to mention the possibility of leaving her beloved Europe.

Robert got up and said, "Let's go down to the balcony. We can see the piazza better from there and it's out of the wind and will be warmer. You take the pitcher and glasses and I'll get the rest." Robert felt that the last thing in the world they needed was a discussion about going back to Michigan and he hoped that by the time they got relocated, it wouldn't come up again.

Ten minutes later they were settled on a small, comfy love seat that he had moved from their living room to the balcony. Bonnie had brought out a woolen cover-up that her mother had knit for them before they came to Italy, a bottle of champagne and two glasses. They'd both had plenty to drink and the last thing that they needed was to split a bottle of champagne. But in those days, they could put away a pitcher of martinis, down a bottle of champagne and still enjoy a good bottle of red wine over a late night dinner without much of a regret the next day. Once they had the champagne opened and poured, Bonnie said, "Robert, that material you put together on the insider dealing ring, do you have a copy here in Rome?"

"No, but there's actually not much in it, you know that."

"Yeah, but they don't. Maybe that's what that guy called Foster wants. Maybe they think we have a copy here and they sent Foster to look for it."

"Could be," Robert said doubtfully. "But we're not even sure that Foster works for Max Feathers. Maybe Foster is tied to those guys that got crushed by that car and tram in Milan."

"What would they want with us? You were going to help them before they were killed and you did the deal with Feathers."

"Don't know," he confessed.

She thought for an instant. "Do you think they truly intend to clean up the insider dealing in your bank, Robert?"

"Rinaldi is gone and several other senior dealers have given in their resignations. It looks like they aim to live up to that part of the bargain anyway."

"I guess we'll know more in the morning, assuming that Foster reappears."

"Yeah," he said, "try to let me worry about that. Are Paolo and Stephanie coming down for our party?" he asked, trying to change the subject.

Bonnie instantly cheered up. Paolo and Stephanie were among her very favorite people. "I talked to Stephanie today and she thinks they'll be able to. Paolo has been unbelievably busy. The unions are really giving him problems. Stephanie wants him to pay their bosses. She said it's just not worth the hassle and, financially speaking, it would be cheap relative to the costs of the go-slow strikes. I invited them to stay with us for the weekend if they can get away."

"I hope they come. I really miss those two."

"So do I."

"What is the last count for the party?"

"Assuming Paolo and Stephanie come, 90 all together. The caterers are coming tomorrow to begin setting up. They're going to put a tent on the roof terrace so we can dance up there. Louisa has organized a great band and has obtained the local authorities' agreement to everything as long as the music stops by 1 AM."

"Thank God Matra allowed me charge it to the bank. This is going to cost a small fortune."

"I'm certainly looking forward to it. Almost everyone we knew when we last lived in Rome is coming. The few that aren't have moved to other parts of Italy or are living abroad. All the bank people that you invited have accepted, including Jean Pierre and Jane, and your clients and key target clients have as well. Jane said we should be sure to have strolling entertainers and even suggested that the caterers provide champagne and caviar throughout the evening."

"Sounds to me that all we have to do to satisfy Foster, assuming he turns up in the morning, is to invite him to our party," Robert said happily and they broke out in laughter which came as much from the martinis and champagne as from his joke.

They ordered a pizza, finished their champagne with it and made love. Robert was shocked when Bonnie asked him to put it in her bum and even more shocked when she came in seconds. He said nothing but knowing that Ciano had taken her that way, had two large whiskies after Bonnie was asleep just so he could get some sleep himself. He set the alarm for 6:30 AM to have plenty of time to get ready for Foster. About 8 AM he heard light knocking on their door, a sound he found oddly encouraging. Maybe Foster wasn't trying to break in yesterday after all, Robert thought, he's just a soft knocker. "Who is it," Robert asked in Italian.

"John Foster, U.S. Embassy," he replied in English.

Robert opened the door and saw a man who flawlessly fit Louisa's description. "May I see some identification, please?" Schaffer asked quite civilly.

"Suspicious family," he said as he dug out the card with photo that he had shown Louisa yesterday. May I come in Mr. Schaffer?"

"Why not," he replied reasonably. "Give me your coat," Robert said and, when he had done so, he invited him to sit and asked, "Have some coffee?"

Schaffer could see him relax. He had obviously been expecting a hard time that Robert had decided would be counterproductive. "Cream and sugar?"

"No, thanks very much. I'll take it just as it comes."

"You frightened my secretary yesterday, Mr. Foster."

"Your secretary?" he asked incredulously. "I thought she was your wife."

"So I gather," I replied.

"Will she tell anyone?"

"We'll, she's told my wife and I'm sure she'll tell her boy friend who is English and who I gather is in the commercial section at the British Embassy."

"Oh, shit," was all he said.

"My sentiments entirely."

"What a mess. I'm really sorry about all this. It was just that your... secretary," he said regretfully, "was so unfriendly and suspicious."

"What would you expect?"

He shook his head from side to side. "Look, maybe I should write her an apology or something?"

"Maybe," I said. "Let's decide about that after you tell me how I can be helpful. I understand you have a 'little job for me to do.'"

"It's no big deal, we ask American business people like you to give us a hand from time to time, especially new arrivals."

"Who's we?" Robert asked.

"The Commercial Attache's Office."

"OK," he said skeptically. "What can I do for the Commercial Attache?"

"We're concerned about what is going on over at the Vatican Bank. We've heard that they move around a lot of money and we'd like to get a better handle on who it comes from and where it goes. We think that some of it could be funds trying to avoid U.S. tax."

"That's it?" Schaffer asked.

"More or less, yeah, that's it."

"Everyone knows that Chase and Morgan are the Vatican's major international bankers. Why don't you ask those guys what is going on?"

"There are no Americans at Chase or Morgan in Italy. They're either Italians or other European nationals and we know from experience that non-Americans won't help very much, unless, of course, we pay them."

"So pay them," Robert said frankly.

"Hell, if we offer to pay 'em, they'll make up something just to get the money."

Robert thought about that and decided that he was probably right. "If I do what you want me to do, could it be considered breaking the law?"

"What law?" he asked genuinely.

"Italian law."

"You're serious, aren't you?" he asked, with a big grin on his broad, surprisingly virtuous looking face.

"Why shouldn't I be, serious I mean?"

"Ok. I see your dilemma. We don't want you to break the law. Just keep your ears open, out of office hours, know what I mean?" He didn't wait for me to reply. "Like at this party you're giving tomorrow night."

"How do you know about the party?" Robert asked sternly, as he was getting pretty fed-up with the whole routine.

He chuckled. "We didn't have to bug your apartment, if that's what you're worrying about."

"I'm serious. I want to know how you guys know about our party?"

He thought for a moment and then said, "I guess it's no big deal for you to know. Maybe you should know, might even be helpful to you."

"Well?"

"Jane told us."

"Jane?" Robert asked, more than a bit perplexed.

"Yeah, Jane, Matra's wife. She's a good, patriotic American. She gives us a hand from time to time."

Chapter 10

A Little Play Acting

"I'm Robert Schaffer," Robert introduced himself as he swung his club back and forth on the first tee. Their first few months in Rome had flown by and it was now mid-April, just a few weeks after Easter and the weather in Rome was perfect.

"Pavoni, George Pavoni," he responded in perfect mid-American English.

Schaffer raised his driver high above his head, used it to stretch his back muscles and then surveyed the first hole of San Pietro Golf Course, one of Rome's most exclusive country clubs. The guy sounds like he's from Chicago, Robert thought, as he walked over to the tee for his first game of golf since coming to Rome nearly four months before.

The view from the tee was remarkably beautiful as the ancient ruins of Rome could be seen through the trees on the left. If you were even half a golfer, however, the vista faded into insignificance when you faced the challenge of the dogleg left, 417 yard, par four hole. The tee was set slightly below the fairway that rose to a peak roughly 230 yards away where a set of traps began. Tall eucalyptus trees lined the fairway on the left and a lake for the full length of the hole guarded the right side. If you had played the course previously, as he had four years before when he was a student in Rome, you knew that a treacherous stream, which was completely hidden from view, cut the fairway in half at a distance of about 245 yards. Schaffer guessed Pavoni figured he was a newcomer because he said, "hit away, it's a fairly straight-forward dog-leg left."

They had been paired up by the starter only a few minutes before and hadn't had a chance to say more than a few words of greeting as several foursomes were waiting to go off behind them. "Thanks," Robert said, "thanks a lot." He could do what he recommended, hit a long drive and end up in the stream, and probably assure himself of losing the first hole. Alternatively, he could pretend to miss the shot and land in the middle of the fairway, just short of the hidden creek. Robert took a few practice swings, teed the ball up a bit too high for the shot he expected and then started it down the right-hand side, high and over the edge of the lake with just a bit of draw to bring the ball back into the fairway. "Darn it," he said as he bent down angrily for the tee. "I missed it. I'll bet it's in that lake.

Pavoni tried not to notice that it was probably an absolutely perfect shot for this hole. With luck, it would have ended a few yards in front of that hidden creek. If he hadn't played the hole before, it was not a great shot. He looked at me suspiciously and said, "You could be all right. If you live right, it will be in the fairway."

He took out what looked like a three wood and hit it straight down the middle with just enough draw so that it would follow the leftward line of the hole. "This hole always scares the devil out of me. If I hit my driver, I'm usually in the trees or lake," he said by way of explanation.

They were carrying their own clubs and made their way up the fairway together. "Where are you from," Robert asked him.

"Originally?"

"And now as well," he responded.

"Chicago, originally, Rome for the last ten years. Archbishop Machinkos brought me over. I work for him at the Vatican. How about you?"

This is a bit of good fortune, Robert thought. His bank had been trying to work its way into the Vatican scene for many years without much success as the Church only wanted to deal with the big boys from New York. So far they were working only with the diverse religious orders around Rome, like the Fransicans and Jesuits, and neither Matra nor Robert had even been able to get an appointment with anyone close to the now infamous Machinkos. And, in those days, he was the man to see. He was known as one of God's bankers.

"I was born and brought up in a little town in the middle of Michigan. My bank assigned me and my wife to Italy a little over a year ago," Robert told him.

"You've been in Rome the whole time?"

"No, we started in Milan and came down here just before Christmas. This is the first time I've played golf since coming to Rome. As you can see, I'm a little rusty."

They were just rounding the top of the ridges when he said, "Looks like you had a stroke of luck. You just missed going into the ditch."

Pavoni had hit a good, safe shot and was in the middle of the fairway about 200 yards from the green. Robert's ball wound up about five yards short of the stream, leaving him less than 180 yards. "Yeah, lucky is right," Robert said. "You're away."

"How about putting a little money where your providence is?"

"Sure," Schaffer replied. "How about five dollars a nine and another five for the match?"

"Fine by me," he remarked, as he took out a four iron and hit his ball three feet from the cup.

Pavoni was good but Robert kept up pretty well until the last couple of holes when his putting deserted him. He had tied him on the front nine so Robert ended paying him $10. After they showered, he invited Robert to join him in the member's section of the clubhouse for a drink. "How long will you be in Rome," he inquired.

"At least two years and, the way we're settling in, I hope I can persuade the powers that be to let me stay longer."

"Great," he said sincerely. "There aren't too many good golfers in Rome."

Robert wondered if he was a priest but there was no way of telling from his dress or manner so he decided to ask him indirectly. "You married?"

"Me, married?" he remarked, and then laughed aloud. "That is one of the nicest compliments I've had in a long time. No, I'm celibate. The old Roman Catholic Church won't make many exceptions, especially not for the priests that handle the money."

Robert chuckled and took a long sip of his very welcome beer and then probed anew. "So what is it that you do at the Vatican?"

"I handle all of the liquid investments, the cash, securities and the tradable commodities. I like it and it gives me an excuse to travel. How about you?"

"Me? I'm the number two at our branch in Rome. I handle the marketing and the allocation of credit. It's a fun job. Sometimes I think I should pay them to do it."

"Don't say that too loudly," he said, and then they both laughed.

"You'll have to come around for lunch one day. I'll introduce you to Jean-Pierre Matra, our number one. Even if we can't do any business together," Robert said disarmingly, "we have a great chef and you'll at least have a good meal."

"I'd enjoy that. Why don't you have your secretary ring mine and we'll fix a date for sometime during the next two or three weeks," he responded and then he handed Robert his card which was embellished with the Vatican seal.

"You enjoy yourself?" Bonnie yelled to Robert from the kitchen when she heard him come in the door.

"It was great," he shouted back to her. "We going out for lunch or staying in?"

Bonnie appeared from the kitchen and came over and gave Robert a kiss. "We're going out. Stephanie called just after you left this morning. She and Paolo should be here any minute. They came down last evening. Paolo has meetings in Rome on Monday with some of the labor union leaders and they decided it would be fun to spend the weekend here."

Robert was delighted by the news, especially as Paolo and Stephanie had to cancel out of their pre-Christmas house-warming party at the last minute due to problems in Paolo's factories in the north. Schaffer was yearning for a good chat with him, so their visit was extremely timely. "That is wonderful news," Robert remarked to her, "but why aren't they staying with us?"

"Stephanie wanted to pamper herself at the Hassler."

"Fair enough. Let me change and I'll be right with you," he said, as he gave her a quick hug and was pleased by her warm reaction.

"Listen for the door, Robert. I may not hear it from the kitchen. We're having dinner here this evening and I've got a few things to do before they appear."

Schaffer changed quickly and had barely finished setting up the bar when they arrived. They both looked tired and drawn but he pretended not to notice. "Stephanie, Paolo," he greeted them. It's wonderful to see you."

"Robert, it's great to see you. How are you and how is Bonnie?" Stephanie queried him.

He walked over and gave her a squeeze. "We're fine," he said. "Rome has been very good for us. It was like coming home but we do miss you two." Bonnie materialized from the kitchen and she and Stephanie gave each other a hug and Bonnie took her almost immediately on a tour of the flat. Robert went over to Paolo. "How goes it, Paolo?" he asked him as he shook his hand with both of his. They had only known these warm, generous people for a little over a year and yet they had become like parents to them and, in some respects, sort of looked after them as though they were part of their family. They had five children of their own, all of whom already had families. They also had a house full of pets which normally included dogs, cats, birds and the odd reptile. Paolo had three or four factories in the north of Italy and employed a total of about five thousand people, enough for the unions to take a serious interest. He was in his late fifties as was Stephanie but they both appeared to be a bit older as they had to go into hiding in Italy during World War II in order to avoid the concentration camps which had been set up for Italian Jews.

"I'm surviving, Robert, but only just" he responded honestly but, as he said it, his features were not without the broad, happy grin which he almost invariably conveyed.

"Well," Robert said to him as he directed him to a chair in front of their sliding glass doors which opened onto their balcony and overlooked the square, "that's not good enough. Join me for a whisky," which was Paolo's favorite drink, "and tell me about the unions. Maybe I can help."

He gratefully embraced the drink, sat and commenced telling me what the unions were demanding. As Paolo depicted the situation, it was abundantly clear to Robert that if he acceded to their demands, his factories would have been uncompetitive and out of business within a few years. The union leaders knew it but were unwilling to bring the rank and file into line without payments into the leaders' personal Swiss accounts. Paolo concluded, "I'm simply not going to pay them, Robert. They say virtually everyone does, but I'm not going to do it. I'd rather see my factories go bankrupt."

"Paolo, I respect you for that but I have to tell you, I think you're wrong...."

He interrupted me as he stared at me in disbelief. "Robert, I can't believe my ears. You've never condoned any sort of corruption or even been prepared to turn a blind eye. You can't be saying that I should pay them. Even if I did, it would only postpone the day of reckoning for my businesses. I have friends who have paid and eventually the payments alone grow large enough to put you out of business. It's just not the right answer," he concluded.

"Paolo, you didn't let me finish," Robert admonished him. "I was going to say that you're wrong not to look at the alternatives to paying them. There must be other methods to make the unions be reasonable."

"Nothing you or I would care to be involved with. As I see it, about the only people the unions don't mess with is the Mafia."

"OK, what about selling out?"

"That is what I'm going to tell the union leaders, Robert. If they don't shape up, I'm going to sell out to an Italian State company, one of the big ones, like IRI. Those guys don't pay the union bosses, they just let them go on strike and fund the losses with taxpayers' money. I'll have to take a knock down price for the companies but I'd rather do that than agree to pay the crooks."

"Out of curiosity, Paolo, is there anything the Commercial Department of the US Embassy in Rome can do to help you?"

He eyed me carefully "Why do you ask?"

"I've been helpful to them during the last few months so I think I could ask them for assistance."

"Robert, those people are treacherous. You should forget about them and definitely avoid them. You might have met the same fate as those two guys in Piazza Cordusio if it weren't for your dossier and your Italian uncle." In any event, please," he implored him, "for your and Bonnie's sake, avoid all your government's people, except and only if it's absolutely necessary, pure functionaries in the embassy."

Robert pondered whether to divulge what had been going on the past few months and decided he should have told him long ago, if for no other reason than the role he played for Schaffer with

Feathers and his band of spies. "Paolo, I didn't want to bother you with it. They approached me within a few weeks of our arrival here." Robert saw Paolo become tense and realized he had been very stupid indeed not to inform him previously. "The first contact came from a guy called John Foster who had I.D. showing he was from the Commercial Department. I verified his identity through people I am confident I can trust and he checked out."

Paolo got up, slid open the glass doors leading onto our terrace, went out and motioned for me to join him. When he was outside he said, "Robert, you can assume that your apartment is bugged from head to toe. Let's go up to your roof terrace, that ought to be reasonably secure."

When they arrived Paolo walked around the perimeter and then carefully examined the TV antenna. When he completed his inspection, he ambled back to Robert and whispered "They've put a powerful transmitter on your TV antenna. It's rigged to pick up conversation inside and then passes it on to a receiving point. It's the same as broadcasting over a radio."

"I've been an idiot, Paolo, I'm sorry."

He looked at Schaffer and gave him the biggest surprise of his life to that point in time. He smiled and whispered, "Your U.S. Embassy friends can help me and, you, Robert, he stressed, more than you ever imagined." And then he began to laugh. At first, he giggled but the more he thought about what he planned to do, the more his laugh turned into a guffaw. It was infectious and even though Robert had no idea what Paolo had in mind, he understood the possibilities pretty well and begin to laugh more than he had for a long, long time. Robert left Paolo on the roof terrace, chuckling still to himself, to bring Stephanie, Bonnie and, at Paolo's suggestion, a bottle of champagne back for a momentous celebration.

They finished their champagne and went out for a long, leisurely lunch during which Paolo revealed his plans. He had Bonnie and Stephanie in such a state of laughter that tears literally rolled down their cheeks. That evening they assembled before dinner in the sitting room where Paolo had found a miniature listening device wedged under a corner of the centrally situated coffee table. Over lunch they had gone through all the "what ifs." What if it's the Americans? What if it's the Italians? What if it's the Chianos, the Mafia, the bank, the Vatican and, over their second brandy, Paulo suggested, Jean-Pierre Matra's boyfriends. Now was the moment to start the performance. Paolo had stressed the importance of being natural and having some fun and, for that reason, Bonnie, Stephanie and Robert were tight as a drum.

Paolo broke the ice when he got up, went to the kitchen and returned with a large paper sack. He inflated the sack with three deep breaths, tip-toed over to the microphone, bent down and then smashed his fist into the bag. The explosion reverberated throughout the apartment and when Paolo topped it off by producing and using a small sack that made a rude sound when squashed, Bonnie collapsed in uncontrolled laughter. After that, they enjoyed one of the best evenings of Robert's life. Paolo told one joke after another for the next hour, sparing no one, and they all intermittently took large gulps of champagne from a magnum Paolo had purchased on the way home from lunch.

After several hours their sides were aching from their hysterics and they were all famished. "We're eating peasant style, Bonnie announced. Lots of cold meats, an enormous selection of cheese, a salad and a great red wine that Paolo and Stephanie brought with them from Milan. If you're still hungry, we have Bonnie-made apple pie."

Paolo had found tiny listening devices in virtually every room of the apartment so it made no difference where they dined. "Why don't we eat in the study? We can have a fire in there to take the chill out of the air," Robert recommended.

"The study it is," Stephanie and Bonnie spoke together. "You guys set up the table and chairs and build a fire. We'll get our dinner ready so that we can eat whenever we want," said Bonnie.

When Paolo and Robert were alone in the study building the fire, Paolo initiated the first phase of the game they had planned earlier in the day. "Robert," he begin as seriously as he could while he leaned close to a tiny device which had been placed under the mantle, "if anything happens to me will you be sure that my family receives these documents."

As he feigned handing over some papers, Robert said "Of course, Paolo, but don't be silly, nothing is going to happen to you."

"I'd like to agree with you."

"Is it the unions you're worried about?" Robert asked as solemnly as he could, trying to follow the script that Paolo had plotted with them.

"The unions are only one of my problems and, frankly, they, and the payments that their leaders want, to persuade the workers to be realistic in their demands, pale into insignificance compared with what I'm faced with now."

"Paolo," Robert said with as much terror in his voice as he could muster, "what is it?"

"You can't help, Robert. Just be sure my family gets those documents if I'm not around."

"OK, Paolo, but listen to me. I tried to tell you earlier. Those guys at the U. S. Embassy owe me. I've given them some important information and I'm sure they'll help if they can." He smiled and almost laughed aloud as Paolo gave Robert a silent round of applause and nodded his head in approval.

"What can those idiots do?" he said it as a statement that I wasn't meant to answer. "I tried to tell that fool Feathers what was really going on but he wouldn't listen. Frankly, Robert, I think that guy has crossed over, he's working for the other side," he said brutally.

"Feathers?" Robert said incredulously.

"Yeah, Feathers. When I was performing the role of intermediary on your behalf at the end of last year, I gave him the gist of an incredible piece of intelligence as a sign of good faith. If he had pursued it, we wouldn't be facing the increasing likelihood of a communist government in Italy. Do you know what he said to me in response to my offer?" Again no answer was expected. "He told me I was a trouble-maker and a liar and he threatened to go back on his deal with you if I even mentioned it to anyone else. He didn't want to know, Robert."

Schaffer was getting caught up in Paolo's story. He was starting to believe what he was saying, Paolo was that convincing. Paolo was mouthing his reply. "Sorry," Robert mouthed back at him. "Paolo, I have every reason in the world to agree with you. I hold him responsible for a lot of what happened to me and Bonnie in Milan. But, I've got to say, I just can't picture him as a traitor."

Bonnie and Stephanie had come in on cue and were ready to play their roles. Who's not a traitor, Robert?" asked Bonnie.

"Max Feathers," Robert explained. "Paolo is convinced that he is working for the communists. I just can't believe it."

"Have you told Paolo about that incident in Paris?" Bonnie enquired.

"What incident?" Paolo commanded before Robert could answer.

"Robert and I were studying in Paris at the same time Max Feathers was," she begin somberly. "There were a lot of student demonstrations at the time and Max got caught up in a violent left-wing riot which landed him and a number of other leaders in jail."

"Feathers was a leader?" Paolo cross-examined her.

It was Robert's turn now. "Yeah, he was a leader in that one riot, Paolo, but I thought it might have been because he was drunk or something."

"How do you know he wasn't involved in other demonstrations and riots?" Paolo continued to quiz them.

"I guess we don't really," Robert reported to him as candidly as he could.

It was Stephanie's turn now. "Paolo, pass on what it was that you tried to divulge through Feathers."

"Bonnie and Robert have been through enough, Stephanie," he admonished her. "I don't want to involve them in this."

Stephanie was playing the director now and pointed to Bonnie. "We're not only involved, Paolo, we're submerged, you know that. Besides, we want to help you in any way we can and maybe help ourselves as well. I'd give a lot just to purge ourselves of all of them, to return to a normal life."

"What Bonnie says is true, Paolo. Maybe if I pass the intelligence to the people in the Commercial Department, they'll help remove your union impasse and agree to leave us alone."

"Please, Paolo," pleaded Bonnie. "We owe you and Stephanie so much. Let us help."

Paolo congratulated us with one of his hushed rounds of applause and then decided it was time to embrace our offer of assistance. "All right," he said, "let me furnish you with the same information I provided to Feathers and then you can convey it to your friends, hopefully in exchange for some help for me and for a guarantee that they won't bother you two anymore.

Paolo pointed to me. "Let's hear it, Paolo."

"It's not a major bombshell, at least for me it isn't. Initially, Robert, you thought that you had uncovered a foreign exchange insider-dealing ring that had been set up for the benefit of the dealers. A bit more probing and you discovered that an important Italian family was intimately involved and you begin to wonder whether there was more to it than pure personal greed. Circumstances were such, however, that you really couldn't do much about it and so you quite rightly did your deal with Feathers. That is about right, isn't it?"

"That is about it," Robert agreed.

"Well, my friends, the people that you saw as the beneficiaries were only the tip of the iceberg. The real beneficiaries, the people who were and are making the big money, are the Italian communists."

"And you told that to Feathers?" Robert asked in amazement.

"And I told Feathers that," said Paolo, as he grinned from ear to ear.

Chapter 11

Sicily Comes to the Rescue

The balance of the weekend flew by. On Monday mornings, it had become Robert's habit to arrive at their palatial offices before anyone else. This provided him an enormous benefit in his dealings with colleagues, not only in their own branch but also with their branches in Milan and Genoa, as Robert had ample time to study any missives which came in from New York over the weekend before anyone else did so. He also found it advantageous to be able to pore over all the leading morning papers and to reflect on the notices from the regulatory authorities in peace and quiet and before his clients had done so. Schaffer had just finished evaluating Antinori's weekly strategy paper, which called for boosting interest rates to all clients across the board, when Matra came into Robert's office. He was breathing heavily, as though he had been running or doing heavy exercises, and perspiration was running from the top of his baldhead down into his horrified eyes.

"Robert, hurry, come with me, please, hurry," he said anxiously.

Schaffer got up instantly and ran after him as he charged toward the back of the building and down a staircase that lead into their back office systems and transaction processing area. Matra had direct responsibility for this segment of the branch's activities, so Schaffer seldom bothered coming down here, except to show his face and let them know that the credit and marketing people cared about them. Most of the staff had arrived but there was still very little actually going on in terms of work as they were chatting about the weekend, chewing on breakfast rolls and drinking cappucino. Matra went straight to the back of the large, open plan room where a small team of people sat in a separate section, charged with the task of issuing and policing documentary transactions such as letters of credit, bankers drafts and the like. The deputy head of the section, a young, not unattractive woman in her early 30's called Adele, stood guard over a desk which was usually inhabited by her boss, Carlo Rodolfo. "Have you found him, Adele?" Matra asked weakly in Italian.

"No, and I've tried everywhere I can imagine," she replied in Italian. Scarcely anyone down here spoke English. The systems and transactions' people were all very bright, and easy to train, but they tended to come from the blue-collar districts of Rome. As a result, they did not have the occasion to learn English or, for that matter, any other foreign language. Robert saw that Adele was attempting to appear disconsolate but, despite her efforts, she conveyed an impression of smug contentment.

Matra was beside himself. Schaffer hadn't seen him terribly concerned about anything much less terrified. He was in a state that Robert had never witnessed in anyone, other than Matra, before or since. He was a walking, talking, cliche of a panic-stricken mortal. "But, Adele," he implored her, "you must find him, for me, for your Jean Pierre," he pleaded now in French, his native tongue.

Thank god he was speaking French, I remember thinking. "Jean Pierre, I don't think she understands you, you're speaking French," Schaffer said, as he saw the blank look on the young woman's face.

"What?" he questioned me in French, as he turned and stared at me as though he had never seen me before.

"Jean Pierre, let me handle this," Robert ordered him in English. "Go back to your office."

"But, you don't comprehend what has happened, what Rodolfo has done,"
He said to me still in French.

I could see Matra was in a state of shock. "Just do as I say," Robert said softly but sternly in Matra's native language. "You don't want the staff to see you this way," Robert whispered to him.

He looked at Schaffer but his eyes weren't focussing properly. "You want to deal with it, Robert?" he finally asked.

"Yes, Jean Pierre, don't worry. Whatever has happened can't be all that bad."

"Oh, it's bad all right," he said in a profound Gallic manner.

I finally took him by the arm and led him to the stairway. "Go on up there, I'll take care of it. I'll work it out with Adele. Don't worry."

"Yes, good idea," he said, "with Adele. She's a good girl, she'll help you."

Once he was out of sight, Robert returned to where Adele remained on guard. Schaffer's Italian had improved a thousand fold since coming to Rome so he was able to barge right in. "Miss?" Robert asked her in Italian.

"Sposini," she helped him.

"Miss Sposini," Robert started again. "Tell me precisely what has happened."

"As I explained to Dr. Matra, Mr. Rodolfo has stolen some money."

"How much money?" he asked her.

"Five million U.S. Dollars," she informed Robert calmly, "and the proof is here in his desk drawer," she said triumphantly as she pointed at the drawer.

In the early 1970's, five million dollars was a hell of a lot of money, even by Wall Street standards, in fact, it was Global's entire profits for the year, so Schaffer begin to fathom why poor old Jean Pierre was feeling more than a bit under the weather. Robert had begun to speculate about Rodolfo a few weeks previously when Schaffer had gleaned from his secretary, Louisa, that Rodolfo owned a villa about an hour and a half's drive north of Rome at the very chic Mediterranean resort of Porto Santo Stefano. And just this weekend, his new acquaintance from the Vatican, George Pavoni, had inquired whether Robert knew a guy at his bank called Rodolfo who had a beautiful 65-foot sailing yacht that he kept at the same resort. Robert had planned to check Rodolfo's compensation package this week, as he knew that even a senior clerk who had been with the bank for many years could not afford such luxuries. "Excellent, Miss Sposini, well done for being vigilant," Robert told her, more as an example for the small crowd of people who were now surrounding them than anything else.

"Thank you, thank you very much," she said proudly. "I was only doing my duty."

"Yes, good...very good" Schaffer said. "Could you tell me exactly what has happened? I mean, how did Rodolfo pilfer the money? Can you show me the evidence?" Robert interrogated her, as he steered her aside, out of the hearing of the other staff members.

"With pleasure. As you know I must check all incoming and outgoing transfers of money."

She was waiting for Robert's acknowledgement and so he said "Of course."

"When I arrived this morning I proceeded directly to our accounting department and requested a record of all transfers last week, a sort of checking that I have been asked by Dr. Matra to carry out periodically. It's just like balancing your cheque book," she offered by way of explanation just in case he hadn't understood what had happened.

"And you spotted the payment?"

"Yes. I noticed one unusually large disbursement that I had not been asked to validate, of Five million U.S. Dollars made after hours, our time on Friday. Rodolfo was not here and so I asked our accounting department for a copy of the payment instruction which I have here," she stated proudly as she reached under her sweater, where she had hidden it for safe keeping, and brought out a copy of the bank's standard payment form. "I saw Rodolfo's signature on it but not that of Dr. Matra, which should be there for such amounts. I became wary and, when Mr. Rodolfo was late for work, I looked in his desk and found the details of the payment order, including a tested telex that he personally sent to New York authorizing the funds to be paid."

"Excellent, Miss Sposini," Robert complimented her. And where did the money go?"

"To Switzerland," she responded.

Robert reflected for a moment. Even though he seldom became involved in the mechanics of such transfers, Miss Sposini seemed to be efficient and knowledgeable. The amount was very large, the destination was suspect, Miss Sposini had not been asked to check the instructions that were made after hours and, most important of all, Matra had not signed off on it. "Maybe a client ordered the transfer," Robert suggested.

"Perhaps, but I doubt it."

"Why?" he asked reasonably.

"There is no documentation to support that and because the money has been transferred to the account of a company controlled by a man that all Italy knows is a crook."

"And who is that, may I ask?"

"Dr. Ciano, Dr. Roberto di Ciano," she answered me.

A shiver went straight through my spine. "How do you know, Miss Sposini?"

"That he's a crook?"

Robert deliberated for an instant and said "Yes, of course, that as well. But I am puzzled about how you know that the company is controlled by Ciano?"

"Rodolfo once told me that he had an offer to work for that company and I investigated it with my uncle, because Rodolfo said he would pay me double what I make here to join as well."

"I see," Robert said. "What did your uncle tell you?"

"Oh, he said the company was controlled by Ciano and that I should not even contemplate going there."

"But how did he know that Ciano had an interest in the company?"

She looked surprised by Robert's question and her face turned a bright red. "My uncle is a chauffeur for someone in the Italian Government." She anticipated my next question and said "For a government minister."

"I see," was all Robert could think of to say.

"Would you like me to draft a report, Dr. Coleman?"

"Yes," Robert responded, "please do, and address it to Dr. Matra." Robert paused for a second and then asked, "Have you advised anyone else of this, Miss Sposini?"

"No, not yet. Only you and Dr. Matra have the details. The staff knows we've got a big problem.

"OK. Let me see your report as soon as possible. Dr. Matra and I will take care of letting everyone know."

Schaffer made his way back to Jean Pierre's office and discovered from Louisa that he had gone upstairs. He had given Robert a key to the little lift next to his office and so a minute later he found Matra standing by one of the room's grand windows silently sipping what looked like a brandy. He had his back to Robert and did not seem to be aware of his presence so Robert said, "Jean Pierre, are you all right?"

He literally flinched at the sound of Schaffer's voice and turned and said "Robert, I'm finished. And it won't be helpful to your career either," he added ominously.

At least he was speaking English, Robert thought. "Listen, Jean Pierre, there is a chance that we may be able to get the money back but I'll need your and Jane's help and, we'll have to move rapidly."

"Get the money back?" he said in disbelief. And then he begin to laugh. "Come on, Robert, that money is gone. Let's not kid each other. I'm sure a few calls will confirm that Rodolfo has sold his flat in Rome and his villa and boat at Porto Santo Stefano. He's probably already in South America. Yeah," he begin to talk to himself, "I'm sure I'm right. I'll bet he's gone to Brazil or Argentina. He's got family there, in both countries."

"Jean Pierre," Robert shouted at him to break him out of his useless speculation. "Get a hold of yourself, man. Your career will only be finished if you stand around here drinking brandy and staring out the window. I have a plan and I need your and Jane's help, now, like yesterday," Robert said again.

The shouting seemed to have the same effect as shaking him. Robert could see his eyes begin to focus and finally gaze into his. "Don't humor me, Robert. I've seen things like this in banking but, thankfully, never on this scale. I can tell you one thing from experience, the odds on ever seeing that money again are minuscule if not zero. The authorities will tell you that the moment we inform them." He stopped for a moment and then added, "So will our colleagues who will be checking the old insurance policies to make sure the premiums have been paid."

He consumed another long drink of what was unquestionably brandy and begin to shuffle around in a little circle as he scratched his baldhead with his watchband. Schaffer could see he was losing him again and so he tried a new tactic to keep him from becoming a totally useless basket case. "Jean Pierre," he begin in an ominous tone of voice. "Did you know that Jane is a spy for the American Government?"

He froze in his tracks and slowly turned his head to scrutinize him. When he was satisfied from the expression on Robert's face that he was deadly serious, he said, "Don't be a fucking idiot."

Robert had never heard him curse before so he was on new terrain. "She could use her leverage to get them to lean on Ciano to return the money," Schaffer suggested. "I know that the Americans have cultivated and worked with him and that they have influence over him."

He wasn't moving at all now and was continuing to peer at Schaffer intently. His eyes were alert and Robert could see that he was thinking about what he had told him. "Even if what you say about Jane is accurate, and I don't think for a second that it is, she can't be valuable enough to the Americans to get them to put any meaningful pressure on a guy like Ciano."

"That alone won't be enough. I don't disagree. But a friend of mine has some intelligence that proves Ciano is actually a communist sympathizer and financial backer, the exact opposite of what the Americans think. Also, I have a relative, an uncle by marriage, that can put special pressure on Ciano," Robert said, and paused for emphasis before adding, "if I want him to."

Signs of hope returned to Jean Pierre's countenance. His demeanors begin to reflect a man who saw more than just a faint, proverbial glimmer of light at the end of the tunnel. "Robert, if you're being less than completely truthful with me, I'll never forgive you."

"Frankly, Jean Pierre, I'm being dead straight, mid-west, American honest. This whole situation could actually be helpful to me in resolving some unrelated but significant issues, like my crusade to eradicate the insider dealing ring that led to me being sent down here." Robert could have added helping a friend to bring some corrupt, Italian labor unions into line and settling some scores with the Cianos but Matra was in no condition to deal with that data. Instead Robert said, "I have more than eradicating a blot on my career at stake as an incentive to help in retrieving our $5 million."

Robert saw Matra transform himself right before his eyes. His stooped shoulders were replaced by his more customary, shoulders back, proud Parisian air. He tightened his belt in an effort to hide his plump stomach and ran a comb through his disheveled hair. "OK, Robert, I'm ready to go to battle with these felons. This is my problem and my responsibility," he admitted, "but I need and accept your offer of help. If you can clear up other issues in the process of helping me recover the funds, so much the better."

Schaffer was sure that Matra viewed his little speech as a call to battle. Robert didn't need the motivation but decided his response would be critical to Matra's dedication to the task at hand, and so he reacted in a way that he hoped would remove any of his lingering reluctance. "Jean Pierre, I just want you to know that I don't care much for criminals, even petty crooks rub me the wrong way. I mean, I don't even like the guy that smuggles the odd extra bottle of scotch through customs or the lady that bribes the clerk at the telephone company $20 to process her request for a new extension rather than the fifty or so that would get done before hers. Even though the money that Rodolfo and Ciano have conspired to pilfer isn't mine, I want it back. I want it back badly."

Robert's comments seemed to be just what the doctor ordered. "All right, Robert lets move into action. You said Jane could be helpful. I'll ring and ask her to come here as soon as possible."

"Good idea, Jean Pierre. Maybe you should forewarn her that I learned from John Foster of the Commercial Attaché's Office at the U.S. Embassy that she has been helpful to them, and that we could really use their help now in getting our money back. You might also mention that I have some very valuable information for Foster on Roberto di Ciano."

"I'll do that," he replied. As we walked over to the elevator he stopped and said "Robert, I'm grateful for what you've done so far. Frankly, you saved me from making a complete fool of myself. If nothing other than that comes out of this, I owe you."

Robert smiled back at him and said "No sweat, Jean Pierre."

Robert had been looking for an excuse to use his uncle Mark's offer of help if Robert ever got into difficulty in Italy. It's not that he relished trouble. It' just that he wanted to see if his uncle had any real influence, if the stories he had heard in his childhood years were just stories or if they had some substance. As far back as he could remember, his father used to tell him about his uncle-in-law's father and mother coming to the States from Sicily during Prohibition and how their eldest son, Robert's uncle, smuggled booze into the States from Canada. The family legend was that against all the odds, including armed opposition from other bootleggers, he successfully ran liquor filled boats across the deep, moonlit waters of Lake Michigan and built up enough capital to go into the legitimate liquor trade after the repeal of Prohibition. He put his younger brothers and sisters through school, including college, provided his parents with the best living style money could buy and sent substantial sums back to his relatives in the old country.

All Robert had was a phone number in a little village in Sicily which bore his uncle's family name, Casateri, and his uncle's instructions to call it, use his name and say he needed help. Schaffer dialled slowly and felt guilty that he had not contacted them a year earlier. At least Sherri had written to them several times before and since coming to Italy, he thought to himself. "Pronto," said the voice of a young girl or woman.

"This is Robert Schaffer, the nephew of Mark Casateri. I am living in Rome and I need some help," I said in my best Italian.

"Just a moment," she answered me.

Robert timed the wait at two minutes before hearing the next voice, which was deep and masculine. "This is Umberto Casateri. If you are Robert Schaffer, you will know Marco Casateri's eldest daughter's middle name." He said no more. It was a question.

Robert didn't have to think long about that. "My uncle doesn't have any daughters," Robert informed him.

"I see," he said. After another moment, he asked "But he has sons." Another question.

"Four sons," and Robert gave him their names.

"How are you enjoying Italy, Robert?" he asked in broken English.

My Italian was better than his English but I wanted to compliment him by speaking English. "Wonderful, until the last few months," I told him honestly. "With whom am I speaking?" Robert inquired.

"I am your cousin, Umberto Casateri," he returned to Italian. "I am sorry about my English but I've only been able to practice when our uncle visits every year or so."

Robert had no idea that his uncle had visited so frequently. "Have you received my wife's letters?"

"Of course. We all want to meet you both sometime soon but you said you need help. What can your family do for you?"

He insisted that Robert go to a pay phone where Robert rang him and he called back. They talked for over an hour and, when they finished, Robert knew the bank would get its money back and that Paolo and Stephanie's problems with the unions would be resolved. Robert also was fairly sure that he would have few, if any, difficulties with Max Feathers, John Foster or Roberto di Ciano ever again. These were clearly powerful and influential people and Robert was fortunate to have them at the other end of a telephone.

Chapter 12

A Challenge for Louisa

Robert didn't want to seem unappreciative of the Casateri's assistance but to this day he laments that he agreed, in return for their support, not to mention their involvement and not to take any credit whatsoever for the return of the bank's $5 million, the resolution of Paolo's problems with the labor unions or for getting Feathers, Foster and Ciano off his family's back. At the time his cousin mentioned it to me, it seemed entirely reasonable. His life and the lives of those closest to him were coming apart at the seams and all of a sudden everything was going to be all right. Who wouldn't have agreed to the Casateri's proviso?

As instructed, immediately after their telephone conversation, he left the bank, went to the local health club and made a scene about wanting to a have a female masseuse when none were immediately available. The Casateri's wanted him to have proof of where he was and what he was doing for the rest of the day and this was the best he could think of on the spur of the moment. It took the club over two hours to produce a masseuse, during which time Robert had a swim, a sauna and a snack of fresh fruit and yogurt. By the time he returned to the bank late in the afternoon, he had a little stack of messages from Jean Pierre, Bonnie, Paolo, Stephanie and Max Feathers not to mention colleagues from around the bank's European network. Instinctively, Robert knew that his topsy-turvy world had been put back in place. As he was thumbing through the neat little mound, Louisa peered in and came over to his desk. "You've missed all the fun," she announced quietly.

"The money is back?"

"You know it's back."

"And Rodolfo, any news of him?" Robert replied, ignoring her reply.

"I doubt that we'll ever hear of him again. I'm sure Jean Pierre is right. He's gone to South America where he has family." She saw Robert eying the pile of messages and said: "I'm dying to talk to you but you'd better make the important calls first. Bonnie is extremely anxious to tell you her news," she revealed and then grinned and left.

Louisa's confirmation of what he was certain would happen with respect to the money made little goose bumps pop out all over Robert's skin. From where he was seated, if he leaned slightly to the left, he could just see Matra across the corridor taking one phone call after another. He was bestowing a few seconds on each well-wisher and then moving on to the next one in what appeared to be a never-ending stream. His more normal grin was pasted into a smug smile of satisfaction. Robert picked up his phone, dialed their home number and was pleased to hear Bonnie's voice after scarcely one ring. She must have been waiting by the phone. "Where have you been, Robert? I've got the most incredible news."

“I had a few things to do. You've heard from Louisa about the $5 million, I presume?"

"Yes, it's an amazing story. Louisa's convinced it was all your doing." When Robert was silent, she pressed him, saying "Well?"

"No comment."

"Robert!" she said his name loudly, the way she did when she wouldn't take no for an answer.

Schaffer could hear by her tone he'd eventually have to say something. "I'll tell you all about it when I get home, which shouldn't be more than an hour and a half or so from now," he assured her after glancing at his watch. "These phones may not be secure," he added by way of explanation. "Louisa says you have some news for me?"

"Yes," she said breathlessly. "It's like I've been a part of a Hollywood film since a little after mid-morning. A team of people from the U.S. Embassy, led by that guy Foster, came to our apartment. I think they would have come in even if I hadn't been here."

Robert’s pulse had already been elevated about the return of the $5 million but the mention of Foster and a team of people from the embassy coming to their apartment that morning had it up so high that he could feel himself flushing. "What happened?" he interjected.

"Foster and all the other people, including a woman whom I think was there just to make me feel comfortable, produced their U.S. Government I.D.'s and explained that they had instructions from the bank to search for bugging devices. I tried to ring you but you were out. Louisa suggested that I just let them have a look around. Neither of us could see any harm in it."

"Go on," Robert encouraged her.

"Well, they found all the ones we had discovered, and a few we hadn't. I could tell they knew where they were although they went through the motions of using electronic equipment to find them."

"Did they explain who put them there and why?"

"Initially, Foster claimed that it happens frequently in Italy, particularly to American bankers. He said the devices were typical of those used by the Mafia to gain inside information so they can make informed investments."

"And later?"

"Well, just before they left, he called me aside and made a personal apology. He said that if they had been properly briefed about us, he was sure that the devices would never have been allowed to be planted."

"It's not an admission of guilt but it is damn close to it, isn't it?"

"As close as we'll ever get, Robert."

"Unbelievable," was all he could think of to say.

"Yes it is," she agreed, and then asked "Have you heard anything from Paolo about his meetings with the unions?"

"Not yet, but he has a call into me. If it's good news, I'll call you back. Are you going to be around?"

"Absolutely. I'm just doing a bit of prep for my classes tomorrow."

When he finished his call with Bonnie, he swiveled his chair toward the west so that he could relish the glorious Roman sunset while he savored the moment. When he turned back to telephone Paolo, Jean Pierre was hovering in front of his desk. Robert started to get to his feet to congratulate him but Matra wouldn't let him get up. "Just sit there and relax," he insisted. "Louisa is convinced that we would have never seen that money again if it weren't for you and somehow I know she is right. I'm grateful for whatever you've done and I'm also grateful for the way you took over this morning. When it comes time for your next assignment, I'll kill myself to get you anything you want, including my job here in Rome."

There wasn't much Robert could say to that. The guy was offering him his job and, Robert thought, considering that Matra would have been more than content to finish his career in that position that was saying something. Robert finally said "I'm just thrilled that it has worked out, Jean Pierre."

He beamed at Schaffer and said, "Lets have a celebration. I'll meet you upstairs in fifteen minutes. The entire staff is invited. Paga la banca!"

Robert laughed and said, "Be there in a minute. I just have to return a few of these calls."

"OK but don't be late. You're an important part of a little toast I want to make."

When he had gone, he rang the Hassler and found Paolo in the bar with Stephanie. The staid ambience that normally pervaded the five star luxury hotel had been replaced with noise that was more customary at a New Year's Eve Party.

"What is going on Paolo?" It doesn't sound like the Hassler I know and love.

"I'm throwing an impromptu party. Champagne for everyone."

"Good news from the labor union leaders?" he inquired.

"Good news, Robert? That is the understatement of the century. Those guys nearly kissed my feet this morning. For the first two and a half hours, we remained at an impasse. Then the head of their delegation was called away urgently. When he returned about ten minutes later, everything begin to change. They started to make concessions and eventually we agreed on a sound and fair basis for our future labor relations. Frankly, I still can't believe it."

"That is fantastic news, Paolo. I can't wait to join the celebrations."

"We're seeing you later for dinner, our treat."

"That's great," he said, "see you later."

Several days afterward Robert received an invitation from George Pavoni to join him and what his note characterized as several other people for a day of discussions on the Italian economy. A charitable organization called "Friends of Rome," or something like that was sponsoring the conference, which was to take place at a small hotel near Porto Ercole. This ancient fishing village is on the opposite side of the peninsula that holds the more posh Porto Santo Stefano.

Robert had Louisa ring Pavoni's secretary to get details and, when he learned that most of the people were bringing wives and staying for the weekend, he rang Bonnie to try to persuade her to come along. Ever since the Ciano party, she had become reluctant to accept weekend invitations, he thought, because she subconsciously feared a repeat performance of what had happened previously.

"Isn't it odd that a priest would be organizing an event involving wives?" she asked me reasonably.

"Maybe he's got one in hiding somewhere," Robert said maliciously.

"Robert, don't be an ass. George Pavoni is a very respectable Vatican official. I'm sure he doesn't have a wife hidden away in a little fishing village, or anywhere else for that matter."

"Maybe he has a girl friend."

"Robert!"

She was getting cross now and that wasn't his intention. He just wanted her to lose some of the seriousness that had afflicted her, even more than himself, since the advent of what he had decided to describe to himself and others as the "Ciano Disaster."

"Talk to Louisa about it. She thinks it's completely on the up and up."

"Well, all right. But what am I going to do while you're in your conference?"

"Louisa thinks you will be happy just enjoying the hotel. It's apparently one of the most beautiful in the world, even better than the San Marco at Positano."

"Nothing could be better than the San Marco, Robert. But, if it's in that league, Louisa's right. I'll be happy just enjoying the hotel."

"Great. Shall I accept then?"

"Let me have a quick word with Louisa; not that I don't trust you."

"What a suspicious girl you are," he said, and passed her to Louisa.

Schaffer turned his attention to a pile of letters, telexes, faxes and messages that had accumulated in the wake of the $5 million episode. If they had been able to brush the whole event under the carpet, few if any of these communications would have arisen. Unfortunately, the staff leaked the incident to friends, who leaked it to the press. Most Roman newspapers and even the influential Milan paper, "Corriere della Sera," splashed their front pages with stories describing the occurrence. As a result, clients wanted explanations and assurances that nothing similar could happen with their funds and reporters used any excuse they could think of to try to get an interview with Matra, Robert and other staff members.

There was one odd communication from Tako Mitsuki, the Managing Director of the Italian subsidiary of Japan's second or third largest trading company. Robert had done an incredibly complicated deal for him just after arriving in Rome, and he had come to think that Robert could solve any problem of any type whatsoever. He saw that Louisa was off the phone and buzzed for her to come in. "Do you know anything more about this than what you've written?" he asked, as he handed her the message she had scribbled for him.

"Only a little. He wants to send two colleagues to see you as soon as possible. I got the impression that it's too confidential to discuss on the telephone."

Robert thought for a moment. The Japanese had never wasted his time before, especially if they wanted to come and see him. "Ring his secretary and tell her that I'll see them this afternoon." As Louisa turned to go Robert said, "How did it go with Bonnie?"

She looked a bit surprised by his question. "Oh, fine. She asked me to have lunch with her and to help her select a wardrobe for the weekend at Porto Ercole." She laughed when she saw the expression of shock on his face and, before he could say anything, she said, "Don't worry. If you're very good to me, I'll only take her to the medium priced boutiques."

Matra and Robert decided to go out to lunch together, "paga la banca." They actually did this about once a week just to catch up and discovered that they got more done in this relaxed atmosphere than they ever would have sitting around a conference table in their offices. In addition to thanking him all over again, he sounded Robert out on joining his club that was the best one in Italy. As Schaffer knew that he had not even offered to do this for his former boss, he was very complimented. Robert ran the weekend at Porto Ercole by him, hoping he would insist on letting him write it off on his expense account. He thought it was a great opportunity and insisted that the bank would pick up the tab. Robert offered to request an invitation for him and Jane and, even to stand down in his favor. But he declined, as Robert knew he would, saying "Just try to get Pavoni to bring Machinkos along here to lunch one day. I'd really enjoy that."

The Japanese arrived within minutes of returning to the office. They went through the ritual of exchanging cards and a few minutes of small talk. Then the senior of the two, a Mr. Matsu, turned the conversation to the reason for their visit. "Mr. Schaffer," he begin, "I know you are a very busy man so I will not waste your time. May I state the purpose of our visit?"

"Of course," Robert responded.

"The chairman of our parent company in Japan is coming to Rome for a series of most important meetings with some of the largest companies in Italy. We have to make certain arrangements for him and we would like your help on some of the more difficult aspects of the visit."

"I would be honored to assist," Robert replied.

"I must warn you, Mr. Schaffer, that our chairman is considered to be a god in Japan and so he is accustomed to special treatment, very special treatment indeed."

"I understand," Robert assured him, even though he didn't really, "what can I do to be helpful?"

Matsu turned to the other fellow whose name still escapes Schaffer. Perhaps what he had to say simply shocked it out of him. "Mr. Schaffer, our chairman wants to play golf at the San Pietro Golf Club. Can you arrange that?"

Robert thought for a moment before making any commitment. The San Pietro didn't like Americans much less Japanese, but he figured that something could be arranged. Paolo Mancini had interceded on his behalf and he knew he would for someone he recommended. "Yes, I'm sure I can."

"Excellent," said Matsu but he nodded again to his colleague to continue the interrogation.

"Because our chairman is a god, he cannot be allowed to walk. Can you arrange for a golf cart for him and perhaps one for the members of his party?"

Schaffer had never seen a golf cart in Italy. "I must check."

Matsu volunteered, "We know that will not be easy. There are only two in Rome. One belongs to the American Ambassador and the other to Archbishop Machinkos of the Vatican. If you cannot arrange it, we will have a big problem as we are not allowed to bring one from Japan."

"I see," Robert said. Schaffer was beginning to understand how important their chairman was.

"There is more, Mr. Schaffer," said Matsu's helper. "Because our chairman is a god, in Japan," he added quickly, "there can be no one else on the golf course while he is playing."

Robert stared at them to see if they were making a joke. When he could see that they were in earnest, he asked, "On the entire course or just on the hole he is playing?"

"Matsu answered himself "On the entire course."

"That is tricky."

"Twicky?" Matsu asked. "What is twicky?"

"It may be very difficult. I'll have to make a few calls and let you know. Is there anything else?" Robert asked out of courtesy, not dreaming there would be.

Matsu took over completely now. "Yes," he announced, "there are several very important matters. Our chairman needs to be entertained."

"That will not be a problem. I am sure that Mr. Matra, our branch manager, and I will be able to provide suitable entertainment."

"He likes women when he is away from Japan. Can you arrange that in the strictest confidence?"

"What do you mean he likes women?"

"He likes the company of pretty young women when he goes to bed at night. They must be tall, blonde-haired, blue-eyed, and white skinned."

Robert had done a few favors for his clients but this was the first time he was being asked to be a pimp. "Let me think about it."

"When can you tell us if you can help in these matters?"

"Is there anything else?"

"One other small request. My chairman wants to take one of the women to a villa in Sicily for two weeks following his business meetings. It must be the type of villa suitable for European royalty. Money is no object in any of these matters."

It took great restraint not to laugh. Here Robert had the representatives of one of the most powerful companies in the world asking for the most banal favors he could imagine for a man who was considered a god in their country. "I'll let you know if I can help."

"Can you tell us by this evening?" Matsu asked.

Robert figured he would know either way within a few minutes, as the only person he knew who would have a chance at organizing it all was Louisa. "Yes, I'll telephone your boss by six pm, would that be all right?"

Matsu considered momentarily. "That will be fine."

When they had gone, Robert asked Louisa to come in. He was embarrassed by the whole thing but had no choice but to seek her help if he wanted to meet their request. When he finished explaining what had transpired, he asked her if this was something he should do.

"Are they an important client?"

"Yes, they are, very important, especially to our colleagues in Japan."

"Then you should do it," she said clearly and succinctly and without hesitation.

"But I have no idea where to begin, Louisa."

"I do."

"Will it cost a lot?"

She thought for a moment. "No, probably nothing at all, but I cannot promise."

"Do you mind doing it, Louisa? If you do, just say so, and I will tell them we cannot help."
She looked at me carefully and said, "You cannot do that. You must at least try; besides, I have an old aunt who has the perfect villa in Sicily. Tell them you will do it for them but that they should only talk to me about it, at my home, in the future." And then she got the managing director, Mr. Akio Okuda on the phone and listened while Robert gave him his answer. When he had hung up, she asked, "What did he say?"

"That if I ever need anything, anything at all, all I have to do is ask."

"Good," she said and went out and begin to make some calls.

Chapter 13

Cultivating People that Count

Within a week Schaffer's business life reverted to the normal Roman style. The conference at Porto Ercole was not scheduled to take place until late May, roughly a month distant, so Robert decided to see if George Pavoni was available for lunch. He was pleased when he took his call. "George, I'm really looking forward to the conference next month. Thanks very much for including me."

"Not at all. There will be some interesting people there and I think you can bring fresh views to a stale conversation."

"I know you're busy. I just wanted to follow up on my offer of lunch when we played golf together. I'd like you to join me and Jean Pierre Matra, our number one here in Rome, sometime in the next couple of weeks?"

"I've been looking forward to your invitation, Robert," he responded, sounding a bit down. "Some of our traditional bankers are beginning to take our relationship for granted. Maybe you can help light a fire under them and make some money for your bank in the process."

"I can assure you of some new ideas and, as I promised you on the golf course, marvelous cuisine," trying to sound positive and upbeat to be sure he was left with a good feeling about their call.

"Great. May I ask a colleague to join me?"

"Sure, we'd be delighted. Should I get my secretary to arrange a date with yours?"

"Yes, perfect," he replied, sounding better than he had initially. "Before you go, I may have a lead for you on a piece of business. Do you know Cardinal Pelli?"

Robert thought for an instant and had a blurry recollection of being introduced to him at a big reception that Matra held just after Robert and Bonnie arrived in Rome, but he wasn't certain. "I've heard of him and may have been introduced to him at a bank function a few months ago."

"How's your Italian?"

"It's actually pretty decent," I was pleased to inform him.

"Good. The cardinal doesn't speak any English but he's very bright and helpful to me from time to time. He needs somc advice. I'll call him to introduce you. Give me until tomorrow afternoon and then ring him."

"Will do, George, and thanks, thanks very much."

"No problem. See you soon."

Louisa came in when she saw that I was off the phone. "Good conversation?" she asked, as she smiled, probably because he was undoubtedly sporting the largest grin in Rome, if not Italy, at that particular instant.

"Not good, Louisa, great, maybe even fantastic."

"And?"

"And, you need to call Pavoni's secretary tomorrow afternoon and arrange a date for him and a colleague to join me and Jean Pierre for lunch, here. He's agreed to do it sometime in the next two weeks or so. Whatever is good for them."

"Do you know the colleague's name?"

"He didn't say, Louisa. I just assumed it would be one of his assistants. Will you ask and also ask her for the telephone number of Cardinal Pelli? Pavoni thinks he may have some business for us."

She raised her eyebrows in acknowledgement of the progress I was making with the Vatican and then said "Of course, and then she immediately changed the subject to matters at hand. "You have a busy day ahead of you. I've typed out your schedule."

Conveniently for Robert, she had typed it on a piece of paper that would fit perfectly into his inside suit-coat pocket. As he looked it over, he wished he could just take the day off and enjoy his little triumph with Pavoni. No one in the bank had ever even had lunch with a Vatican employee of the level of Pavoni and no one had ever been introduced into a piece of business by them. Schaeffer knew from his brief but rapidly growing experience that a business day in Rome or for that matter anywhere else doesn't get much better than that, unless you're collecting a big fee, of course. "Everything looks pretty routine, Louisa, except this meeting with Jean Pierre and Mr. Lupo. Who is he?"

"He was introduced by Dr. Antonori. I think he's a representative of the company that is building the road through the Gran Sasso."

"You mean they're building a road through that granite mountain down south?" Robert asked. You are joking, Louisa, aren't you?"

"If they can build the road, it will make it much easier to travel to the southeastern part of Italy," she told me defensively.

"How much of the road has been completed?" he interrogated her.

She thought for a moment and her brow wrinkled. When Louisa finally answered, she had on her haughty, socialist look. "It is a very important project. The company employs a great many people. I believe the road is only just started and it will take another ten years to finish."

"If they can finish it," Robert said, reminding her of the challenge of digging through granite.

"If they cannot go through it, they will go around it," she assured me.

"OK. I'll see what I can do," he said as he already begin to dread the presentations he would have to develop for the bank's assorted credit committees in Milan, London and New York in order to procure consent to grant the loan. He knew the company building the road would never go bankrupt, because another company that was owned in turn by the Republic of Italy owned it. The guys in London would groan but approve the loan because it would inevitably look to be so profitable. But the jerks in New York could well turn it down in order to throw more money out the window on some metal bender in the America whose days were numbered. It was tough to get enthusiastic with all that in the back of his mind. It would have been easier for him to make an advance to the Italian subsidiary of the mid-west metal bender, which was near bankruptcy, than to furnish money to an Italian company that would continue to exist even if it couldn't dig a whole in a granite mountain. As Louisa smiled and turned to go back to her desk, Robert decided now was the perfect moment to remind her that she still hadn't managed to secure an appointment he had been hoping for ever since he came to Rome. "Oh, Louisa," he called out to her when she was almost out the door, "would you mind trying Tom Sugar again?"

She turned and smiled. "If you make the loan to the road building company, I'll get you the appointment with Mr. Sugar."

Robert laughed and said "Other way around. Appointment first, loan second."

"Deal," she responded.

Ten minutes later she was back in his office and, seeing that he was on the phone, she took a piece of paper from a note pad, wrote on it, handed it back to him and left. When he read it, he nearly leapt out of his chair. "Appointment with Mr. Sugar, tomorrow, at ten am." He couldn't believe it. As soon as he was off the telephone he went out to her desk. "Thank you so much. How did you manage it, Louisa?"

"Oh, it wasn't terribly difficult."

"Tell me," he asked, as he just couldn't imagine how she finally persuaded Sugar to see him.

"He's been pestering me for months to have lunch with him. He just happened to ring again a few minutes ago and, I said 'yes'."

"Louisa?" Robert said sternly.

"Only lunch. He wants more, but that is all he's going to get," she said matter of factly.

He looked at her, again admired her beauty and smiled. He knew that there was no question about that and felt just a little sorry for Mr. Sugar.

Antinori surprised them by turning up for the meeting with the road building company. He arrived with Lupo, who looked alarmingly like the meaning of his name, 'wolf'. He had a long, gangly torso and his legs were not much longer than his arms. Facial hair, which had been groomed meticulously into a combined flowing beard and mustache, blended into his bushy eyebrows and the rest of the hair on his head. "Marco, Jean Pierre greeted Antinori. We didn't know you'd be introducing Mr. Lupo personally. It's good to see you."

Antinori looked slightly embarrassed. Robert figured that he had probably told Lupo that his presence at the meeting was critical. Schaffer knew Antinori had a girl friend in Rome and figured that was his real reason for coming down from Milan. By attending the meeting with Lupo, Antinori could charge the whole trip, including a gift for his friend, to the bank. "I didn't want you to make any special preparations, Jean Pierre." He nodded to me, introduced Lupo to both of them, and then they went to Matra's entertainment center.

While Matra showed Lupo around, Antinori took me over to one of the windows overlooking Rome. "I gather from Jean Pierre that without your intervention we would be out $5 million. I just wanted to let you know that we're all grateful. Well done, Robert."

Schaffer had come to know Antinori reasonably well and praise of this nature was not without its price so he was not surprised when he said "I also gather you're getting close to the Vatican. I'd die to be in the luncheon you'll be having here in a few weeks."

How could Robert say 'no' to the country manager? "If you're in Rome, I'd love to have you attend," was all he could say to him, even though he knew that he would now take credit for organizing the whole thing.

"Oh, I'll fly down especially for the luncheon, Robert. This is a real break- through. In a way, it's more important than getting back that $5 million, at least as far as the bank is concerned. For Jean Pierre, and you, bringing in the Vatican will help the guys in New York forget about the lax controls which prevailed here."

Robert didn't know what to say. It was an odd way for Antinori to be thanking him but more in keeping with his style than his initial unequivocal praise. "I would have thought that $5 million in hand is worth more than the prospect of doing business with the Vatican," he said.

"No question, Robert, but one way or the other the bank would have obtained its $5 million. The insurance companies would have had to pay up, less a small deductible."

Looking back on his career this single, two or three minute conversation had more to do with his leaving the bank than any fifty other events combined. It said it all really, especially coming from an outsider like Antinori. An insider would never have been able to articulate the problems of the institution so clearly and succinctly.

"Robert," he heard Jean Pierre paging him from near a grouping of impressionist paintings. "Come and tell Mr. Lupo about these artists. You know them so much better than I do."

Lupo and Schaffer hit it off. Robert happened to know a bit more about the Impressionist period than he did and they both loved Renoir. The details of the loan became insignificant and, just after he discovered that Schaffer would be attending the Vatican sponsored conference at Porto Ercole, Robert did a superb deal for the bank, subject only to the approval of the good old boys at head office.

Over dinner that night Robert told Bonnie about some of the things going on in the bank. This violated a self-imposed cardinal rule, but he needed to share the reasons why he knew they should begin a medium to long term search for another job for him in banking or a related field. She asked all the right questions, as he knew she would. After almost two hours of relentless interrogation, she said "sounds like everyone in the bank is a crook of one type or another," she concluded, "and if you haven't become one already, you will if you try to make the bank a career."

He hadn't thought of it that way. "I knew I should violate my own edict," he told her, "you are absolutely right."

"But, lets be practical," she emphasized, as she took a sip of her wine, a lovely red Dolcetto Robert had selected to celebrate the decision they were about to make.

"Let's let the opportunity come to us. Make a name for yourself, do some great deals that will establish your reputation and make you valuable in your own right," she advised.

"No question," he agreed.

"If you conclude definitively that the bank is not a long term career, can you avoid becoming one of them?" she asked sensibly.

That didn't take much thought. "Absolutely, and, more importantly, I'll be able to have fun."

"What do you mean by that?"

"Well," he mimicked her and watched her giggle, "I'll always put the client first, I'll take more time off, I won't work quite so late and, most meaningfully, I will torture the bastards with honesty."

She gazed at him, smiled and said, "To honesty," and felt very guilty when she thought about Carlo and Alberto.

"To honesty," he replied.

The next morning he arrived at the bank at eight am in order to prepare for his meeting with Tom Sugar, the European Chairman and Chief Executive of one of America's oldest, largest and most profitable consumer products companies, HRH Brands, Inc. Tom's office and apartment were literally next-door in a recently renovated palace that was manifestly only a few decades newer than their own. Before he relocated from the suburbs of Rome to the new building, he had a ten minute drive from his flat to work and everyone who knew Tom at all figured that he took the new building in order to save 20 minutes a day in travel time. That Tom Sugar was a workaholic was beyond doubt. Whether he relaxed much at all was the question most people asked, although it was clear that he did have time for the odd lunch with pretty young women like Robert's secretary.

Just the fact that Tom was a busy man made it difficult to obtain an appointment with him, even if you had a great transaction to lay before him on a silver platter and you represented one of the world's largest banks. Louisa's success in securing a meeting for Robert deserved far more credit than met the eye, as Tom's company despised Robert's bank. The feelings had nothing to do with individual personalities. That sort of problem can eventually be resolved just because people move on, up or out. In their case, their company got royally shafted by Schaffer's bank during World War II, when the bank refused to make good on a large deposit that one of HRH's European subsidiaries had placed with a branch of theirs in Berlin. The bank had encouraged Tom's company to put the money with their German branch, and as their New York based parent company had no legal obligation to honor the deposit when the Germans expropriated their assets, it didn't.

Over the years, a paragon challenge to all officers in the bank was to be the first one to do any kind of business at all with HRH since World War II. It was understood that whoever achieved this objective would prosper. Robert had already decided on his fundamental strategy for the meeting, so he had planned to use this time to peruse public information and to think about what Tom would be troubled about from a business viewpoint. Robert wanted to get inside his mind so that he could relate to him, his problems and the challenges he was facing. The parent company's public financial information offered little insight into the European business, other than where they had offices and factories. The pile of magazine and newspaper clippings would at least give Schaffer up-to-date data, so he began to sift through a stack that Louisa had gathered. Most of it was innocuous, except for one article that claimed that HRH had refused to pay bribes demanded by several labor union leaders. The reporter, who was known for his gutsy commentary on highly contentious issues, claimed that industrial strife was, therefore, a foregone conclusion.

"Good morning, Robert."

"Morning, Louisa," Schaffer said without looking up. "Did you have an enjoyable evening?"

"Lovely," she replied. "Friends from London who are visiting Rome stopped in for a drink and then took us out to dinner."

"Lucky you," he said as he continued to read the article.

"Ready for your meeting with Mr. Sugar?" she inquired.

"Just about. Have you ever heard of a reporter called Gianni Rosa?"

"Thought you'd like that article," she said, and then replied to his question. "Yes, I've even been at a British Embassy dinner party which he attended. He's very bright."

"But what type of reporter is he? Can he be trusted, is he honest?" Robert questioned her.

"Yes, he can be trusted. He's quite a well-known investigative journalist. Supposedly, not even the Mafia has been able to get to him. Several attempts have been made on his life."

"I'm surprised he's stayed alive," Robert said candidly.

"He has a twenty-four hour a day, two man team assigned to guard him. His newspaper pays for one and his father picks up the cost of the other."

"Unusual," he opined.

"Yes, but it's understandable. He and his family have no economic interests that depend on which political party is in power. His father is a prominent eye surgeon at a medical institute which the family founded here in Rome."

"I see," he told her and, for once, he actually did. "Thanks very much, Louisa. You did a great job putting all this together for me."

"My pleasure. Want to go over your agenda for the day?"

"Good idea," Robert responded, and about an hour later he left for his meeting with Tom Sugar, taking only a scrap of paper and his elegant gold pen. Robert figured most bankers would go armed with an attaché case full of glossy covered presentations and he wanted Sugar to know that he was dealing with Robert as an individual and not just with the institution he represented.

Robert timed his arrival to be precisely five minutes late, a trick he had learned from a British colleague at a conference the previous year. He always arrived late for chairmen and chief executives and early for more junior officers, simply because everyone else tended to do the exact opposite. The tactic tended to make senior people remember you and junior personnel grateful. Robert realized that he was pushing his luck given the history of the relationship between HRH and the bank. Predictably, Sugar's secretary looked at her watch when she arrived at reception to bring Robert to her boss's office.

"I'm terribly sorry I'm a few minutes late," he said in response to her gesture.

"I'm afraid Mr. Sugar only has a few more minutes for you, Mr. Schaffer. Please come this way," she instructed me.

As Robert followed her up the palatial spiral staircase to Sugar's office, he wondered momentarily why he was bothering Louisa as his own secretary was probably even more shapely and attractive than his own. But then he calculated that Sugar was probably so career oriented that he'd never mess around with his own employees. When they finally arrived at his office, she knocked once on the closed door, opened it in almost the same motion and announced him "Mr. Schaffer, Mr. Sugar."

His researches had forewarned him about Sugar's size and age but Robert was still a bit surprised by his Napoleonic build and youthful looks. He was standing behind his desk wearing a starched white button-down shirt with a plain grey tie bearing the letters "HRH" in bright red. "I'm Robert Schaffer," Robert said, as he looked him directly in his deep blue eyes. "Sorry I was a couple of minutes late."

He studied Robert carefully and then extended his hand and said in a high pitched but not unpleasant voice "Tom Sugar. Have a seat," he responded, as he pointed to a small, uncomfortable-looking, armless chair positioned squarely in front of his desk. No one would want to sit there for very long which was undoubtedly precisely why he had selected the chair and the position.

Robert sat and said "I won't waste your time," but, before I could go on, he interrupted me.

"Nor I your time. There is not a chance in hell that we can do business together. I'm sure you know the history between our two companies but, I thought that as we are neighbors, it would be important to tell you that in person. It's nothing personal. At least you didn't waste any paper." When Robert feigned a blank expression, he added "I assume you haven't produced the normal glossies as you haven't brought an attaché case."

"I did my research and figured that was a waste of time," he replied honestly.

"Good," he said as he stood up and begin to come out from behind his desk, presumably to usher me out the door.

Robert didn't budge and said "Sit down for three minutes. I have something to tell you which may make or break you career."

He froze and eyed me angrily. It was clear that he wasn't used to that kind of treatment. He held his ground and said "I'll stand," and then he glanced at his watch and told me "three minutes."

"Thanks," Robert said, as he remained seated. "Sometime in the future you're going to have a problem that no one else can solve. When that happens, call me and give me a chance to figure it out for you. If I do, you open an account with our branch here in Rome or, if you prefer, with our head office in New York, and put in a meaningful deposit for one year or more."

He thought for a second. "OK," he responded, "but don't hold your breath. We never have banking or financial type problems and, even if we did, there has to be someone else somewhere in the world who could work it out for us."

"I said any kind of problem, like a strike at your factory south of Rome." Robert didn't want him to take the comment as some kind of threat, so he added, "I saw Gianni Rosa's story."

Sugar's entire demeanor changed abruptly. He stood there for a few seconds and then returned to his chair behind the desk. "What do you know about him?" he asked.

"Only a little," but Louisa's briefing enabled him to fill in a few blanks for Sugar. Half an hour later he walked Robert down stairs.

"You've been very helpful to me, Robert. I hope I never have to make the call but, if I do and you solve the problem, I'll open an account with your branch here in Rome. All they can do is fire me."

When Robert got back to the office he was on cloud nine and couldn't hide it. He walked straight over to Louisa and, much to her chagrin; he gave her a kiss on the check. “Thanks, Louisa. Your preparation really helped me in that meeting. You're an angel."

"What happened?” she asked as she followed him into his office.

When he had explained the meeting, she smiled and said, "Very clever of you, but what are you going to do if he does call with a real problem you can't solve?"

Assuming you make can make the arrangements required by Mr. Matsu's chairman, I'm going to ask my favorite Japanese trading company to solve it for me."

"I'll expect a big bonus this year, you know," she said with a smile on her lovely face.

"I know, and if the bank won't pay it, I'll find a way to pay it myself," he promised her, and he meant it. She looked embarrassed so he quickly changed the subject. "Any developments while I was out?"

She nodded. "Yes, you won't believe your luck. Pavoni's colleague won't be his assistant. He's bringing Archbishop Machinkos with him."

"You're teasing me, Louisa."

"No, it's the truth," and then she paused before adding, "I told Dr. Matra. I'm sorry, it's just that I was so excited." She looked more than a bit guilty. "I hope you don't mind."

"Not at all," he lied. "How did he react?"

"He's going to find a way to exclude Antinori. He's thinking of inviting our chairman to fly over especially for the luncheon but wants to discuss the whole thing with you first."

"Good day so far," Robert said with a chuckle.

"That is not all that happened. You're seeing Cardinal Pelli this afternoon and, to answer your next question, I didn't tell Dr. Matra."

Chapter 14

A Very Dangerous Deal

Robert looked on his upcoming appointment with Cardinal Pelli as an opportunity to begin to form his own personal client base one that values his honesty and integrity and creative banking. When Matra discovered that he was going to see Cardinal Pelli, he insisted that Robert use his chauffeur driven Renault, even though that meant he would have to take a taxi to see one of their existing clients. It transpired that Pelli wanted to meet Robert at his private apartment in the Vatican, a venue which Matra's driver, Guido, found impressive. "Do you know where to go once we get to the Vatican," Robert asked Guido in Italian.

"Yes, it's around the left-hand side," he answered authoritatively. "Before coming to the bank, I drove for a wealthy Roman who did all of his foreign exchange transactions through the Vatican."

"You're joking."

"Not at all. Everyone knows they have a bank that will buy your Lira and give you foreign money or buy your Dollars or whatever. You don't even have to have an account there as long as you have the cash."

"Is it legal, Guido?" I asked him, bearing in mind that for as many years as he could remember, it was illegal to take all but small amounts of Lira out of Italy.

"Legal?" he said, and gave me a big grin in his rear view mirror. "I never really thought about it, but I suppose it was and still would be. There are no borders between Italy and the Vatican and I don't think there's a law saying you can't make a contribution to the Catholic Church, is there?"

"What's that got to do with it?" Robert asked as he failed to hide his anger over being ridiculed.

"Everything, Dr. Schaffer. You see, we used to fill the trunk of my former boss's Mercedes with suitcases full of Italian money, bring it to the Vatican Bank and make a contribution to the Church, usually 5 or 10 per cent of what was in the boot. In return for the donation, the Vatican Bank would exchange the balance of the funds for U.S. Dollars that they transferred out of Vatican City to Switzerland. He even let me do a bit for my son, who was going to school in the Italian part of Switzerland and needed money for his living expenses."

"Very interesting," Robert commented wryly. "Do you know what Cardinal Pelli does for the Vatican, Guido?" Robert asked, thinking that his former employer might have had dealings with him. All Matra knew about him was that he had a magnificent Villa in Parioli, a wealthy Roman suburb, and that he often acted as an intermediary for the Vatican, kind of an ambassador without portfolio and that he had a well known and gorgeous mistress.

"He runs all of the Vatican's businesses outside of Italy, at least that's what my old boss, he used the word 'capo', once told me." Guido swerved to avoid three tourists who stepped right in front of the Renault. "Idiots," he hissed as he shook his fist at them and almost hit another group of sightseers. "We'll be there in a minute," he announced.

The exhilaration Robert felt as a result of this pivotal call was now clouded by Guido's outrageous report but he discounted it heavily and nearly put it out of his mind as they pulled in front of the famed cathedral. Guido weaved expertly through the early spring throng and made his way around the side to an entrance which was hidden by a Bernini arch. A uniformed Swiss guard stood off to the side with a medieval spear in his hand. "Is this it?" he asked Guido.

"Yes, this is it. Go through those double doors," he pointed off to the right, and a receptionist should be just inside. How long will you be, Dr. Schaffer?"

"I really don't know, Guido. I shouldn't think it would be very long."

"OK. I think they'll let me stop over there," he motioned to a little group of cars about a hundred feet up the road. "I'll be watching for you from over there."

"Fine," Robert told him as he got out. Alone on the steps he suddenly felt intimidated by the aura of the place. The Swiss Guard nodded to him as though he was expected and another appeared from out of nowhere as Robert mounted the short flight of stairs, his spear momentarily barring his path. For no specific reason that Schaffer could fathom, the weapon was pulled away and he told me to proceed.

A priest met me just inside the double doors. "Dr. Schaffer?" he asked in perfect American-accented English.

"Yes," I replied in surprise.

"I am Father Costa, one of Monsignor Pavoni's assistants. I will introduce you to Cardinal Pelli. I understand your Italian is good?" he said it as a question.

"Yes, I am comfortable in Italian," Robert replied.

"Good, please follow me."

He led Schaffer up a wide marble adorned corridor, the left side of which was lined with glorious stained glass windows depicting the life of Christ. As they approached a rather grand hall, which looked like it could be for private audiences with the Pope, he turned sharply to the right and made his way up a narrow, spiral staircase to the floor above. When they came out, they found themselves in a passageway similar to the one below and Costa turned to the right and led Robert to a large door at the end of the hall. "The Cardinal's apartments are just through here Dr. Schaffer.

Please follow me. His eminence is waiting for you in his study."

The room just inside the corridor housed a secretary, filing cabinets, a fax machine and the normal paraphernalia associated with the office of an important businessman. The next chamber was a small, elegantly furnished waiting area that opened onto a large conference suite, whose door was ajar. A separate door led into Cardinal Pelli's office. Costa knocked twice and let himself in when Pelli's deep, masculine, booming voice beckoned him to enter. "Your Eminence," he greeted him solemnly in Italian as he bowed slightly, "may I present Dr. Robert Schaffer."

"Dr. Schaffer, please come and sit," he said affably, as he pointed me in the direction of a comfortable looking seating arrangement situated in front of three large windows which opened onto the Vatican's interior gardens and courtyards. "Will you join me for coffee or perhaps you would prefer tea?"

His deep, resonant voice did not match his tall, rather fragile frame but Robert was not too surprised as many clerics he had encountered had voices that did not match their looks. He assumed it was due to the voice training they must all receive "Coffee please, Your Eminence," Robert responded.

"Thank you Fr. Costa," said Pelli and we both watched as Costa reluctantly left us to talk alone together.

"If you require anything at all, Your Eminence, I shall be here in the reception area," he said in parting.

Pelli looked as though he might say something else to the departing priest but he was gone before he had time. "The man is completely useless," he said as he turned to me. "I don't know what will become of the Church in the next century. We can no longer attract any quality people. It's the marriage thing, Dr. Schaffer. We're simply going to have to follow our Anglican colleagues and allow a man to take a wife, have a family and still be a priest. You're not a Catholic are you?"

"No, Your Eminence, I'm one of your Anglican colleagues."

"Well done, you're ahead of us then," he said cheerfully. "Dr. Schaffer," he said in a serious tone of voice as he turned to business matters, "I believe Monsignor Pavoni mentioned that we may have a business proposition for you?"

"Yes, Your Eminence. I am sure you know that my bank is most interested in developing a relationship with you."

"Yes, Dr. Schaffer, most people are," he said it matter-of-factly. "The situation we have in mind is complex and will require a," he paused while he searched his mind for the right words, "fresh approach."

"I am capable of that, Your Eminence, and so is my bank."

"Excellent. Let me start from the beginning. Several years ago, about ten I believe, we begin to invest in a variety of small, high technology companies on the West Coast of the United States. You do have offices on the West Coast, Dr. Schaffer?" Robert nodded and he continued. "I assumed you did. These companies were engaged in activities aimed at improving human living conditions. The businesses ranged from a manufacturer of low cost modular housing to biomedical research. One of our first investments was in a small company producing advanced health care devices. Quite recently, we learned that this company had diversified several years ago into birth control products."

Pelli cleared his throat at this point in his revelations and Robert used his apparent discomfort to ask "How did you learn, Your Eminence?" he wanted to discover indirectly who might know of their investment.

"We read about it in the newspapers," he confessed. "We have so many investments that it is difficult to follow them properly but that is a discussion for another day and could be another business opportunity for you, Dr. Schaffer. In any case, this company is apparently making a large portion of its profits from these devices so we need to sell out, preferably in the next several weeks if not before. The key objective is to avoid disclosure of our ownership. Receiving a fair price for our shares is important but not critical. Can you help us, Dr. Schaffer?" he inquired, as he took out a pack of Marlboros, offered Robert one, and lit one for himself.

From a professional point of view, there were a thousand questions that he could and should ask. Pelli had made it clear from the outset, however, that they were looking for a fresh approach. "Your Eminence, may I suggest a simple and very quick solution which should meet your requirements, although it is not terribly professional?"

Pelli thought for a few moments and then said "Of course. It could be refreshing."

"I will give you a note, a personal note," Robert added with emphasis, "and you will give me the shares. I assume they belong to whomever has possession of them."

"Yes, of course, they are in bearer form," he answered Robert's question without commenting on the solution.

"Perhaps it is much too unprofessional," Robert interjected in order to allow him to easily reject the idea.

"No, no, not at all," he said quickly. "I'm just thinking. It's so simple. There must be something wrong with it," he said it more as a question than as a statement.

"There is the question of price, Your Eminence."

"Yes, of course. How do we deal with that?"

"We leave the note blank and you fill in the price when I sell the shares."

"You are prepared to do that?"

"Yes, of course," Robert said quietly and with a calm that Schaffer did not feel.

Pelli got up from his chair and walked over to the window, opened it and took a long, deep breath of the crisp Roman spring air. "What a brilliant idea, Dr. Schaffer, what an absolutely fabulous solution to our quandary."

"Thank you, Eminence," Robert said graciously as he felt the goose bumps of success spread over his entire body. This was the first time that he felt the true high that comes from these moments, a physical feeling as good as the best red wine you have ever tasted combined with a night after in the arms of your lover. The feeling was so good that you get seriously hooked on it and will do anything to have it again.

"When can we consummate the transaction, Dr. Schaffer? Will you require a lawyer?"

"A lawyer would mean one unnecessary person being made aware of the deal. I do not require one but if you do..."

"No, I only thought you might," he cut me off swiftly. "What do we do next, then," he inquired.

"I've never done this before," he admitted. "I guess you give me the shares and I'll write out a personal I.O.U., if you have a piece of paper."

Pelli smiled broadly, crossed his study to a small cabinet and extracted a bottle of what turned out to be the best Armagnac Robert had ever tasted. He filled two glasses, returned to where Schaffer was seated, handed him his glass and said "To a long and mutually profitable relationship, Dr. Schaffer," he toasted me.

"Eminence," Robert said as he touched his glass to Pelli's.

They both drank and then he said, "May I call you Robert?"

"Of course," he responded.

"Please call me Enrico," he said as he raised his glass again.

A half hour later Schaffer was in the back of Matra's Renault on his way to his apartment in

Trastevere basking in glory. "Did you have a good meeting, Dr. Schaffer?" Guido broke the silence and begin the process of helping him to return to the real world.

Robert resisted the overwhelming temptation to say "The best meeting of my entire life" and said instead "Yes, Guido, it was a good start, but these things take time."

"Oh, I know Dr. Schaffer. My former Roman employer always used to complain about how much time the Vatican takes over even the most simple business."

"Oh, well, Guido, we'll do something with them one day, I'm sure."

"Of course, Dr Schaffer, of course."

"Robert, you signed your life away to them," Bonnie pointed out when he had finished briefing her.

"I guess I did, didn't I," he admitted.

"They could put any number at all on that note and put you into bankruptcy."

"I suppose they could, Bonnie, but they won't. How are they going to collect it?"

I could see her mind racing through the possibilities as she thought about it. Finally, she said "They could sell it to a third party and let them collect from you."

"It's non-transferrable," and before she could ask anything else he said "Bonnie, that was the most important deal I will ever do. It will change our lives one way or the other and I know it will be for the better."

She pondered what he had said and then the phone rang. Bonnie was perched next to it. "Pronto," she answered and then quickly switched to English. "Oh, hello, Jean Pierre. Yes he's right here. Just a moment, please," she said and handed Robert the phone as he went over to her and gave her a peck on the cheek.

"Trust me," he mouthed to her and then turned his attention to Matra. "Hello, Jean Pierre."

"Robert," he said anxiously. "How did it go?"

"Great," he replied. "In fact," he added, "it was the best meeting of my entire life."

"It was?" he inquired with more than a hint of surprise in his voice.

"Absolutely. I've done a deal."

"But Guido said you looked down and that it would take a long time before anything happens."

So much for Guido, Robert thought. "I'm glad that is what he said. I don't want him or for that matter anyone other than you to know what happened in that meeting."

"I see."

"Jean Pierre, we can't talk about this on the phone. I'm going to the bank in a few minutes and could meet you there if you'd like to be briefed."

"You're going to the bank tonight, now?" he asked incredulously.

Matra couldn't stand the thought of working at night or on the weekend so Robert said, "Jean Pierre, you don't have to. It can wait until morning. It's just that I want to put my thoughts down on paper while everything is still fresh in my mind." Robert didn't want to tell him on the telephone that he wanted to put millions of dollars worth of shares into their vault.

"Oh, good," he said, "see you first thing tomorrow then."

"Tomorrow," Robert responded and hung up. "Bonnie, come with me to the bank and then we can go out to dinner and celebrate."

Robert could see she was still unconvinced that a celebration was in order but she put on a brave face, smiled and said "Why not."

Bonnie decided to have a leisurely bath and a nap to feel refreshed, as they could not arrange a table for dinner until 10 pm. They arrived at the bank at about 9:30 and found it to be a circus of lights, inside and out. It looked as though every single light had been turned on inside and the outside was surrounded by the flashing blue lights of both normal police cars and the para-military, Carabinieri. When Robert attempted to enter the front gates, Carabinieri leveled a gun in the direction of their car. Both Bonnie and Robert instinctively raised their hands and he opened the door and got out very slowly. "I am an officer of the bank," Robert told him.

"Show me some identification," he ordered me.

Robert carefully reached inside his blazer, extracted his wallet and then his bank identification. "Here, check this," he said, as he handed it over to him. "I am Dr. Schaffer, the number two officer in the bank."

He looked at the I.D. and him several times. "All right, Dr. Schaffer, you may enter. Who is the woman with you?"

"My wife," Robert answered him. "We were on our way to dinner and I saw all the lights and decided to check. What is happening?"

"The alarm went off about fifteen minutes ago. We were here within minutes but when I last checked, we have found nothing. My captain is over there," he said while he motioned to a tall man near the front entrance. "Maybe he has more information."

Schaffer got back in, drove carefully inside and explained the situation to Bonnie as he tried to find a place to park the car. "I'll bet our house still has bugs in it."

"It could be a co-incidence," Robert said lamely.

"Or your friend Cardinal Pelli wants to have his cake and eat it too."

"What are you talking about?"

"He has your blank note and maybe he sends someone along to collect shares which can be negotiated by the person who has them."

Robert finally managed to wedge the car between a police van and the side of the building. "A year ago I would have said you are going mad. Today, I think it's very unlikely, but I wouldn't rule it out. The sooner those shares are registered in the name of the bank, the better."

The captain was a sensible man. Once he had discharged the formalities of checking Schaffer's I.D., he wasted no time. "They breaked in strongbox, Dr. Schaffer," he struggled to inform him in English.

Now that Robert had collected his thoughts, he was just as anxious about his chairman's art collection, and his own on-loan Renoir, as he was about the contents of their vault. Robert was impatient to learn as much as he could as quickly as possible and couldn't cope with the man's failure to grapple with the English language. But he was rational enough to find a way to change to Italian without offending him. "Please, Captain," he answered in his native language, "I must practice my hopeless Italian, if you will allow me."

The policeman's expression of relief was conspicuous and he proceeded in rapid Romano, a language that is as distinct from Milanese Italian as a Boston twang is from a Fort Worth, Texas drawl. "They only had about seven minutes in the vault but they managed to break into quite a few safety deposit boxes and to make a general mess of the files you store in there. The tellers' cash boxes, of course, are gone."

The chance that his note for shares transaction with the Vatican was not the motive for the break-in and that it was a straightforward robbery actually made Robert feel relieved. The concern, however, of having to deal with complaints from their clients about the lost contents of their security boxes, especially so soon after the embarrassment of the missing $5 million made Robert feel ill. "What about our art collection?"

"Art collection?" he questioned Robert with a vacant expression on his face.

Even though there was no basis why the man should be cognizant of it, his lack of knowledge aggravated Schaffer. "Yes, Captain," he said testily, "we have an exceptional selection of Impressionist paintings in our entertaining center on the top floor and our chairman keeps a portion of his personal collection there as well."

"We'd better have a look," he said gloomily. "Please show me the way."

Robert led him up the marbled stairs, through the principal banking hall and then up again to the floor housing his and Jean Pierre's offices. For the first time Robert noticed that the main alarm system had either not functioned or had been turned off. "What happened to the alarms," he interrogated the captain as they approached the top of the stairs.

"The primary and secondary systems were not on or the robbers found a way to disable them. They never sounded. We were only alerted when one of your back-up systems was set-off by the opening of a dummy box in the vault," he informed us.

Robert had an almost overwhelming urge to peek into his office but resisted and took him to the little elevator that led to the entertaining center. The door to the lift was closed and there was no sign of forced entry. Robert extracted his keys and quickly found the silver one that unlocked the lift. The Captain stood in front of them as it opened. "Stay here," he ordered Bonnie and Robert as he drew his gun and called out to one of his men "Franco, come with me."

The man called Franco, whose face looked like a retired prizefighter's, drew his gun and followed the captain into the lift. When the door closed, and Bonnie and Robert were alone Robert said, "If it's untouched, I'll be more rather than less worried."

"Me too," she replied. "Let's check your office for the Renoir."

They went back along the little corridor, turned left, entered his office and turned on the lights. The walls were bare. "Thank god," Bonnie whispered.

"Amen," Robert concurred. "Let's take a look in Jean Pierre's office," he remarked and led the way across the open space that housed our secretaries' desks. Robert went in before Bonnie. "Same here."

When they came back out, Franco met them. "The captain wants you to join us upstairs, Dr.

Schaffer. Anything obvious missing here?" he inquired.

"They grabbed all our art work. I haven't had time to see if anything else has been taken."

He shrugged without saying anything and led the way back to the elevator. The three of them went up together where the captain met them. "The walls have been stripped bear, Dr. Schaffer."

As they entered the large room, he could also see that the door to their chairman's storeroom was open and that the compartment appeared to be virtually vacant. "Have you inspected that room?" he asked, as he pointed toward the open door.

"Nothing much in there," he replied. "Why?" he asked with evident surprise in his voice.

"That is where our chairman kept most of his European based art work," he apprised him. "Altogether there was about $15 million in art housed in these two rooms."

The looks exchanged by the captain and his deputy said more than any words could about the situation. Finally, the captain broke the silence and said "Better come with me to the vault and then we'll have a careful look around the whole building."

He led the way down the stairs and through the main banking hall to the little winding passageway that led to the secure area. A squad of men, wearing what seemed to Schaffer to be white surgical gloves, hovered around its entrance. They were inspecting four holes that had been drilled in a half moon shape adjacent to the main locking mechanism and seemed perplexed by the method of entry. When the leader of the team saw the captain he said, "Rarely see anything like this, Captain. It's like they had a blueprint of the electronic bolt."

The captain nodded and motioned for them to follow him into the vault. Papers were strewn around the little chamber and about two dozen of the two hundred safety deposit boxes had been pried open, without inordinate damage, and emptied of their contents. All the raided boxes were on the left-hand side. "It looks as though they planned to go through the lot," commented the head of the investigative team who had come in behind us. "Whoever was in here was being methodical. They would have gone through them all if they hadn't opened one of your dummies."

"That is the second time I've heard that word, Robert," Bonnie whispered to him. "What's a dummy?"

"Out of the two hundred boxes, there are five dummies which, if opened, will trigger a back-up alarm system if all else fails. The only way to avoid triggering them is to know the number of each, and only Jean Pierre, one staff member and I have those numbers."

The captain had understood me. "We will need to know the numbers of the others, Dr. Schaffer, to complete our work," he explained.

"Of course, Captain.

Robert called Jean Pierre when they had finished inspecting the vault. "Jean Pierre," he commenced in a despondent manner, which Robert regretted but couldn't overcome, "you had better get down to the bank right away. We've had a burglary. All the art is gone and they managed to get into the vault as well." He waited for a response but, when there was none, he kind of shouted down the line "Jean Pierre, are you there?"

"I can't deal with it, Robert," he finally said in a desperate voice. "Tell me it isn't true. If it is, then I am finished. The chairman will never forgive me."

"The insurance will cover it, Jean Pierre," Robert replied miserably, knowing that if for some reason it could be proved that the alarm system wasn't on, the insurance wouldn't cover anything at all. His voice sounded so awful that Robert just couldn't raise that possibility.

"Insurance can't replace the chairman's collection, Robert. He'll never get over it."

"Come on Jean Pierre, he'll be able to replenish it with some great pieces. Prices are down for impressionists. He'll have a great time rebuilding it," Robert said as he tried to cheer him up.

"Robert," he begin again woefully, "he called me about the alarm system only a week or so ago. He was worried about it and asked me to bring in a new firm to evaluate it. He thought we should add additional sensors." Robert didn't know what to say so he decided to remain silent. "They're supposed to be coming in tomorrow morning to go over it in detail," he added.

"I'm sorry, Jean Pierre," Robert replied.

"I guess I better come down, huh?"

"Yes, the police need to interview you."

"The police?" he asked, showing that he had not really focused.

"Yea," Robert responded. "The place is crawling with regular police, Carabiniere, and special investigators. You name it, and we've got it in the way of police."

"Who else is there, from the bank I mean?"

"No one, other than Bonnie. We were going to stop here for a few minutes before going on to dinner." When he didn't say anything, Robert added, "It will only take a few minutes of your time, Jean Pierre. I'll have finished a thorough check of the building by the time you get here. Why not bring Jane and we'll all go out and get drunk afterwards?"

"I'll be there in a few minutes," he said, and then all Robert heard was a dead line.

An hour and a half later Bonnie and Robert dropped Jean Pierre at his home. He was too shaken to drive when he learned that the insurance might not cover the losses. "Poor Jean Pierre," Bonnie said when he got back to the car after they literally helped him up the steps to his house.

"It won't help us either," Robert answered.

"No, but we're leaving. It's only a matter of time and the right opportunity. The Bank was his career, his life really, and, he's right, the chairman will never excuse him. I've heard from Jane that the old man loved every piece of that art collection. Some of it had been in his family for decades."

"I didn't know that. That's terrible."

"Robert, cheer up," she told him happily. "We could have been in there when the burglars broke in, and we might have been killed. Anyway, believe it or not, I'm famished," she announced honestly. Bonnie was and is like that. She loves to eat in a crisis. Some people drink, Robert used to smoke, but Bonnie munches. Italy has that kind of effect on most people and, it certainly did on Bonnie. After a while you're either up or down the vast majority of the time. It's only the level of the peaks and valleys that varies from person to person.

Robert looked at his watch. "It's nearly midnight and I'm nervous about these share certificates," he said as he patted his sport coat inside pocket for what must have been the hundredth time in the last few hours. The police couldn't get the alarm system to function so he had no choice but to keep them with him. "Let's go somewhere I can park right in front. I'll relax more." He usually loved walking the darkened, often gas-lit Roman streets in search of a restaurant but now was not the time for that.

"I know the perfect place," Bonnie said excitedly. "I read about it only last week. It's just across the river from our apartment, in a refurbished tavern. The article said they have superb food and a marvelous guitarist."

A few minutes later they left their car with a parking attendant and a twenty-dollar bill got them a great table near the piano and guitar players. A waiter was with them in seconds and they ordered spaghetti with virgin olive oil, garlic and hot pepper seeds and a bottle of 1986 Chianti Classico Reserva. Robert gave the guitarist a few dollar bills and, in the face of his prodding and against his better judgment, he agreed to his request to play a World War II Partisan song that the Italian Communist Party had tried to adopt as its own. The song was actually a favorite of all the groups that joined during the war to resist the Nazis and Fascists. Bonnie and Robert had adopted it as their song of protest against the corruption inherent in all of Italy's political parties and they enjoyed the commotion among the locals that it's playing inevitably caused.

When the guitarist was about half way through the third chorus and really into the most rousing part of the song, a familiar face came into view. This time Robert placed it immediately, leaned over to Bonnie and said "Max Feathers is here." Robert had his arm around the back of her chair and could feel her whole body stiffen.

"My God in heaven," she said, and went absolutely white. "That's no coincidence, Robert. I'll bet he was behind the burglary tonight and I'll bet he still has bugs in our apartment. Let's get out of here," she said and started to collect her things.

"No, Bonnie, we're not going to run. We have a lot more going for us now than we did last year. He knows about my Italian relations and how influential they can be so I think he'll behave himself. Besides, there are one or two other people I can call on to be helpful that I couldn't have last year."

"Robert, I hate that bastard. I know he's responsible for a lot that went wrong last year and this as well."

Robert smiled at her and said "I'll bet he'd say the same thing about us."

She thought momentarily and then begin to laugh, at first surreptitiously and almost silently and then more loudly and openly. The tension that had built up in her face dissipated and, when she had settled down, she said, "I never thought of it that way and now that I am, I know you're right. We're probably not exactly his preferred people, are we?"

"Not exactly at the top of his list, darling. Try to stay calm; he's on his way over. Just let me handle it."

"Robert, Bonnie," he greeted them with his, hale fellow well met style. "What a coincidence to find you two here."

Schaffer was more than slightly tempted to make the world a better place by inviting Feathers outside to push him in front of one of the many cars racing down the Lungo Tevere. At this time of night, if a foreigner with alcohol in his blood stream were found dead by the side of that treacherous road, the inquiry wouldn't last very long. "Tell us what is on your mind, Feathers, and then leave us in peace."

Bonnie added, "We've had enough of you to last us forever."

"It's nice to feel wanted," he remarked, as he held up his hands in mock self- defense. When they said nothing, he continued "All right, I'll say my piece and get out of your hair but it's probably best if I don't have to shout it."

There was a spare chair at the table next to ours and, with a nod of agreement from the occupants, Robert withdrew it and pushed it toward Feathers. "Make it quick," Robert ordered him.

He gave Robert one of his disdainful looks, sighed deeply, placed the chair opposite both of us and sat carefully, as it didn't look very sturdy. "Look, I've got a job to do and you two aren't making it any easier," he begin seriously.

Bonnie's great mood had done a flip-flop. "Whatever job you've got, I wish you'd get out of our lives. I hold you responsible for a lot of the ugly things that have happened to us ever since we saw you at Ciano's party last year."

Feathers adjusted his chair so that he was directly opposite both of them, leaned forward over the middle of the table and glared first at Bonnie and then at Schaffer. "Robert, you have given me and a lot of other people in this country a royal pain in the ass from almost the first moment you took up your post in Milan. If you had just minded your own business, done your job in the normal way and enjoyed the better things this country has to offer, you and Bonnie would be a lot happier and not in the trouble you are now."

"Don't preach to me or to Bonnie, Feathers. We're fed up with you and the common criminals you associate with. Whatever job it is you are supposed to be doing, I think you're in it for old Max Fathers first with your employer a distant second. If you have something to say, do it quickly and let us in peace."

"How dare you, you little twerp," he shouted, as he reached back and started to launch one of his ham-hock fists at Schaffer.

But Robert was two steps ahead of him. Schaffer had hooked one of his chair's spindly legs with his foot and, as his weight shifted backwards in order to launch his punch, Robert jerked his foot abruptly toward him and studied Max as he struggled to keep from plummeting over backward into the piano. Robert's maneuver caught him like an ambush and his head smashed into the side of the piano first and then one of its legs, just before it collided with the marble floor. It didn't take a doctor to see that Feathers was in bad shape. He was out cold and blood begin to trickle from under his head. He had taken most of our wine with him so he looked as though he had been the victim of a Viet Cong raid. "Call an ambulance," Robert shouted in Italian and then he leaned over him to see if he were breathing. Bonnie was next to him and Robert turned to her and whispered "He's out cold but breathing. Probably just cut his head on the piano."

"What has happened here?" demanded a man who behaved like the proprietor.

Before Robert could respond, the piano player volunteered, "The guy was drunk and fell over. He looked like he was giving these people a hard time."

When Robert looked up at him, he smiled and said "Ciao Bella, Ciao," the name of the World War II Partisan song Schaffer had asked him to play.

Robert mouthed "Thank you" and allowed the crowd of inevitable gawkers to jostle Bonnie and Robert away from Feathers and the ruckus that surrounded him. Someone came running by with smelling salts and bulldozed his way through the throng. Robert held his breath when he put it under Feathers' nose and heaved a sigh of relief when he begin to come around. "He's OK," he said to Bonnie. Let's get out of here."

"What a night, Robert," she said, as she made her way toward the front entrance.

The attendant recognized them and brought their car around in minutes. Robert gave him a few bills and let him help Bonnie in, while Robert went around to the drivers' side. "You OK?" he asked her.

"Barely, but I'm not going home until I'm fed."

"You're amazing, Bonnie," Robert responded. “All I want is a triple scotch on the rocks."

"You'll be hungry after that," she warned him.

"Maybe," Robert replied skeptically, as he checked inside his jacket pocket to be sure the share certificates were still there.

"I know the safest place in town, Robert."

He glanced at his watch and then at the road as he searched desperately for a gap in the speedway's traffic. "At 1 am in Rome, there is no such thing as a perfect place when you're walking around with the equivalent of millions of dollars in cash in your coat pocket." He spotted a gap, floored the little car and made a reckless right turn into the fray, narrowly missing a van that had slowed to take the next exit.

"Just tell me where to go. The further we are from Feathers, the better."

"Take the next left over the river," she instructed him.

There was a stream of traffic on his left, so he slowed markedly, darted into a little break and then accelerated to avoid being smacked from behind. Horns sounded but he had made it unscathed and was pleased to see the bridge he wanted to cross coming up on his left-hand side. When he looked rapidly in his rear view mirror, he saw a car in the lane he had just exited urgently trying to make it into his lane. "I think there's someone trying to follow us, Bonnie. Take a look to your right."

"The blue sports car?"

"Yeah."

"Don't worry, the people behind us don't want to let him in. Take the bridge exit; turn left on the other side of the river, and then the first right into the Old City. Unless he knows where we're going, he'll never be able to follow us."

Robert followed her instructions and as he headed into the winding roads of the Old City, he was delighted to see no sign of the blue car. "Don't see him, do you?"

"Not a sign. It was probably a friend of Feathers."

"Where to now?"

"The Casino Club," she declared proudly.

"An illegal gambling club is your idea of the safest place in town?" he asked dubiously.

"Absolutely. They have a huge safe, which I'm sure you can use temporarily for the shares, great bar and good pasta. You can also leave the car with their doorman."

She was right. "Good idea," he conceded.

"Perfect idea," she countered, they'd never let Feathers in," and then we both begin laughing together.

Five minutes later they were safely tucked behind a pleasant table in a small dining area adjacent to the roulette room. They had thought better of the idea of leaving the shares in the vault, on the grounds that with the way things were going, the Club was sure to be raided and we'd never see the certificates again. "Same as before?" he asked Sherri.

"Why not? It sounded good then and it sounds even better now."

When the waiter brought them their drinks, including a triple scotch for Robert and Bonnie's always favored Bloody Mary, they duplicated the order they had made less than an hour previously at the refurbished tavern. Bonnie then lifted her glass to Robert and made a toast "To survival."

"I'll drink to that" he saluted her and then he downed his scotch in one long gulp.

Two hours later, they drove back to their apartment in Piazza Santa Maria in Trastevere. As soon as they rounded the bend and entered the road that lead into the square, they encountered a large black Cadillac limousine, bearing small American flags on the tip of each front fender, parked by the side of the narrow road. A Carabinieri vehicle sat protectively behind it with its small blue light making lazy turns. "They can't be here for us, can they, Robert?" Bonnie asked.

He surveyed the scene carefully and slowed the car to a snail's pace. When he observed a door to the limo begin to open, any lingering doubts evaporated. "Afraid they are, sweet, but at least they seem to be devoid of cloaks and daggers." But he had spoken too soon.

"It's Feathers," Bonnie said breathlessly.

And then a second man got out of the sleek black Cadillac. "And that's John Foster with him," Robert remarked.

"Well, at least it's all out on the table now. They definitely work together and there is not even a shadow of a doubt that they're spooks," Bonnie pointed out.

Robert had little option but to halt the car, as the bulk of the two big Americans permeated what remained of the road. "Stay in the car and lock the doors after I get out, Bonnie. Before I say a word to Feathers and Foster, I'm going to check them out with the police. Get behind the driver's wheel and, if anything funny develops, just get the hell out of here and go to the police station on the Lungo Tevere."

"OK, but be careful, Robert."

"I'll do my best," he told her with a smile, as he got out and slammed the door quickly behind him.

"We need to talk to you, Robert," Feathers greeted him seriously.

"Not till I check you guys out with the police, Feathers," he cautioned him. "Stay where you are and don't go near Bonnie or she'll run you both down." Feathers and Foster just shrugged and, as he passed them on his way to the Carabineiri car behind them, he noticed that Feathers had a large white bandage taped on the backside of his head.

When the police perceived that Robert was making his way to their car, the one closest to him got out and gave him a miniature bow and salute in the normal, courteous manner of the Italian paramilitary security forces. Schaffer noticed that he was wearing the uniform and insignias of a colonel. "Good evening, Dr. Schaffer, he said in perfect, American accented English. May I be of service?"

"Good evening, Colonel," Robert replied, "I believe you can. Are these men officials of the U.S. Government?"

"Yes, Dr. Schaffer, they most certainly are," he answered him.

"Are they members of the intelligence services?" Robert asked and studied him very carefully when he did to see his manner of reply and not just to hear the words.

"Yes, Dr. Schaffer, they are. They need to ask you some questions and I would advise you to cooperate. They can do nothing to harm you in any way in Italy but they could make your life a misery in the States."

Schaffer looked the man over carefully and, even though there was no doubt in his mind that they were Italian officials, he decided to confirm it as best he could. "Please do not be offended, Colonel, but I would be most grateful if I could see some form of identification."

He smiled. "Very wise, Dr. Schaffer. I fully understand your caution," he told him and produced a badge and several bits of official looking documents.

When Robert had finished perusing them, he said, "Thank you, Colonel, I am most grateful."

He smiled, gave him another salute, got back in his car and, a few seconds later, his driver backed their car into the piazza and left. When Robert turned around, Feathers and Foster awaited him.

Chapter 15

The Spies Come Clean

"The colonel said you have some questions to ask me. He also confirmed that both of you work for U.S. intelligence."

Feathers and Foster exchanged a brisk look. "Robert," Feathers begin, "you really got under my skin back there, but that's still no excuse. I was out of line."

"This is a ridiculous place to have a sensible conversation. Let me park our car and then we can go up to our apartment. Do you need to speak to Bonnie as well or can she get some sleep?"

Foster took over. "She ought to be there as well. Hopefully, we won't need to bother either of you again but we can't promise anything."

Ten minutes later Feathers, Foster and Robert were in their living room while Bonnie made coffee in the kitchen. Foster had brought an electronic gadget with him that he said would verify whether there was any eavesdropping equipment in the apartment. He had found and removed one from the sitting room, which he assured Schaffer and Feathers was now safe for conversation. With Robert's blessing, he was going from room to room, carefully inspecting the instruments' dials for any indication of further bugs. That left Feathers sitting across from Robert, whose bandage made him look a little silly now that they were in the light. "Robert, we're never going to agree on some of the issues we've been hassling over. For better or worse, our government, yours and mine," he said with emphasis, "has made keeping the communists out of power in Italy the single most significant strategic foreign policy objective for the United States in southern Europe. Foster and I and others have been charged with carrying out that policy outside of the normal channels."

"Even illegally?" he asked naively.

"By Italian law, mostly illegally," Feathers admitted.

"So even though people like Bonnie and I try to clean out an illegal insider dealing ring from an American Bank, you guys will try to stop us if it causes you a problem."

"That's about it," he said as he looked down at the coffee cup Bonnie was now filling with her own special jet-black brew.

"Why didn't you just tell us that a year ago?" Bonnie demanded.

"I tried, more than once, but possibly not as candidly as I should have. Still, I'm not convinced it would have made any difference."

"He's probably right, Bonnie," Robert remarked frankly. "I doubt that I would have behaved other than as I did if Max or anyone else, including the President of the United States, had told it to us straight."

"Especially if that charlatan had told us," she stated, as she sat down next to him.

Robert paused for Feathers to rebut Bonnie's reproach and was shocked by what he said. "Frankly, I'm not one of his fans, but I'm not at all sure that we'd be better off with anyone else, especially looking at Italy in isolation. As long as communism is seen to be a threat to our society, regardless of who sits in the White House, our policy will be more or less the same."

"But why support people like Ciano, especially if he's really a front for the communists?"

"We knew about his links to the Italian Communists long before you talked to your friend, Paolo Mancini about it."

"You mean you're supporting a guy who's tied to the communists?" Robert asked. "That is crazy."

"Ciano has to pay everyone something in order to give him and his family some sort of chance at long term survival. He can't be sure the communists won't gain power one way or another, so he gives them enough money to blackmail them if they do takeover. It's kind of like advance protection money. He does the same with the other key political parties in Italy. Virtually all big, wealthy Italian families do the same."

"Good Lord," was all he could think to say.

"The real problems in Italy center around corruption at all levels of government and in every single political party, Left, Right and Center. The Mafia couldn't exist without it."

Bonnie and Robert gawked at each other. It seemed to him at the time like they had been unwitting actors in a complex play. Bonnie broke the silence just as Foster returned from his surveillance of the rest of the flat. "What do you need to ask us, Max?" she questioned him in a half-repentant manner.

"First let's hear from John," Feathers responded and, at the same time, he relaxed noticeably.

"It was lit up like a Christmas tree, Max. Some rooms had two or more taps and the bedroom had four. Needless to say, they weren't all from the same maker."

"Holy shit, Robert," Bonnie said involuntarily, and broke the tension completely as we all caved in with laughter.

When we had all eventually recovered, Feathers asked "Is the place clean now, John?"

"I'd say the odds are one hundred to one that I spotted everything. But it would probably be a good idea to have some music on while we finish our talk. It will be just that much safer."

Robert put on the 1812 Festival Overture and turned up the volume. "Right, let's hear it, Max."

Feathers finished his coffee and commenced the questioning. Foster periodically broke in, usually seeking more conclusive data about times and places. They were principally anxious to go over the twenty-four hour period encompassing Bonnie's departure for St. Moritz with Alberto Ciano, Robert's late night dinner in the Old City piano bar, the slaughter in Piazza Cordusio, and Robert's trip to St. Moritz and Lovingo. Schaffer was astounded that they knew about and were equally interested in his recent meetings with George Pavoni, Cardinal Pelli, and the wolf man, Signor Lupo.

Feathers focused in particular on what he thought had been a chance pairing with Pavoni at Rome's San Pietro Golf Club. It was nearly light outside and Bonnie had gone to bed about half an hour earlier. "What made you decide to play golf that day, Robert?" he inquired.

Schaffer had to reflect a while but finally remembered. "It isn't easy to get on that course. My friend Paolo Mancini had intervened on my behalf several weeks before they finally gave me a date and tee time."

"How far in advance were you notified?"

"I'm not sure, but I'd say a couple of days."

"Time enough for the 'chance encounter'," he said the words in a way that conveyed precisely the opposite meaning, "with Pavoni to be arranged well in advance."

"You don't seriously believe that Pavoni actually arranged for us to play together?" Robert asked skeptically.

"If I had to speculate, I'd say he did, but it's just as possible that someone wanted you two to meet and made the arrangements off their own bat, as the English would say."

"And I suppose you totally discount the possibility that it was a 'chance encounter, ' as you put?"

Feathers reflected for an instant and then made a pronouncement which Robert recalls to this day, and he is sure he will continue to recall for as many years to come as he is blessed with, "The one thing that I have learned as a result of my training by Uncle Sam over the last several years is that 'chance encounters' which end influencing or substantially facilitating important events are about as probable as a sunrise or a sunset."

Robert thought for a moment. "Max, if I wanted to be a spy, I would have joined the CIA or whoever it is you work for when you gather intelligence. For the time being and, for that matter, for the foreseeable future, all I want to be is a damn good banker. Maybe one day I'll want to become something else, maybe even help old Uncle Sam, but not now. How do I get everyone off my back?"

Feathers studied him carefully. Robert couldn't tell from his expression what line he was going to take. After awhile he got up and walked over to the windows fronting onto the Piazza and then turned to face me. "To be completely honest, I think you'd have to leave Italy to stand a chance of being left in peace. You're too involved in the critical issues facing this country to be left totally in peace. Besides," he said, as he walked back to where he had been sitting, "by virtue of the bank you work for and the position you occupy, there's always going to be someone, on one side of the fence or the other, that will want to know what you're up to."

Feathers had a way of getting the old adrenalin flowing. Schaffer was getting his second wind and, looking at him and considering everything, there was no way Robert was suddenly going to walk away and go back to the life he had led before coming to Italy. Even if he wanted to, he knew Bonnie would be miserable assuming she agreed to leave, and that was an assumption Robert knew he could no longer make. "Then it looks like I'll have to be more than a damn good commercial banker, Max, because I'm not leaving."

"Somehow, Robert, I didn't think you would be."

Robert caught Louisa just after her morning shower. "Sorry to bother you at home, Louisa."

"No problem. Sorry to keep you waiting. My hair is still dripping wet."

"I'll let you dry off in a moment. I've been up all night and need a few hours sleep before facing what is going to be a horrible day. I won't be in until about noon," he told her.

"What's happened, Robert," she asked solicitously. Is Bonnie all right?"

"She's fine physically and better than me mentally. The bank was robbed last night and we just happened to get there only moments after the police. Jean Pierre just couldn't deal with it so we had to."

"Dear Lord in heaven," she said in Italian. "You poor man. You've been through so much."

"I'm just thankful no one was injured, Louisa."

"Who else in the bank knows, besides you and Dr. Matra?"

"Unless Jean Pierre has said something, no one but Bonnie."

"May I speak frankly?" Louisa asked.

"Of course. I want you to Louisa," he told her sincerely.

"I think you should have a cold shower and come into the office. You can sleep this afternoon. Someone has to deal with the staff and with Dr. Antinori. If Dr. Matra...."

"Louisa," he interrupted her. "You're right. I'm exhausted but I have to be there. You're absolutely right."

"I should not have said anything but I thought I must," she said formally.

"Please, Louisa, don't apologize. I'm more than grateful for your advice. With any luck, I'll be there before you are."

Chapter 16

Enjoying Life in Rome

Bonnie slept until just before noon and decided to have coffee and a cigarette on the balcony overlooking the square below. It was going to be a beautiful, unseasonably warm day and she fully intended to enjoy it despite the extraordinary events that had occurred in the previous twenty-four hours. She reflected on Robert's deal with Cardinal Pelli, the discussions she and Robert had with the US intelligence people and on the robbery at the bank. She instinctively knew that they were all inter-linked but she was fed up with worrying about such things and with dealing with the issues and problems that their lives now seemed to embrace. She wanted to spend much more time enjoying the cultural aspects of Italy and learning more about the country's artistic treasures. She also admitted to herself that she missed the excitement and physical joys that had accompanied her affair with her art teacher in Milan. The very thought of him kissing and licking her breasts and between her legs and penetrating her with his tongue and enormous penis made her wet and in need of physical relief. She knew that for the moment she needed to stay with Robert but admitted to herself that he was no longer much fun to be with and that she found at least one other man infinitely more exciting in bed. Bonnie realized that she had married her best friend and that it turned out he was really much more of a friend than a lover. She looked down at the square beneath her and wanted to partake in the light-hearted atmosphere-taking place there. She was tempted to call her former lover, Carlo who only recently ceased trying to see her. But instinctively she knew that would not satisfy her needs.

"Hi darling," Robert interrupted her thoughts.

Bonnie literally jumped out of her chair. "Robert, you frightened me."

"Sorry, I just let myself in. I'm exhausted, Bonnie. I've got to crash for a few hours," he said, gave her a kiss on the top of her head and left the balcony to have a shower and some sleep.

She thought for a moment and then called out to him: "Everything OK at the bank, Robert," but he had not heard her and by the time she made her way to the bathroom, he was already in the shower. She was still wet and in need of sex but she knew that at the moment at least doing it with Robert would be little better than using the dildo she had bought out of desperation a few weeks previously. Bonnie went back out to the balcony and lit another Marlboro. "I need Carlo's tongue and cock," She whispered to herself "or, even better," she giggled, "Marco's."

When Robert finished his shower, he went straight to bed. Bonnie knew he would sleep away the afternoon and decided to invite Marco for a drink in the square. Marco Ronza was one of five students, three young men and two young women, she was teaching drawing, an art that few people were capable of teaching or learning. Shortly after their transfer to Rome, Carlo had recommended her to the prestigious Verdi Istituto d'Arte di Roma and, based, Bonnie thought on Carlo's praise for her abilities, they had immediately offered to send her as many students as she could handle. She had interviewed and tested 30 and limited the number of her class to five who came to her Trastevere flat every Tuesday and Thursday afternoon from 3 until 6 PM. On most days class could be held out on the balcony or up on the roof terrace and one of the beautiful parts of Piazza Santa Maria would serve as a model for the day. As the skills of her students had progressed, on several occasions Bonnie had employed young nuns from a nearby convent as models for her students. They would pose nude in the sitting room that fronted onto the balcony and the background beauties of the church spires of Rome. On one recent occasion, one of the young nuns scheduled to model felt ill and had to excuse herself and Marco had volunteered to replace her as a model for the rest of the class. He had a gorgeous, athletic body, fine stunning facial features, and jet black her on his head, under his arms and surrounding his enormous penis.

"Marco, è Bonnie. Come stai oggi?" she asked him in her now nearly fluent Italian when he answered his phone.

"Sono molto bene, Bonnie. Come stai?"

They spoke in Italian for a few minutes and agreed to meet for a glass of wine and a drawing session in the square in mid-afternoon. Bonnie checked on Robert who was now snoring loudly, had a shower, put on deep red, sensuous lip stick and then slipped into a skin tight, low cut, v-neck jumper and a pair of snug jeans. She brushed her blonde hair back and put gold clips on each side at the back to hold it in place, grabbed her sketch book and a handful of cash and made her way down to the square and took a table at a cafe that best caught the late afternoon sun. Before Marco arrived she ordered a half bottle of Gavi di Gavi and began to sketch three French tourists who were enjoying a mid-afternoon plate of pasta. She was on her second glass of wine when Marco arrived.

"Bonjourno, Bonnie," he greeted her as she stood up to kiss him on both cheeks in the Italian fashion.

"Buon giorno, Marco. Si prega di sederti," she returned his greeting and offered him a chair next to her own.

"Bonnie, let me practice my English today," Marco suggested. "It is getting rusty. What have you drawn there?" he asked when he saw her sketch.

When he was seated next to her she let her legs touch his under the little table and was pleased when he did not move them away. "I was just beginning to draw those three French tourists," she commented and nodded toward them. "I'm fond of the French and seeing and drawing them brings back memories of my time in Paris when life was simple and fun."

"You sound nostalgic," he chided her. "How can Paris compare with this beautiful place and with my company?" he noted as he leaned toward her and gave her a squeeze with the arm he had placed behind her chair.

She leaned toward him and let her head fall momentarily onto his shoulder and then turned and looked up at him. "Would you draw me, today, Marco? I'd like you to have a sketch of me. I have one of you. It's only fair."

"Here, Bonnie, while you draw the French tourists?"

She paused, looked up and giggled when she said "It's a bit public, Marco."

She watched him, as he understood what she was suggesting. "We can use my studio, if you like. You've never been and I would love to show it to you."

"What are we waiting for, Marco?"

Fifteen minutes later they made their way the final hundred yards up a windy passage to Marco's studio that doubled as his flat. Like so many formally educated Italian artists of the day, they came from wealthy families that provided them with whatever they needed to be successful. Marco's flat was small but charming and had outstanding views over the ancient part of Rome. He had a fabulous terrace adorned with pots of flowers. His bedroom and studio looked out over the terrace and beyond it over the ancient part of the city. Once he had shown her around, he settled her on the terrace and fetched a bottle of white wine from the small kitchen that also opened onto the terrace. He filled their glasses and toasted her: "To the most beautiful lady in all of Rome."

She smiled and said: "To the man with the most gorgeous body in all of Rome."

"He threw his head back and roared with laughter and commanded her "Now young lady, it is time for me to draw you as you drew me. Off with your clothes!"

Bonnie could hardly restrain herself. She was desperate to take him in her mouth and have him between her legs. She knew she had never wanted any man more in her life and sensed that once she had him, her life would never be the same again. In fact, she believed it would be so much better even if this were only one fleeting moment in time and was never repeated again. She needed his youth, his artistic bent, his incomparable smile, his sense of humour, and his ability to make her happy and relaxed even when she was so blatantly seducing him. Most of all, she needed his magnificent body and his enormous cock.

She stood up, drained her glass of the calming liquid and stood back so that he could admire her while she undressed. She kicked off her shoes, unbuckled the belt on her jeans and slipped them down and stepped out of them. She did a little turn and with her back toward him, pulled the jumper over her head and cast it aside. She had not worn a bra so the only clothing on her body was a sexy pair of lacey knickers that she slipped down to the ground. She cupped her breasts to cover the hardness of her nipples and turned to face him and gasped when she saw him equally naked with the most magnificent erection she had ever beheld. His cock looked to be a foot long and was standing tall, plastered against his taught, muscle-laden stomach. His enormous balls hung between his parted legs.

"Sorry, I just couldn't wait. I'll have to sketch you later," he announced and opened his arms to her.

Bonnie came to him, kissed him passionately on the lips and let his tongue probe the inside of her mouth and then dropped to her knees and began to lick his cock and balls from top to bottom. She was leaving a little puddle on the floor but didn't care. This was the most sensual moment of her life and she was determined to let her body and its needs have their way. She turned him around and began to kiss his bottom and then pushed him forward and licked his little hole until it was open and allowed her to insert the middle finger of her left hand while she stroked his cock with her right hand. "I love your body, Marco," she told him.

Marco extricated himself from her embrace, knelt down and began to kiss her face softly and then her mouth with passion. "I love you, cara," he told her and then his hands were all over her breasts and ass and then between her legs. He inserted three fingers in her pussy and used his thumb to massage her wonderfully erect clit. She came within seconds of the plying of her clit and when she did he lifted her off of her feet and carried her into his bedroom where he laid her on the bed, spread her legs, lifted her ass off of the bed and inserted his enormous throbbing cock into her incredibly open pussy. Bonnie came again, this time with an uncontrolled moan as his full length filled her completely. "I love you, my darling," he told her again and he meant it with all his heart.

Bonnie allowed his swollen cock to lift her off of the bed and began to moan with every stroke. "I love you too, Marco," she finally replied to him and knew that she did. "Give it to me, darling, give it to me hard, she begged him."

Marco looked down at her and as he pledged his undying devotion did as she asked and shoved his throbbing dick deep into her again and again and, finally, as she came one more time he emptied himself into her and cried out: "I need you so much, Bonnie, so much, my darling."

Robert awakened as the sun was setting over the ancient city. He used the loo and went out to find Bonnie. "Darling," he called out. "I want to take you out for dinner. Let's go to Sabatini, Bonnie. I want to celebrate. Bonnie, darling, where are you?"

As Robert searched the flat for his wife, Bonnie was coming one last time as Marco took her from behind. When he had finished, she turned over and pulled his head to her tummy and stoked his beautiful black hair the way she would have stroked a small child. "I knew my life would never be the same once I was with you, Marco. I was right and I will never look back, my darling. However, I do have a husband and need to return to our flat. Will you be alright, my love?"

Marco let her continue to stroke him and eventually said with love in his voice. "As long as you are happy, I will be fine."

Half an hour later, she let herself into their flat and found Robert pacing the living room. When he saw her, he rushed over and put his hands on her shoulders and demanded, "Where you have been, Bonnie. I have been so worried about you?"

Bonnie felt like saying: I've been in the arms of my new young lover and my life will never be the same again but could not do that to Robert. He had been too important a part of her life to hurt him in such a way and, he was her friend. "Sorry, Robert, I needed to feel the life of Rome. When you went to sleep I went for a stroll around the Old City and ran into some of my art students at a little Bistro. We spent the afternoon drinking wine, drawing and enjoying the vibrant life of Rome."

Robert wanted to be angry but she looked so happy and content that he just took her in his arms and gave her a squeeze and said: "You look so happy and content, darling. I was really just worried about you. Let's celebrate. The powers that be have removed poor Jean-Pierre as Branch Manager and put me in his place subject of course to a complete review of the circumstances surrounding the robbery. We will have a huge increase in pay, a bigger flat or, if we wish, a villa, no questions about expenses, and, darling, we can stay in Rome for at least another 3-5 years."

Bonnie could not believe what he was telling her. "Robert, that's unbelievable. Will it make you happy?"

"I know how much you love living here, Bonnie so it's an easy decision. It's a great career move for me whether I stay with the bank or find a job outside and I know it will make you happy. So, yes, darling, it will make me very happy."

Bonnie knew marriage to Marco was impossible no matter what he might think at the moment. His family would never permit it and her own would be shocked beyond belief. But, knowing she could be with him for at least three years was a dream come true. "Let's do celebrate, Robert. I'll have a shower and change and then let's go to Sabatini."

"It's already booked, Bonnie."

Jean Pierre Matra stood in what had been his entertainment center and the home of his Chairman's offshore art collection. He looked out over the ruins of the Roman Empire and of his own career. Everyone in the bank was blaming him for being lax with the staff in respect of security. The powers that be in New York told him that he should have been more vigilant and none of the troubling events that had transpired would have occurred. Jean-Pierre could not help wondering why people had not yet focused on the fact that all of the troubling events had occurred since Schaffer's arrival in Rome. Robert had escaped scrutiny in respect of the illegal transfer of the $5 million that Rodolfo sent to Switzerland because he had been credited with getting it back. Matra was surprised that Schaffer was not a serious suspect in the theft of the art treasures, especially as it was rumoured that his Italian family had ties to the mafia; and he was shocked that Schaffer had already been promoted to Rome Branch Manager. His own fate of being assigned to the incredibly dull job of Head of Marketing for Global's Canadian operations, which were located in Toronto, was less surprising. In fact, he had been amazed that he had not been replaced as Rome Branch Manager after the $5 million illegal transfer.

Jean-Pierre considered the police report that the bank's alarm was not fully switched on. It appeared, the report said, that was not possible to blame Robert for anything deliberate as Matra had told him to go directly home from his appointment with Cardinal Pelli and it was clear he had done so. In the absence of Rodolfo, who had not been heard from since the $5 million fiasco, and in the absence of Robert, responsibility for the alarm system rested with him. The police had uncovered evidence that he had personally turned the alarm on and was the last one to leave the bank but initial inquiries showed it was not switched on at the time of the burglary. So, the police wondered who had turned it off. The burglars would have required two keys and a code known only to Matra and Robert now that Rodolfo was gone. The keys had been changed following Rodolfo's departure and the code was changed daily by Matra who then told Robert the secret four digits. The police had asked Robert and Matra for their keys and both had produced them so unless the burglars had obtained the keys and the code from one of them and after the burglary had returned the keys, they reasoned, there was simply no explanation. Unless, the report went on, duplicates of the keys had been made and the burglars got the code from Matra or Robert or another party who had somehow discovered it. The police had correctly noted the normal procedure that was for Jean-Pierre to decide a new four-digit code and to tell Robert that code before they opened the bank's vault using the previous day's code at 9 AM. When the vault was opened, a new code had to be entered. Until a new code was entered, the vault could not be locked. If Jean-Pierre did not turn up before 9 AM, Robert had the authority to select and enter a new code. He would then tell Jean-Pierre the code when he arrived. If neither Jean-Pierre nor Robert came into the office, the vault could not be opened.

The decision to replace Matra was almost instantaneous and had been taken by the Chairman personally within hours of the burglary. Jean-Pierre knew that he had almost been moved out of Rome following the $5 million transfer by Rodolfo and that the Canadian job was one of several they were looking to move him into at that time. Jane was not unhappy as she was born and raised in Buffalo, New York, a short drive from Toronto, and her parents and many cousins still lived there. However, Jean-Pierre had absolutely no intention of taking up the post and was quietly confident that with a little help, the police would eventually find that Robert Schaffer was a crook and was totally to blame for the burglary. Jean-Pierre even thought that the powers that be might reappoint him as Rome Branch Manager once Schaffer was found to be culpable.

Bonnie was on cloud nine. She had been quietly savouring her afternoon of bliss with her new, exciting, devoted, caring, young, adventurous and gorgeous lover while Robert went on and on about their good fortune. "I can't believe our luck, Bonnie," Robert begin once they were seated at Sabatini's sipping champagne and enjoying their first cigarettes of the evening. "Less than a year ago we were in New York learning what it would be like to be in hell, as you have so often said, and here we are responsible for the bank's activities in Rome. I know what you're thinking, Bonnie, please don't say it. This time I just want to feel what it is like to be on top of the world."

"I wasn't going to say anything negative, Robert," Bonnie said calmly. "I'm thrilled for you and for me. I just want to enjoy this incredible city. Let's leave the heavy thinking until later or, better yet, never."

This is not the Bonnie I know, Robert thought. No matter what I have achieved, there has always been a question, a doubt, and a negative comment. Finally, he praised her saying "Bonnie, I have never seen you so relaxed, content and happy. Success obviously agrees with you, baby."

Bonnie took a deep drag on her cigarette, looked at the bubbles rising to the top of her champagne glass and turned to Robert and looked him in the eyes. "Robert, I have never felt so content and happy. Just enjoy yourself. We are going to have a fantastic three years and hopefully more, here in Rome."

Robert was on a high. He was not even 30 and manager of one of the most important non-Italian bank branches in Rome. His predecessor, Jean-Pierre Matra was promoted to this position at the age of 45 so Robert quite rightly was pleased with himself. The fact that his wife was drop dead gorgeous and drew gazes from any straight male in Rome was a bonus. "Bonnie, I think we deserve a break. How would you like to spend a few days on the Almafi Coast? Annarosa told me about a great hotel that I know you would enjoy."

Bonnie was in a different world, one she had not been in before. She decided to tell him how she felt without telling him the real reason for her feelings. "Robert, I really don't need a break on the Amalfi Coast or, for that matter, anywhere else. I just want to enjoy Rome. I love our flat, this beautiful square, my art classes and students, and your success at the bank because it makes you happy. I really don't need anything more than that at the moment."

Robert was shocked. This was a side of Bonnie he had never seen. She looked and acted truly content. He looked at her as she sipped her champagne. She looked stunning. He hoped she would be in the mood after dinner. "I'm more than happy just vegging out in Rome, Bonnie. I'll take a few days off so we can get to know the City better and," he added after a pause, "each other again."

Bonnie looked over at Robert, smiled and thought: What I really need, Robert, darling, is a few days with my gorgeous, young lover and his enormous dick. Instead she said: "Hey, Robert let's just chill out and see if we can get bored with life."

When Matra arrived at his Parioli villa, which bordered on the incomparable Villa Borghese and its lush tropical gardens in the most elegant part of Rome, Jean-Pierre decided to have Jane ask her friends at the American Embassy for help in discovering how the burglars had obtained entry to the bank.

Guido deposited Jean-Pierre in front of the villa and waited until he was safely inside, a practice they had adopted following knees cappings by militant groups, including the Red Brigades and the Italian Mafia, on bankers who would not play the protection money game. Matra found Jane, who was a 35 year old, good looking, dark haired, brown eyed, American of French decent, in the kitchen preparing supper for their 12 year old twin boys who had been chatting to their mother. "Hi, darling, hi guys" he greeted them cheerfully. Everything OK?"

The apron she wore did not hide Jane's fabulous figure and when she turned away from her cooking to offer Jean-Pierre a kiss, he gratefully accepted it, gave her a little hug and then turned to his sons. "Guys, you alright?"

George, the elder of the two boys by 10 minutes, tried to be pleasant but the thought of having to leave Rome and all their friends had begun to sink in and both he and his brother were quite down. "We'll be fine, Dad," George said. It's just a bit of a shock."

"Michael?" Jean-Pierre queried George's brother.

"I'm OK, Dad, just a little down," he noted honestly. "I suppose I'm holding out hope that the art will suddenly materialize and everything will be back to normal, the way Mr. Schaffer got the $5 million back for you."

"Who told you that Mr. Schaffer got the $5 million back, Michael?" Matra demanded.

"I did, Jean-Pierre," Jane admitted. "It's no big secret, darling. Everyone knows he was responsible for its return."

"Everyone?" Matra asked calmly.

"Well, yes, Jean-Pierre. Everyone that matters. Even my friends at the US Embassy confirmed it to me just last week."

Matra whispered: "They did, Jane?"

"Boys," Jane turned to the twins and announced: "Dinner will be ready in about 15 minutes. You can watch a video until then."

"Thanks, Mom," they said in unison and adjourned to the family room which was down the corridor past the dining room.

Once they were gone, Jane returned her attention to Jean-Pierre: "Well, yes, Jean-Pierre, they did. In fact, Anna Ciano, John Tremarco's wife called me to let me know."

Jean-Pierre's heart started to beat faster. "I thought Tremarco worked out of the US Consular Office in Milan."

He used to. Anna actually called to let me know they have just been transferred down here. John's been appointed Commercial Attaché. During our chat she asked me about Robert and Bonnie and it came out."

"It came out?" Jean-Pierre said as he began to pace back and forth in the kitchen with his head bent forward while his eyes searched the floor like an American bald headed eagle hunting for prey.

"Yes, Jean-Pierre. She said that Robert has family in Sicily and that they intervened."

"Does he, Jane, does Robert have family in Sicily?"

"He does, Jean-Pierre and I hear that they used to be main stream Mafia. Apparently Robert's uncle by marriage immigrated to the States many years ago and made a fortune which has allowed the family there and in Sicily to develop normal businesses."

"Normal Businesses, Jane. A Mafia family with normal businesses?"

"Yes, Jean-Pierre, normal businesses. I think one of the family member's deals in art here and in New York, for example," she said.

And then what she had said hit her like the proverbial ton of bricks. "My God, Jean-Pierre. Do you think Robert could have been involved in the burglary?"

Matra had fallen to his knees in the middle of the kitchen floor and was looking out the bay window at the sky and the heavens beyond. "Thank you, God, thank you," Matra told the heavens and then he looked up at Jane and said: "I knew it, darling. I knew it. The way things have gone since they were transferred down here from Milan had to have something to do with them. Our lives were really pretty normal until they got here. I had decided to ask you to have your friends at the Embassy do a little research into Robert and Bonnie and their families. It looks like that won't be necessary."

Jane was a very savvy woman and spent a few minutes considering what had come out about the Schaffers. When she was comfortable with her conclusion she said: "Jean-Pierre, it could be that Anna is trying to set them up. Remember, she is Anna Ciano and Robert had a hand in dismantling a part of the insider dealing ring that her father is said to be involved in."

Matra interrupted his wife. "But Jane, darling," he implored her, "just think, if his Sicilian family is involved, we could be seen by the bank as victims of a conspiracy and we might be able to stay here in Rome. After a few years of the old way of life, we might even be restored to prominence and elevated to the Country Manager job here in Italy or in France."

"Darling, I hope it is true but even if it is, it will be very difficult if not impossible to prove unless...."

"Unless?" he asked.

"Unless my friends can help us find the proof!" she exclaimed.

Chapter 17

One Down and Several to Go

Carlo Rodolfo sat in the heart of Buenos Aires in a little bar off of the main lounge in the 5 Star Hotel Faena sipping an outstanding Chilean red wine, a case of which he had donated to the hotel's owner on arrival on the condition that during his stay he could drink two bottles on the house and that he would be given a free upgrade to a sea front room. He had been given the 1966 Vina Cousino Macul Reserva Merlot the previous day by the owner of the hotel Isla Seca in Zapallar, Chile, a luxury boutique hotel on the Pacific Coast of Chile where he had been staying as a guest of Count Roberto di Ciano since his attempt to relieve his employers of $5 million. Carlo had flown to Buenos Aires via Zurich within hours of transferring the money from the Rome Branch of The Global Banking Corporation and then had driven a rental car to Zapallar and had been cooling his heels in the luxury boutique hotel since his arrival. His masters had paid a substantial sum to the hotel's owner to register Carlo Rodolfo in an assumed Chilean name.

By now Carlo had expected to receive $500,000 in cash in his Buenos Aires account and was not happy that the funds had not arrived. He had called Count Ciano on three occasions and each time a low level functionary had told him to sit tight. He decided to try again. He called to the bartender: "Necesito llamar a Italia. Tienes un teléfono?

"Un momento, señor."

A few minutes later, the bartender produced a telephone and connected him to an international line. "Just dial the number, Dr. Rodolfo. The call is on the house."

"Many thanks," Rodolfo responded happily and then dialed Ciano's number which he had committed to memory.

"Pronto," a voice across the Atlantic replied.

"Conte Ciano è lì, per favore?"

Rodolfo heard Roberto Ciano's voice in the background ordering the person who had answered the phone to find out who was calling. "Un momento, prego. Chi sta chiamando?"

"Sono Carlo Rodolfo."

Carlo heard the responder telling Ciano who it was and heard Ciano telling him to get rid of Rodolfo.

When the responder came back online, Carlo stepped in and said: "Informa il conte che, se egli non parla a me, mi fgo alla polizia."

Carlo heard the responder exclaim to Ciano: "He's going to the police if you don't talk to him!"

A minute later, Roberto di Ciano came on the phone. "Carlo, where are you, my friend? I tried to reach you at the hotel we are paying for and they said that you had checked out," he said calmly and with concern is his voice.

After cooling his heels in the small hotel in Zapallar for several weeks and with no sign of his cash, Carlo was furious. He shouted: "You bastard, Ciano. You promised me my money would be available within days of the transfer and I have not seen a penny and you have been ducking my calls. I'll tip off the Italian police about you sponsoring the entire operation if you don't transfer the money to me here in Buenos Aires within 24 hours."

Ciano was extremely calm and deliberate in his reply. "Carlo, my friend, I am sorry that you have not heard but we had to send the money back."

"You what?" hissed Rudolfo as the bartender hovered and made signs for Carlo to stop shouting.

"I am sorry Carlo but this Schaffer man has powerful friends in Italy, the sort that come from Sicily. We simply had no choice. But do not worry; I have another operation underway that will enable me to send you the money in a week or so."

Rudolfo tried to remain calm. He understood the problem but did not like the sound of the solution. Whatever it was Ciano was up to could easily fail, he thought, and there was no way Rudolfo could ever return to Italy so he was desperate for the money. "Listen, you son of a bitch" he hissed at Ciano. If that money isn't in the account we set up in Buenos Aires within 24 hours, I am going to send the Italian Financial Police and the main Italian newspapers, including that investigative reporter, Rossi, a copy of the dossier I have on you." There was no response from Ciano so Rudolfo said, "Did you hear me, Ciano?"

"I heard you, Carlo," Ciano responded evenly. "I'm just making arrangements for the transfer on another line. Give me a minute please." Several minutes passed and then Ciano came back on the line and told Rudolfo: "The money will be in your account in Buenos Aires tomorrow just after 3 PM Buenos Aires time." The line then went dead.

Carlo was relieved. He put the phone down and signalled to the bartender who came straight over. "Sorry about the commotion."

"No problem, Sir. What can I get you?"

The second bottle of Merlot, please. I'd like to share it with you. It's a little celebration.

The next day Carlo arrived at the front entrance of the bank that held the agreed account just before 3 PM. When he got out of the taxi, a young, short, dark haired man in a dark suit wearing a white shirt and tie man came up to him and asked: in Italian: “Are you Mr. Rudolfo?”

Carlo looked down at the man who looked like the proverbial bank teller and was pleased that Ciano seemed to be making sure that he would get what was due to him. “Yes, I am,” he responded pleasantly.

“Good,” the man responded. I have a little present for you from Count Ciano and with that he reached inside his jacket, quickly withdrew a Baretta pistol and pumped three slugs into Carlo’s chest. When he had fallen to the ground, he put another bullet into Rudolfo’s head and calmly crossed the street to get into a black Ford saloon that sped him away.

After dinner with her family, Jane Matra went to her study that was swept regularly for listening devices and called her regular contact in American intelligence, Max Feathers. Max had been her contact ever since his masters at the Central Intelligence Agency assigned him to Rome. Jane had provided him and his predecessors with invaluable information over the years and they had done her little favours including providing her information on Jean-Pierre’s love life away from home and covering up her own indiscretions. She was confident that Feathers could shed some light on the burglary and the role Schaffer played in it, if any. The question was, would he be willing to do so. She dialed his private line at home and when he picked up said: “I need some info, Max. Can we have breakfast tomorrow?”

Feathers paused and thought. This must be important as she rarely calls me at home. “Sure, Jane. 8 AM, usual place?”

“See you there,” and then she hung up and found Jean-Pierre in the living room fixing himself a large brandy. “I’ll know something tomorrow morning, Jean-Pierre. In the meantime, I’d love to join you for a brandy, a large one,” she added as she wanted to get a good night’s sleep so that she would be fresh for her meeting with Feathers.

The next morning Jane took a taxi to the bottom of the Via Veneto, paid the driver off and strolled past the US Embassy to the top of the famous road. Their normal meeting place was any one of the Via Veneto cafes that Feathers randomly selected in order to minimize the likelihood of being overheard by listening devices. She surveyed each café fronting the street for any sign of Feathers and when he was not in any of them, crossed over the road and started down toward the bottom. Finally, she spotted Feathers sitting just inside the front window of the Café de Paris sipping coffee and reading a copy of *La Repubblica,* a daily that covered local news. Had he been reading *Corriere della Sera,* she would have continued her stroll to the bottom of the Via Veneto and returned home as Feathers would have been under surveillance.

“Good morning, Max,” she greeted him and took a seat with her back to the road.

"Morning, Jane. Are you well?"

"Very, thank you, Max. Can we talk?"

"Think so but keep it indirect," he replied as he filled her cup with steaming black coffee and offered her a croissant from the pastry basket.

"OK and thanks for the coffee.

Feathers nodded and was all ears. "What's so urgent?"

Jean-Pierre is convinced that his deputy has had something to do with the transfer to Switzerland and with the burglary. Everyone except poor Jean-Pierre knew that Schaffer used influence with his family down South to get the transfer back. Will he do that again for the things that were just taken?"

"Doubt it as we think his Sicilian family were involved in the burglary."

"Wow," Jane exclaimed. "On their own or with others."

"Not sure but probably with others. We have one finger that points at the Vatican and another at Ciano."

You're joking."

"Wish I were, Jane. We are as puzzled as anyone with an interest."

"Any idea what happened with the burglar alarm system?"

"Anyone with a listening device in your husband's office would know the daily code as he always tells Robert the code in the same place every day. Also, anyone with half a brain could figure it out as since he took over as Rome Branch manager he uses the four digits that comprise the day of the month and the month of the year. So, when it is 18 October, the four digit code is 1810."

"Give me a break Max; even Jean-Pierre would be more creative than that."

"We think he does it that way just in case he forgets the code."

"Oh, my God, Max, how incredibly embarrassing."

"Hey, Jane, that's nothing. The manager of one of the most important banks in Rome used to use the same code every day, '1111'. When he was told by his auditors that was too easy, he changed it to "1234'."

Jane shook her head in disgust, paused and then began a new line of questioning. "Why would the Vatican be interested?"

"There might have been some things in the vault that could have been of interest to them," he volunteered as he took out his handkerchief to blow his nose.

"And Ciano?"

Feathers finished wiping his nose and then said mater-of-factly: "He owes a number of people for the successful $5 million transfer even though he had to agree to allow it to be returned. He doesn't have the cash readily available, mainly because Schaffer screwed up a big chunk of his illegal foreign exchange earnings." Feathers then began to rub his hand over his already brushed back hair and periodically pinch the tip of his nose, actions that Jane knew from experience were indications of discomfort.

Jane had her machine gun going and just kept firing: "And Robert Schaffer's Italian family?"

Feathers now started to cough and got out his handkerchief again. Finally, he said, "It cost them a lot to get the $5 million back. Some people are saying that they may be recouping their investment."

"I suppose you are now going to tell me that our bank's Chairman conspired to steel his own art work."

"Never thought of that," Feathers responded too quickly for Jane's taste.

Bull shit, Max. If there is one thing you guys would know about, it's that," she commented definitively.

"We don't spy on people in the US," he said without much conviction.

Jane guffawed and looked feathers in the eye. "Hello, Max. It's Jane here. Halloo?"

He looked at her intently and finally noted: "Our US cousins claim that among real friends and family, he was quoted at a very recent dinner party as saying: 'Every shitty art purchase I have ever made was stuffed into our Rome Branch vault which I hope anyone can break into. With any luck, I will collect the insurance money and buy some decent paintings.'"

Jane leaned back in her chair, took a drink of the fizzy water that had suddenly appeared and told Max: "Sounds like the leadership of the entire Christian world had a motive to break into the bank."

"It does make it difficult to pin-point the culprit," Feathers agreed.

Jane's American background simply could not be contained and she exclaimed: "My God, Max, you guys must spend a small fortune accumulating all this information."

"A very large fortune, Jane, a very large one indeed."

Jane leaned back in her chair and looked at the time. "It's only 8:30, Max but I could use a Kir. Join me?"

Feathers didn't even hesitate. He had some things he needed Jane to do for him and always tried to be accommodating to his informants. "Sure, love to join you, Jane." He hailed the waiter, ordered the Kirs, turned to Jane and asked: "Are you still seeing the cardinal?"

She knew this was coming the moment Feathers mentioned potential Vatican involvement in the burglary. "You know I am. We like each other," Jane paused and added, "lots."

"Sure, sorry but I need you to ask him a few questions," Feather responded as his hand once again began to pinch his nose and brush back his hair.

Most everyone in Rome that mattered, with the possible exception of Jean-Pierre Matra, knew that Jane Matra was Cardinal Raffaello Saperla's mistress. "I figured as much. What do you need to know?" asked Jane.

"If I remember correctly, Saperla works fairly closely with Cardinal Pelli. Try to find out what happened in the meeting between Pelli and Schaffer on the day the burglary took place."

The question got Jane's attention. She sat straight up in her chair and leaned toward Feathers and asked: "Robert Schaffer had a meeting with Pelli on the day of the burglary, Max? That's quite co-incidental, isn't it?"

"That's what we thought. It could be a very important piece to the puzzle, Jane. We would be very grateful if you could shed some light on it."

Jane looked down at the table and lifted the Kir to her lips and took a sip. "No problem. I'm seeing him at lunchtime at his villa. Want me to plant a bug so you can hear the answer personally?"

Feathers laughed out loud and commented: "Wouldn't that be fun."

"Ass hole."

"Sorry I couldn't resist," he responded and became serious again. "Unfortunately, Saperla is super cautious. His villa is checked daily for listening devices. As far as we know, no one has penetrated his security, except you, of course."

"OK, but only on the condition that you keep me informed of what you learn about the burglary. Neither Jean-Pierre nor I are exactly thrilled about leaving Rome for Toronto. I have let Jean-Pierre think I am as I think he would go around the bend if he thought otherwise."

"No problem. I will keep you posted but can we meet again later today," he asked apologetically. My masters are desperate to know who was behind the burglary as they think it is tied into other, shall we say, unusual events. Eliminating the unknowns will help them put the bigger puzzle together."

Jane quickly checked her diary. "I need to be home today by 4:30 for the boys so shall we say 3:30?"

For Feathers, the debrief was top priority so all he said was "Perfect. Just use the normal routine."

Jane returned to her villa to prepare for her time with Saperla. She had been seeing him for about two years and just the thought of having such a powerful man as her lover man her ache all over with need. The fact that he was also a magnificent, well endowed, unselfish lover was icing on the cake. She looked in the mirror and studied her face and body. Saperla loved both and spent hours telling her exactly that and giving her little kisses all over. Just the thought of it made her wet. At 11:30 she got into her Alfa Romeo GTA 1300 Coupe and drove the one-mile distance to Rafaello's magnificent Villa that lay on the other side of the Villa Borghese also in the Parioli area of Rome. A footman welcomed Jane by opening the door to her car and guiding her to the entrance where the butler welcomed her to the inner splendors of Saperla's villa whose foundations dated back to the time of Christ.

"Boun journo, Marco, come sta?

"Boun journo signora, sono bene, grazia come sta lei?" the butler responded with a broad smile and led her into the formal sitting room where Saperla would join her from a door that lead into his private apartments.

A few moments after Marco had departed, Saperla entered wearing a pair of hand-made, dark brown slacks and a light orange coloured Gucci button down sports shirt. His shoes were brown and from Saville Row. He was a tall, stately man in his late 50's and his jet-black her was just flecked with grey at the temples. As was their custom, he greeted her in English, a language in which he was bilingual as a result of his years at boarding school in the UK and then at Harvard University. "My darling Jane," he said to her and held open his arms for the embrace that they both so enjoyed.

Jane literally ran into his arms and kissed him passionately while he lifted her off of her feet and took her into bedroom where they made love for an hour. Saperla made her come often and to her great delight was the only man she ever had who could make her fluids run. When they were sated, they showered, dressed and made their way out to his private terrace that had a view of most every historic building in Rome save the Vatican. 'Out of sight, out of mind' was Saperla's explanation to Jane when they initially begin to see each other.

Marco had laid a simple bar and places for two, next to each other, at the dining table. Saperla poured their customary, generous portions of Gordon's Gin into tumblers and topped them up with ice, lemon and tonic water. "To Rome, my darling, may it last forever."

"To Rome," Jane said and clinked her glass against his and retorted: "May God's Kingdom last forever," Raffaello.

"Of course," he said and after a pause added: "I won't let you leave Rome, Jane. I would be miserable without you. I will find a way to prevent it," he promised her.

"I cannot desert my family, Raffaello, surely you know that, my darling."

"I know and I would never let you do that. What I have in mind could reinstate Jean-Pierre at Global here in Rome or, at a minimum provide him with a new platform to allow him to stay and live well," Saperla assured her.

Marco materialized from doors that lead from the kitchen to the terrace. "May I serve lunch, Eminence."?

"Of course, Marco, what are we enjoying today?"

I believe Madame Matra enjoys caviar which will be followed by a lovely white fish done in a bag, Roman style."

"Indeed I do, Marco. That will be splendid," she exclaimed.

"Excellent, Marco, please serve us the starter now perhaps with a glass of Tattinger Champagne."

Marco bowed and took his leave to retrieve a huge bowl of Beluga Caviar together with saltine biscuits, chopped onion and egg as well as cream cheese together with a bottle of Tattinger, all served on the best Sterling Silver money could buy.

Jane and Raffaello had worked up a huge appetite and devoured the entire bowl of caviar but only after the Tattinger was complimented with an ice-cold glass of the finest Russian Vodka.

While they feasted on the caviar and drinks, Jane picked her lover's brain for information about the burglary. "My friends at the American Embassy have asked me to find out if the Vatican might have been an unwitting accomplice to the burglary, Raffaello. Would you mind giving me something I could pass on to them?"

"Why do you associate with them, Jane," he asked her reasonably. "They are not the brightest sparks in town, especially Max Feathers."

"You know very well why I need to humour them, Rafaello. They do whatever needs to be done to be sure that my indiscretions with you are kept out of the papers among other useful services I ask them to perform."

"Such as?" he asked her with raised eyebrows.

"Such as my other indiscretions," she teased him.

"Ha, ha," he laughed with her as he munched away at the caviar. "You know no one else could satisfy your lust, darling, at least not the way I do."

"You are a very naughty boy, Rafaello but you are fantastic in bed so I forgive you!" she laughed with him as she washed down the last bit of caviar with the chilled vodka.

Jane needed another session with Saperla following lunch after which she was finally sated in body and mind and when she met Feathers at 3:30 she had lots to tell him.

"Well, Max, this information will really cost you, my friend," she stated with glee as she sat down once again with her back to the Via Veneto but this time on the opposite side of the street.

"You know we will take care of you, Jane but, please, is it good news or bad news?" he said with fear and dread in his manner and voice.

Jane paused for effect. "Depends on your perspective, Max. I suppose there are some very good news and some very bad news. You know what Italy is like, a big roller coaster."

"Tell me the good news first, Jane. Several other," he paused to search for the most appropriate word 'projects' shall I say, that I am working on have come apart at the seams. I'm not sure I can take more bad news without a quick adrenalin fix," he commented as his slumped over the table, head down posture betrayed how down he really was.

Saperla claims it was most probably a freelance job set up by the firm that had been hired to review the alarm system. They were due to go in and spruce things up beginning Monday morning. Knowing there were weaknesses, they contracted with a professional outfit from abroad, SAS types, to rip off the bank. So, Max, it seems it was only about money."

"God, Jane," Max groaned, "I just can't wait to hear the bad news."

"Come on, Max," Jane tried to pick him up. "It's not that bad but before we get to it, I did manage to discover what Robert agreed to do for Pelli."

"I'm listening," he said with real interest in his voice.

"Pelli sold Schaffer several million dollars of bearer shares in a company that had become an embarrassment to the Vatican."

"Schaffer doesn't have that kind of money, Jane."

"Robert gave Pelli a personal promissory note for the shares and left the amount blank so that Pelli can simply fill in the amount Robert will owe them when the shares are sold."

"Clever and gutsy," he told her.

"Very," she agreed. "Saperla says that they will be giving Robert lots of business, especially the tricky stuff."

"It's going to be difficult to get him to want to leave Rome, Feathers volunteered miserably."

"If Bonnie really wants to go, Robert will follow her, I am sure. He's like a little puppy dog around her. Probably why she needs other men. That's the good news, Max. Can you bear the bad?"

"I'll have to," he said and then added, "Christ, Jane, how does a guy like Saperla know all this stuff? We more or less have pieced together what you have said but how in the name of God can the Vatican do it? You need huge resources to gather this sort of data."

"For one thing, they have more money than most people think; and among other things, they have a couple of people inside the US Embassy, Max, just over there she pointed to the building that graced the bottom end of the Via Vento not far from where they were sitting. The really bad news is that Raffaello knows several other, much less friendly types, have penetrated your security."

For the very first time in her life Jane witnessed a grown man totally lose it in a public place. Feathers begin to rock back in forth in his chair and to sob uncontrollably. He slumped forward on the table and laid his head on his arms in a little pile in the middle of the table. His sobbing made the table jump up and down; Jane had her hands full just keeping it and Feathers upright.

"Max, Max," she leaned over the table and hissed into his ear. "For God's sake, Max, get it together. You're making a spectacle of yourself! Besides I have more news for you. Maybe I should call Tremarco or Foster?" she threatened him in the hope she would bring him back from the brink.

Feathers lifted his head and said: "You better leave, Jane, leave before the cops get here and link us. Leave now, please, please," he implored her.

"Too late, they've called an ambulance, Max. Let me handle this. Just put your head back down on the table, now," she hissed at him.

Feathers did as he was told and by the time the owner of the café led two paramedics to their table, he was just sobbing into his arms. "Signora," the owner, addressed her in Italian, he seems totally distraught. I have called an ambulance for him."

"I am sorry for all the commotion," she began. "I have just had to tell him that his young son was killed only hours ago on his way to school in America in a car driven by his mother. She is only barely alive and will die soon as well."

"Oh my God, signora, how horrible!" The owner explained. "Can these men help, Signora, please let them help," he pleaded with Jane.

"No, please. Thank you and please thank them for the kindness. I need to take him home to pack so he can fly home to America. Just let me calm him a little here and then we will leave."

The owner told the ambulance men who told everyone in the café the horrible news and almost in unison, they got down on their knees and implored almighty God to save Feather's dying wife.

Jane tried to pay the bill but the owner refused. "Could you just get us a taxi, please?" she asked him and seized the opportunity to get Feathers to his feet and to guide him to the pavement and to the taxi that the owner had managed to hail. "Thank you, thank you so much," she told him and then asked the taxi driver to take them to her Parioli villa.

"Jane, I am grateful," Feathers finally managed to say, "so very grateful."

"Christ, Max, what happened to you?"

"My career is ruined, Jane. I am head of security for the Embassy. A breach of this nature is virtually unprecedented anywhere in the world."

"Well, Max, if you help me and Jean-Pierre stay in Rome, Saperla will help you discover the people that have penetrated the American Embassy's security, not only those loyal to the Vatican but those loyal to others."

"Others?" he mouthed it inaudibly and miserably as though he had not heard before that there were others. "Jane, you must tell me who they are. Please, Jane, I am finished if I personally cannot expose them."

“Max, he wouldn’t tell me. He told me to tell you that he will give you their names if you can figure out a way to have Jean-Pierre reinstated as head of Rome Branch.”

Feathers was finally putting it back together. The intellectual challenge was working its magic as Jane hoped it would. “Let me get us a proper drink,” Jane said to him. “Scotch rocks OK?

“Feathers hesitated and then said, “Yeah, perfect, Jane. Make it a large one.”

In the hope that she might persuade Feathers to devote time figuring out the way forward for both of them, after leaving Saperla’s villa Jane had organized a baby sitter for the boys so that she and Feathers would have quality time to try to figure out a strategy that satisfied their needs. No matter which direction they took, Robert Schaffer seemed to be the key to the way forward. “If Bonnie Schaffer were seeing other men,” Max asked Jane, “how could we use that information to achieve our objectives?”

“If she were seeing several men other than Robert, we could easily use that information to persuade her to have Robert seek a posting outside of Italy or, if we could organize it, to accept a posting outside of Italy if it were offered. On the other hand, if she was seeing just one man and he is here in Rome and she loves him, it will be difficult to get her to leave.”

I feared that is what you would say, Jane. She has been quite a naughty girl since she arrived in Italy. She took a near 40 year old artist lover within weeks of arriving in Milan from New York, screwed Alberto Ciano’s brains out when they spent a weekend at the Ciano villa in mid-December, and has recently taken up with one of her 20 year old art students. Unfortunately, we think she has fallen in love with him and would do virtually anything to remain in Rome so that she can continue the budding affair.

“Christ,” Jane swore. “A bitch in heat is one thing; but one that is in love is a totally different challenge.”

“Yeah, I know, but I think I have an idea that will make her want to leave Rome.

“Great, Max, what is it?"

“We’ll have him discovered.”

“Discovered?” she asked.

“Yeah, we’ll get him a fellowship to attend the Institute of Art at the University of Paris.”

Chapter 18

Moving On

Robert Schaffer asked the bank to allow Jean-Pierre to stay in Rome for one month in order to allow Matra to do a proper hand-over. Schaffer wanted to pick Jean-Pierre's brain for the details needed to run the branch efficiently and also wanted to use the time to have Matra introduce him to all of the bank's clients and to Matra's key contacts in Italy. The schedule Robert and Jean-Pierre agreed was from dawn to dusk and included weekends so Bonnie was pretty much left on her own. She was thrilled initially as it gave her time to indulge herself with Marco and her new found love of the artistic beauties of Rome. However, on the third week of the hand-over period, just after a mind bending lovemaking session with Ronza, her new world came apart.

"You're going to do what?" Bonnie asked Marco incredulously.

"I'm going to accept a fellowship to study art at the prestigious Institute of Art at the University of Paris," he repeated himself.

"Marco, how could you?" she said selfishly.

"Bonnie, I thought you would be happy for me, my darling. It's a life-changing opportunity for me," he said reasonably.

Bonnie thought, I have been such a fool but said "Marco, I am happy for you; it's just a bit of a shock." She gave him lots of kisses and thanked God that she had not told Robert that she was leaving him. It had nearly come out the night before when they were sipping champagne on their balcony overlooking Piazza Santa Maria. But something told her to wait until she was sure Marco wanted her to move in with him. He had asked her more than once but so far she had said 'no'."

"Bonnie, my love, I want you to come with me. You know that I am independently wealthy, darling. I want to take care of you and want you to be with me all of the time."

Suddenly, she no longer felt the fool. "Oh, Marco, I do love you so," she cried out and threw her arms around him and made passionate love to him.

When Feathers heard the tape of the conversation, early the following morning, he called Jane Matra. "Jane, can I see you?" asked Feathers. We have a problem."

"Of course, Max. Same routine?"

"Yes, please. Can you be there by 10 AM?"

A little after 10, Jane spotted Feathers with a copy of the *Corriere della Sera* sitting on his own in the Via Vento's Café de Paris. She passed him by and took a seat in the café next door, ordered a double expresso and started to peruse the *Daily American.* After 15 minutes she left some money for the waiter and hailed a taxi for their fall back venue. "Il Vaticano, per piacere."

Feathers left shortly after her and they met up half an hour later in the Vatican Bank in a queue to make a deposit. "Were you followed?" feathers whispered to her.

"No."

"Good. The problem is that Bonnie's lover wants her to come with him to Paris and we think she may leave Robert and go with him."

"Shit."

"My sentiments entirely. What are your thoughts?"

I think we need to find another platform for Jean-Pierre. If you have accurately portrayed Bonnie's state of mind, I can tell you she will undoubtedly go with the guy to Paris. That leaves Robert here and Jean-Pierre in need of another prestigious job in Rome.

"Unless we pin the blame on Robert Shaffer for the burglary," Max suggested.

"You can do that? Max."

"Possibly. We can certainly create a lot of doubt in the minds of Global's senior management about Robert Schaffer's suitability for the post of Global's Rome Branch Manager.

"What about his Sicilian family?" asked Jane with serious concern showing on her face and also in her voice.

"They will try to protect him. No doubt about that and they are very capable of playing rough."

Jane paused for thought and moved forward in unison with the queue as Feathers tagged along behind her. Pinning the Blame on Robert needs to be a last resort, doesn't it?"

"Absolutely," replied Feathers. "The very last resort."

Robert Schaffer had arranged for the Vatican's bearer shares to be registered in his own name only so that the shares could not be sold or transferred without his signature. That way he could control the price at which they would be sold and to whom they would be delivered. He felt this precaution was more than called for in the light of the crooked behavior surrounding Rome Branch. He also opened a safety deposit box in his name only at the main Rome office of Italy's largest bank and personally placed the shares in the box. Once these security measures were in place, he turned his attention to figuring out how much they were worth and how best to achieve that value. When he was ready with a solution, he went to a pay phone outside his bank and spoke to Cardinal Pelli's assistant to arrange for him to meet with Cardinal Pelli to report. He could have had Louisa make the appointment and Guido drive him to the Vatican. Given their big mouths, he knew that would be stupid.

The next morning he was in Pelli's office just after 11 AM. "Your Eminence," Robert said and bowed his head slightly in deference to the Cardinal when he met him in his Vatican office.

"Please, Robert, I want you to call me Enrico."

"Thank you, Enrico. I thought I had better report to you in person."

"Of course, Robert. Where do matters stand?"

Robert brought him up to speed regarding security arrangements for the shares and then explained the economics first broadly and then in detail as Enrico seemed to have a thirst for the nitty-gritty, perhaps, Robert reasoned, just to be sure that Robert had done his work properly. "So, Enrico, the way I see it," Robert concluded, "we should sell say a third of the Vatican's shares to the people I have discovered are keen to buy the entire company. To encourage them, I suggest we sell this tranche of shares at a relatively low price, say 5% below the market value. That will give them a good base to launch a full bid for the company which of course will have to be at over 50% above the market value in order to be successful. With a fair wind, by implementing this strategy successfully, you could get well over $17 million for all of your shares rather than the current market value of just a little over $10 million, Robert said matter-of-factly. Here is a copy of all my workings in case you would like to review the details," he concluded as he slid a thick book over to him.

Enrico was more than impressed. He was flabbergasted. Other banks most probably would not have thought of this approach. If they had, they would have given him the $10 million and kept the $7 million for themselves and, Enrico admitted to himself, the Vatican would have been thrilled. "You have my sincere thanks, Robert. I am very impressed and wish you the best in bringing this proposal to fruition." The Cardinal stood and thus brought the meeting to a conclusion.

"Thank you, Enrico. I will keep you informed of developments."

As Pelli walked Robert toward the door to his office, he stopped just short of it and said: "By the way, if you bring this off, I will open a Vatican Bank account in your name with a beginning balance of $500,000. I hope that will be a satisfactory commission."

Schaffer thought for a few seconds. "That will be more than satisfactory, Enrico. Thank you very much indeed."

Robert was on cloud nine when he left Pelli's office. The goose bumps were there and he wanted to celebrate what was a great achievement. He was not sure whether he would keep the $500,000 for himself or turn it over to Global. It would be a big decision but there was no reason to make it now. However, bearing in mind the events following his last meeting with Pelli, he decided to say nothing to anyone about the deal or the commission, including Bonnie.

He now needed to implement his plan for the Vatican's shares. Once it was done, he would have plenty of time to celebrate. The question in his mind was who can I trust in Global to do this deal. The answer came back to him and his mind's eye immediately in capital letters, NO ONE! He thought for a few minutes and then the answer hit him right between the eyes. I have some debts to pay to people that have been helpful to me, he thought, and now is the time to repay them. He picked up a taxi outside the Vatican and went to the Calisto, a little bed & breakfast with an 'in' bar just a stone's throw from his flat in Piazza Santa Maria. He ordered a large whiskey and went to the pay phone just outside the entrance to the Calisto, put a handful of coins in, and dialed his cousin Luigi's number.

Luigi answered immediately: "Pronto."

"Luigi, E 'il tuo cugino, Roberto."

They went through a series of questions that they had arranged for future contacts, exchanged pleasantries, and then Robert told him what he intended to do for the Vatican and explained how Luigi and his family could make a lot of money on the deal and be enormously helpful to Robert. When Schaffer had finished, Luigi said: "We will share whatever we make 50-50, Robert, I hope that is satisfactory."

"Not on your life, Luigi. You keep 75% for your family and I will be more than happy with the rest."

Luigi paused and then finally said: "Robert, we are family. You owe us nothing for what we have done for you or will do in the future. It must be 50-50 or nothing at all."

Robert hesitated but he knew he must accept Luigi's 50-50 proposal or risk offending him. "50-50 it is, Luigi and thank you."

"E 'nulla, nulla, Roberto," and then the line went dead.

Robert went back to his table, took a long sip of his whiskey and realised that for the first time in his life he would join the growing ranks of banking industry crooks if he kept the $500,000 commission from the Vatican or if he passed the final bit of information, the name of the target company, to his cousin Luigi. Doing both would make him one of the bigger crooks among his banking industry colleagues. But, he reasoned, I might as well make some money, everyone else does. Maybe Bonnie was right; maybe you cannot have a long-term career as a banker without becoming a crook.

He took another sip of his whiskey and thought he saw Bonnie walking with a man to Piazza Santa Maria. He stood up and saw that the woman was holding the man's hand and decided he must be mistaken. He sat down again and sipped at his whiskey. He had not seen much of Bonnie over the last several weeks but she seemed quite content whenever he did see her. In fact, he thought, she seems downright happy. He looked at his watch and seeing it was just half past noon, decided to go back to their flat to see if she happened to be around and wanted to join him for lunch. He put some notes on the table and made his way to Piazza Santa Maria. The man and woman he had seen previously were sitting in Sabatini sipping champagne and playing kissy-face. "My God," he said out loud "it's Bonnie and one of her students, Marco Ronza!"

He was frozen at the entrance to the piazza. His heart started to beat as rapidly as it had when he saw her get into the Mazzarotti and kiss Alberto Ciano on the lips. This time, he thought, it's one of her fucking art students. He forced himself to relax and after about five minutes his heartbeat had returned to normal. He was still at the entrance to the piazza watching his wife having a relaxed, intimate conversation with a man at least six or seven years younger than she was. A waiter brought them some pasta and they tucked in. Robert watched them for another five minutes and saw that they could not keep their hands off each other.

His mind was in high gear as a result of his meeting with Pelli so he forced the emotions into neutral and let his mind get on with the analysis for him. Robert took a table at the restaurant just across from theirs, ordered a glass of Chianti and a plate of spaghetti with garlic, oil and hot peppers and settled in to watch the show. Robert never came home for lunch so Bonnie had no reason to be worried about him seeing her with another man. Bonnie had told him last autumn that they needed to spice up their marriage. He had not paid attention and she fell into bed with Alberto Ciano. Now she was obviously seeing another man, a young one with time on his hands. As they kissed and touched and cuddled in public, he could not help but think about what they did in private.

Robert paid his bill and sipped wine until Marco paid their bill and then followed them at a distance as they made their way to Robert's flat. He waited 20 minutes at the entrance to their building to be sure that Marco was staying with her and avoided the noisy lift and walked up the five flights of stairs to the entrance to his flat. He listened at the door for ten minutes and then let himself in. He went to the cupboard that had held his camera, retrieved it and checked to be sure it was fully loaded. He marvelled at his cold, ruthless approach to what should have been a totally emotional situation. She had hurt him more than he realised over the last six months and he was fed up with her spoiled brat behaviour. He could hear Bonnie's moans coming from their bedroom and crept up the hallway to the door to their bedroom to be 100% sure that what was obvious was actually happening. They had left the bedroom door ajar and the shutters open so the light was perfect for photos. He could see Marco's ass moving back and forth as his cock penetrated Bonnie's pussy. Her legs were spread wide and her ass and pussy elevated a good foot off of the bed supported by Marco's arms, which were linked under her, and by his enormous cock. He was beginning to move more quickly as Bonnie's moans took on her pre-cum tones. Robert began to take one picture after another and thought, Marco has done this more than once with her. He wants to come with her.

Just as the two of them were about to explode, Robert pushed the door open, took several more pictures and shouted at the top of his voice: "Get out of my life you fucking whore!" And then the emotions took over completely. Robert begin to kick the bed and then he grabbed a lamp and broke it over Marco's head. Marco slumped to the floor and Bonnie begin to scream as Robert said slowly and in a threatening voice: "You have one hour to get some clothes on and to get out of my life. I am going back down to the square. If you or Marco are here when I come back, I will kill you both."

When Robert went back to the flat, Bonnie and Marco were gone. She had packed a few suitcases with essentials and left. He was much less emotional about it than he ever dreamed he could be. In a sense he had moved on and so had Bonnie. The next day Louisa played the intermediary. At midday Louisa came into to see Robert who had said nothing about his break-up with Bonnie.

"Robert, Bonnie has asked me to go to your flat with her so that she can get the rest of her things. I am so sorry about what has happened."

Robert had finished with the tears. "Louisa. It's best for both of us. I am ambitious and enjoy the cut and trust of this amazing world in which we all live. Bonnie just wants to live for the day. We should and are going our own separate ways so by all means use the afternoon to help her move out of my apartment."

"Robert, she asked me to say how sorry she is that you found out in the way you did. She never wanted to hurt you."

Robert paused and then said: "Tell her I want her to be happy and to move on. It was good that I found them together as it makes it so much easier to simply dismiss her from my life. In that sense it was a blessing for us both."

"That is very cruel, Robert. Are you sure you want me to say that?"

"Yes, Louisa, I do. It's true and she needs to know that I will no longer be here even if she needs me. She has to make her own way now."

Louisa left without further comment and wondered if Bonnie understood how ruthless Robert could be if he were crossed.

When Feathers got into his office at the US Embassy in Rome, a clerk brought in a sealed envelope. Max opened it. Inside was a fax that was marked 'Top Secret'.

Robert's not going anywhere. You can just wipe that off the option list, Feathers. DFR, Director Operations.

Feathers immediately called Jane Matra and arranged to meet her on the Via Veneto. When she arrived and had ordered a double expresso, Max passed her the top-secret fax. As she read it, he said: "Sorry, Jane. Reinstating Jen-Pierre as Global's Rome Branch Manager is no longer an option. We are going to have to find a new platform for Jean-Pierre."

"What happened?"

"He's ditched the bitch and is in high gear. It's like the ball and chain is gone and he can do anything. He's got the ear of the senior most people at the Vatican. He is a producer and he is a loyal American. Our top brass has promoted him to super star status. He's an untouchable, Jane.

Jane Matra looked Fathers in the eye and said: "You know, Max, you guys are really flighty, kind of like a pretty 16 year old girl with too much time on her hands and too many guys in search of her honey pot.

"Say whatever you like, Jane. There is no way our guys will do anything now but support Robert Schaffer. He's on a roll, has the Vatican behind him as well as his Sicilian family for God's sake.

"So what's so wrong with another platform, Jane asked with a little smile on her face?"

Feathers relaxed visibly. He had no room for maneuver and hoped Jane would see that was the case. Nothing, nothing at all. "We've hired a head hunter who will approach Jean-Pierre through his friends. We've got three or four suitable positions for him. All offer more money and a better pension plan."

Jane was speechless. She just sat there for a couple of minutes saying nothing. Finally, Feathers broke the silence: "Jane, I thought you would be happy?"

"Happy, Christ, Max I am delirious with relief. Robert has been good to Jean-Pierre since Robert took over as branch manager and last evening called him to assured him of support if he decides to pursue a career in Rome with another institution. If you can deliver, I will be in your debt as will Cardinal Saperla."

"We have one problem, Jane and it is a very big one. Count Ciano wants Robert Schaffer out of Italy."

"So why doesn't he just bump him off. You know, a motor cycle borne hit or something?"

"Count Ciano also wants to stay alive. Robert's Sicilian family would seek retribution. They are much more powerful than the Ciano's."

"What can I do to help, Max?"

"Maybe the Vatican would find it useful for Robert to be transferred to Global's Head Office in New York City? If he were there, their interests would be safeguarded by someone they trust, someone who would be at the heart of power. You more than anyone could make that happen, Jane. If you can, maybe even the Global Rome Branch Manager's job would be back on the table."

She thought for almost a minute. Finally, she said: "I am sure Cardinal Saperla would see the benefits of that."

Chapter 19

Pearl Harbour

Bonnie and Robert's break-up did not surprise Paolo and Stephanie. They learned first from Robert who called Paolo on the day he found Bonnie in bed with her student lover. They counseled Robert to move on as Stephanie knew that Bonnie had taken a 40 year old art teacher as a lover when she was in Milan and also that she had a brief but passionate affair with Alberto Ciano. Stephanie also felt Bonnie was a selfish dilettante and that Robert deserved better, someone who would pull her own weight and contribute to his development as a person. The fact that Robert had found her in bed with a 20-year-old man who was also her student doomed Bonnie to eternal damnation as far as the Mancini family was concerned. Their real concern, however, was that Paolo had heard from people he trusted completely that Roberto di Ciano wanted Robert out of Italy and that if it weren't for Robert's Sicilian family, Robert would already have met the same fate as Carlo Rodolfo.

Paolo flew down to Rome to see Robert just after he and Stephanie learned that he had thrown Bonnie out. "Robert, Stephanie and I feel so badly for you," he greeted Robert when Paolo met him for dinner at the roof top terrace restaurant of the Hassler Hotel.

"I'm not completely over it, Paolo but I am nearly there. I would never take her back but to be honest I am still searching my brain to understand why she was so unfaithful to me. I thought she was my best friend, Paolo, my very best friend. How could I have been so wrong about her?"

"You will probably never know, Robert but you are better off without her. You are a good and kind man. You will find someone else who will be devoted to you and you to her."

"Thank you, Paolo. I value your and Stephanie's support."

They chatted on for over two hours about Italy, Paolo's businesses, the labour unions, and most of all the burglary at the bank. "I am sure the Ciano family was the prime movers behind the burglary, Robert," Paolo concluded after going over all of the possibilities.

"I agree with you completely about the involvement of the Ciano's, Paolo. They are very dangerous people."

"If it weren't for your Sicilian family, Robert, you would be dead. I learned just a few days ago that Carlo Rodolfo was gunned down in the streets of Buenos Aires about ten days after he fled Italy. It is known that the Ciano's had him killed, probably because he was threatening to go to the police unless he received his $500,000 commission from the illegal money transfer. Ciano couldn't pay it because your Sicilian family forced the return of the money.

"Have you any evidence that the Ciano's were behind the burglary, Paolo?"

"No, but I hear from friends and informants that they are at the top of the list of suspects."

"Maybe I should leave Italy, Paolo. It would be better from a career point of view to stay but I would like to live long enough to have children and to enjoy life a little."

"Italy needs men like you, Robert, if it is ever to emerge from the quadmire of corruption but Stephanie and I would understand if you decide to leave."

The talk with Paolo helped Robert focus on the realities of life. Now he had to make a huge decision, to fight or to run and he wasn't sure yet what that decision would be.

Bonnie Schaffer was shocked by Robert's reaction to her infidelity. She never dreamed he would not forgive her much less that he would threaten to kill her. She admitted to herself that she had been a lousy wife to him but felt that her unfaithfulness became inevitable when he did not respond positively to her requests to spice up their marriage. She had not yet had the courage to tell her family in Michigan, mainly because she knew she would have to tell some version of the truth because of the pictures that Robert had taken of her with Marco.

When Alberto Ciano arrived without warning at Marco's flat not long after Robert had thrown her out, she was feeling particularly vulnerable. Marco had gone out to a university lecture so she invited him in for a coffee after Alberto told her that he had some important news for her. She was dressed only in a loose fitting housecoat which left little to the imagination but she felt comfortable as Alberto had been her lover, albeit briefly.

Once she had made them coffee and they had settled themselves at a small table on the balcony, Alberto gave her the news. "We have decided to offer you the position Curator of our family art collection and of our hotel collection as well. Will you accept it Bonnie? I would be good for you and for us."

Seeing Alberto again brought back the memories of the albeit brief but enormously exciting affair and she was flattered to see that the Ciano's saw merit in her artistic abilities. It was the sort of intellectual and emotional uplift that she suddenly realized she was desperate for. "Where would I be based, Alberto? I mean, I wouldn't want to be away from Marco."

"You would need to be in Paris, Bonnie and I believe I have heard that is where you are headed next in any case."

My God, she thought, how would he know that? "That's right, Alberto. Marco has been offered a fellowship to study art at the University of Paris and he wants me to go with him."

"Well, it's settled then. When can you start?"

We will be moving up to Paris in two weeks. I suppose anytime after that would be fine."

"Wonderful, Bonnie. I'm so happy that we will have an excuse to see each other again. I have missed you, darling."

Bonnie could feel his eyes penetrating her house coat like a laser beam and realized that her housecoat had come open and that he could see her naked breasts. Before she knew what was happening Alberto came to her and began to kiss her passionately and to fondle her breasts. His touch was magical and she simply could not resist his advances.

"Let's go to the bedroom, Alberto, it will be so much more comfortable in there."

Ciano bent over, took her in his arms and went to the bedroom. She took off her gown and lay naked before him on the bed. He stripped off quickly and penetrated her moments later. Her response frightened her as she came within seconds and when he continued to pump her, quickly came again. "My God, Alberto," she moaned, "I have missed you, darling" and then he filled her with his come and she squirted all over the bed.

Jean-Pierre Matra had done everything he could to assist Robert in the handover. He had introduced him to his key contacts and to Italian government officials as well. The month flew by but Matra felt it was time well spent. He was able to see everyone he wanted to see with dignity and in fact he received several unsolicited offers of employment from his contacts and friends during the handover period. In fact, however, the last thing he wanted was a new post working for anyone. His dream now was to form his own firm, one that would assist foreign companies to set up in Italy and Italian companies to set up abroad. Only one thing was missing, the $1 million in start-up capital that he had calculated would be needed to be sure of success. As Matra made his way back to his Parioli villa in his new Mercedes, he was confident that the required money would soon be in his numbered Swiss account.

When Paolo took his leave of Robert to get some sleep at about 9:30 PM, Schaffer decided it was time to determine whether he had the option to stay on the side of the angels rather than that of the felons. He got out his contact book and quickly found the page with Akio Okuda's home telephone number and signaled to a waiter to bring him a telephone. When it arrived he dialed Okuda's number and was pleased when he answered.

"Akio, it is Robert Schaffer. I am sorry to trouble you at this time of night but I need to ask you a favour."

"Anything, Robert, anything at all," he responded as the gratefulness Okuda felt for what Robert and Louisa had done for Okuda's chairman flowed clearly down the phone in his tone and his words.

"A burglary took place at the Rome branch of Global a few weeks ago and I need to know who was responsible. So far, my enquiries in that regard have come up with many suspects but with no conclusive evidence. Do you think you could assist me?"

"That is a small favour, Robert, I will still owe as much as I did before you made this call. I am sure that I will be able to help. In fact, when it occurred, I asked my colleagues to look into the matter and we already have a quite conclusive preliminary view. Had you been in difficulty, we would have offered our assistance without being asked."

Schaffer was overwhelmed. In all his dealings with Okuda and his colleagues, he had been impressed with their behavior and especially with their loyalty. Now he was simply speechless.

"Robert, are you there?" asked Okuda.

"I am, Akio. It's just that I have been through a very difficult period in my life and your immediate kindness and the comfort you are giving me have made me quite emotional."

"I see. We'll not to worry, I and my company will provide you with what you need. I will come to Rome tomorrow afternoon with our conclusions and with the evidence to support them. Is 2 PM at your offices OK?"

"Perfect. See you then."

When they had rung off, Robert could not help crying tears of joy. A waiter saw him and asked if he could help. "Yes, please, I need a very large whiskey, an Oban if you have it with some ice and water on the side."

Robert slept well for the first time in months. When he woke up, he quickly showered, made coffee and took it and a croissant to his balcony. He downed the croissant in a few bites and sipped at the steaming hot coffee. He then went into his study and retrieved his contact book and brought a telephone onto the balcony. He found Max Feather's number and got him on the phone after a few minutes of tooing and froing with the switchboard operator at the US Embassy who initially denied that there was a Max Feathers with them.

"Robert is that really you," Feathers said when he finally came on the phone.

"Hi Max, yes it is really me. Are you free for an early dinner tonight? I have some interesting information for you."

Feathers hesitated and said, "Can I bring a colleague?"

“Of course, if I can bring one as well?”

“Deal. When and where?”

“Your choice as you will be paying,” Robert said with a chuckle.

“I see, well in that case why not dine here at the US Embassy? The food is good and we can have some peace and quiet.”

“Perfect. Is 7:30 PM OK?”

“That will be fine. See you and your colleague then,” Feathers said and rang off.

Robert then found Paolo at the Hassler and persuaded him to join him and Feathers and Co. for dinner and then dressed and let Guido speed him out to the bank where he spent the morning at the bank working with Louisa. Thankfully, the month long marathon with Jean-Pierre was over. Robert decided to keep his old office and to make Jean-Pierre’s entertainment centre his own. He planned to give Jean-Pierre’s old office to his second in command when he got around to selecting one of three candidates that had been proposed to him by the boys in Human Resources in New York. When he finished with matters that Louisa considered urgent, he turned his attention to a little pile of telephone messages that Louisa had decided should be dealt with when time permitted. At the top of the pile was a note from Louisa that Tom Sugar had called him the previous day. Wonder what Tom did to her to deserve the second pile, Robert thought and then could not suppress a guffaw.

Louisa looked at him sternly and said: “He tried and failed. Maybe he’s calling to complain!” and then they had a laugh together.

Robert put the numbers into his contact book and got through the rest of the little pile by the time Akio Okuda arrived. He was famished but lunch would have to wait. Akio and Robert greeted each other warmly and then they got right down to the matter at hand once Louisa had served tea.

“Akio, I am sorry to have had to ask you for this favour. I hope it has not in any way inconvenienced you to come here today,” Robert begin sincerely and with thankfulness in his voice.

“It has been my great pleasure to prepare this dossier for you Robert, Akio said as he reached inside a small suitcase that he had brought with him and passed a leather bound, three inch think document to him. Here is the only other copy, Robert, Akio went on as he brought it out from the suitcase. These are with my Chairman’s personal compliments and he has asked me to say that we are still very much in your debt.”

May I look at this please, before you leave?”

"Of course."

Schaffer begin to go through the report which included certified statements, photographs of documents marked "Top Secret", pictures of people in various stages of dress and undress, and a variety of supporting materials. The crowning glory was a succinct two-page summary of the findings referenced meticulously to the documents and supporting materials and to other materials that could be obtained on request.

Schaffer was visibly shaken by the findings and after he collected himself asked Akio: "How can I ever repay this debt I now owe you, Akio?"

"You owe us nothing, Robert," Akio stated sincerely. We are honoured to be of some small assistance to you. Please study the materials carefully and then I strongly recommend that you place one copy in a secure location and that you give the other to Mr. Feathers when you see him tonight at the US Embassy. I wish you well, Robert."

Robert was literally speechless and when Akio stood up he could not resist embracing him in the Roman style, a gesture that Okuda accepted graciously and then returned unreservedly. Schaffer accompanied Okuda out to his chauffeur driven limo that took him straight to Fiumicino Airport and the private jet that would take him back to Milan.

When Robert got back to his office he found Louisa looking though one of the dossiers. "Louisa, please do not read those materials. It will be dangerous for you personally to know what is in them."

"I am sorry, Robert but I have been so worried for you and your safety. These dossiers will keep you safe and so now I can sleep well at night."

"Alright, Louisa but please keep what you have seen to yourself. After I study them carefully, I am going to put them in a secure place, freshen up and brief Paolo before going to dinner at the US Embassy. Can you ring Paolo and tell him I will see him at the Hassler at about 7 PM?"

"Of course. Shall I ask Guido to bring the car around?"

Robert had the dossiers under his arm and was on his way out of the door. "No need, Louisa, I will take a taxi."

Once Schaffer had deposited the original copy of the dossier in his safe deposit box in the bank in downtown Rome, he took another taxi to Piazza Santa Maria and then made his way to his flat. When he opened the door, he could immediately see that something was very wrong. The flat had been torn apart from top to bottom. Someone had been looking for something and did not seem to have found it. There was no way he could stay in the flat so he called Louisa and asked her to call the police and then to join him as soon as possible. When Louisa and the police had come and gone, Robert managed to find what he needed for an overnight stay and grabbed a taxi to the Hassler where Louisa had already reserved a room for him. It was 6 PM by the time he was settled in his room but that was enough time to thoroughly review the dossier. There was no doubt that Robert could stay in Rome if he so chose. There also was no doubt that Robert had the power to put a number of important people in prison.

At 7 PM Robert took the dossier and went up to the Hassler's roof terrace. Paolo was already there and they embraced each other warmly. Paolo was drinking Compari on the rocks and had ordered a large Oban whiskey for Robert. Robert moved the drinks to the side of their table and placed the dossier in the middle, angled so that Paolo could easily see the materials as Robert turned the pages.

As they turned the pages together, Paolo's face gradually became an ashen colour. "This is an incredible dossier, Robert," Paolo concluded when he had been through it. "I am not really surprised that Matra worked with Ciano in pulling off the burglary of your bank but I am shocked that the US government fenced the art work and has promised Ciano protection from your Sicilian family. I am not sure what Max Feathers will say when he sees the dossier but for our own safety, I think only one of us should go to the Embassy tonight and that should be me, Robert."

Robert took a large gulp of his whiskey and washed it down with an equally large measure of water. "I think I need to reward my Sicilian family, Paolo. I am going to need their protection."

"How are you going to do that, Robert?" Paolo asked with concern in his voice.

Robert explained the deal he intended to do for Cardinal Pelli and how his Sicilian family could benefit and Paolo said: "I agree, Robert, you had better make that call to your cousin now."

Robert got out his contact book, hailed the waiter for a telephone and when it had arrived, dialed the number of his cousin, Luigi. When they finished with the coded words that verified who they were, all Robert said was "Please implement Blenheim & Sons Healthcare Corporation as soon as possible."

"I will do it now," said Luigi. "The markets in New York are still open."

When Robert left the branch with the dossiers, Louisa rang Jean-Pierre Matra at his villa in Parioli and explained what she had seen in the dossier. Matra thanked her, called Roberto di Ciano and then went directly out the door of his villa to his Mercedes and sped toward the bank where he picked up Louisa and headed to Fiumicino Airport in an effort to catch the first flight out of Italy. Robert nearly came to blows with Paolo over who should go to the US Embassy dinner but finally prevailed by telling him that he would think of himself as a coward for the rest of his life if he did not go personally.

“Good luck, Robert, if you are not here physically by 11 PM, I will call Rossi and give him the best story of his life.”

“Paolo, take this envelope. It contains the name of the bank where I have the safe deposit box that contains the shares in Blenheim & Sons Healthcare Corporation and the original copy of the dossier given to me by Akio Okuda. It also has the key to the box and a notarized letter of instruction allowing you access to the safe deposit box. I hope you don’t need them,” he told him, “but if you do, I wish you well.”

Robert then took a taxi from the Hassler to the US Embassy where he was expected. The US Marines on duty at the gate checked his ID and sent him through to reception where a young female American diplomat escorted him to a secure room at the heart of the embassy’s underground safe rooms. Feathers was waiting for him with John Foster.

“Robert, good to see you said Feathers. You know my colleague, John Foster.”

“Max, John,” Robert said. “I had planned on bringing my dear friend Paolo Mancini but we decided it was better for him to stay behind just in case I am late for a meeting we have at 11 PM.”

“Ah, you have another meeting this evening, Robert,” Feathers said rhetorically. “Best we get on with it then. Whiskey?” he asked.

“Love one, a malt if you have it.”

Feathers went over to a sideboard which held a wet bar and what appeared to be a selection of salads, smoked salmon, cold meats, cheeses, and fresh fruit. He fixed Robert a neat Oban and poured a glass of red wine for himself and John Foster.

“So, what have we there?” Feathers enquired as he handed Schaffer his drink and nodded to the dossier that was tucked under Robert’s arm.

Robert looked down and placed the book on the dining table just in front of Feathers and Foster. “Oh, it’s a dossier documenting the people behind the insider dealing ring in Milan and Lugano, the $5 million illegal money transfer from our Rome Branch to Switzerland, and the burglary of Global’s Rome Branch,” Robert responded in an incredibly low key, unemotional way. It’s really fabulous reading, Max especially the bits about you and John here. I must say, you guys do get around.”

Feathers begin to brush back his hair and to pick at the tip of his nose while Foster grabbed the dossier and began to turn its pages rapidly. “My God, Max, you won’t believe what’s in here. We are fucked.”

"Shut up, John. We had nothing to do with any of that."

"He's got copies of our Top Secret communiqués in there, Max. He's even got pictures of you and me with Ciano and Matra not to mention some of Italy's criminal elite. You're a dead man, Schaffer. What an ass hole you are to bring that in here."

"Even Feathers saw the ludicrous nature of that statement. He's got to have the original somewhere else, asshole. Let me see it," he ordered Foster.

While Feathers and Foster went through the dossier, Robert fixed himself another large scotch and a plate of smoked salmon and tucked in while he watched the colour drain from each of their faces with the turn of each damning page. Schaffer was on the cold roast beef and salad when they finished.

"What do you want for this and the original and a mutual non-disclosure agreement," Feathers asked.

Robert had expected the question and said: "A total disbandment of the insider dealing ring, a return of all of the art that you guys fenced for the Ciano's, and $1 million in cash to our Chairman's Favorite charity."

"That will cost a fortune, Schaffer," said Foster. "There is no way we are going to agree to those terms."

"Shut up, you moron," ordered Feathers. "He's being very generous. What is you Chairman's favourite charity, Robert?"

Robert paused for effect and said "my back pocket, Max, my fucking back pocket!"

Made in the USA
Lexington, KY
10 March 2019